Soraya Lane graduated with a law  wasn't the career for her and that is the author of historical and c including the #1 Kindle bestsellin and *The Secrets We Left Behind.*

Soraya lives on a small farm in her native New Zealand with her husband, their two young sons and a collection of four-legged friends. When she's not writing, she loves to be outside playing make-believe with her children or snuggled up inside reading.

ALSO BY SORAYA LANE

The Italian Daughter
The Cuban Daughter
The Sapphire Daughter

Soraya
LANE

The
Royal
Daughter

SPHERE

SPHERE

First published in 2023 by Bookouture, an imprint of Storyfire Ltd.
This paperback edition published in 2024 by Sphere

1 3 5 7 9 10 8 6 4 2

A CIP catalogue record for this book
is available from the British Library.

ISBN 978-1-4087-2964-9

Printed and bound in Great Britain by
Clays Ltd, Elcograf S.p.A.

Papers used by Sphere are from well-managed forests
and other responsible sources.

MIX
Paper | Supporting
responsible forestry
FSC® C104740

Sphere
An imprint of
Little, Brown Book Group
Carmelite House
50 Victoria Embankment
London EC4Y 0DZ

An Hachette UK Company
www.hachette.co.uk
www.littlebrown.co.uk

To all my wonderful readers around the world.
Thank you for coming on this journey with me!

PROLOGUE

London, 1973

Alexandra closed her eyes, her breath shallow as she tightened her fingers around her violin. She lifted her chin, rehearsing in her mind, trying not to listen to the impeccable performance of the violinist ahead of her, trying not to compare herself as she prepared for what was to come.

I can't do this.

Fear rose inside of her, a line of sweat forming on her upper lip as her heart started to pound. She thought for one fleeting moment that she should simply gather her things and run, that she should avoid the heartache of what she was about to put herself through. That she shouldn't have been there in the first place.

'Alex.'

A hand closed over her shoulder, gentle and reassuring. She opened her eyes and turned to find Bernard standing there, his thick dark hair falling over his brow, his soft hazel eyes reassuring as she stared back at him; at the man who'd made all of this possible.

'This is your moment to show the world who you truly are,' he whispered, his hands light against her back as he pulled her closer, as she tucked her violin to her chest and stared back at him. 'You *deserve* to be here, Alex. You deserve everything that has brought you to this moment.'

His lips brushed hers, and when he pulled away he pressed his forehead gently to hers, carefully stroking her hair as they stood. His breath was warm against her skin, the feel of him so close reminding her of just how far she'd come, of the opportunity she'd been given, of the gift he'd given her.

'Nothing will ever be the same after today,' he murmured. 'Today is your day, my love.'

She looked up at him as he took a step back, as he reached for the hand that held her bow and gently lifted it, placing a kiss against her skin as she looked into his eyes; eyes that told her she had nothing to fear. Eyes that told her he believed in her.

'Thank you,' she whispered, swallowing past the fear in her throat, choosing in that moment to believe the words of the man who loved her.

Then her name was called, and as Bernard slipped into the background, Alexandra stood tall and took her first step onto the stage, her heels clicking as everything around her fell silent.

Bernard was right. It was time to show the world who she truly was.

CHAPTER 1

London, Present Day

Ella turned the little box over in her hands, brushing her fingertips over the label as she stared at her grandmother's name. She'd thought about it all day, wishing for a quiet moment to open it and discover the contents, and now it was almost dark and she was still none the wiser about what was inside. She hesitated before pulling the string, thinking of how many years the box must have sat unopened, deeply curious as to what she was about to discover.

Part of her wondered if she should have waited until she was with her mother or her aunt, but the other part of her knew she simply couldn't wait a second longer; she'd already had the box in her possession for an entire day.

Ella gently tugged at the string, fibres lifting into the air as the knot gave way, and she carefully placed the name tag on her desk before taking a deep breath and opening the small wooden box. She wasn't sure what exactly she'd been expecting, but inside was a piece of paper folded down into a tiny square. She took it out as tenderly as she might handle the priceless art in her gallery and carefully unfolded it, her eyes travelling quickly across the contents of the page.

It was a sheet of music, with a handwritten note in the bottom right-hand corner.

I know you can make this your own. B.

B? She read it over and over, and although it made as little sense to her as the musical notes themselves, she was still curious about what it could all mean. She looked back in the box and saw there was something else there, something folded in half, and she used her nails to prise it from the bottom where it was partially stuck. *A photo*. It was black and white, but even without colour it appeared vivid. It reminded her of a Greek island, for it showed a view of an endless stretch of water with a glimpse of a stucco-type house to one side, and in it a woman and a child—a girl—were staring back at whoever was holding the camera. She examined their faces, the quality grainy as she squinted and held it closer to her eyes, wishing she could recognise the two people or at least find something in their appearance that was familiar to her. The woman was smiling, mid-laugh perhaps, and the girl was leaning into her, her head dropped to the woman's shoulder, their hands clasped. Her daughter, perhaps?

She looked away from them for a moment and studied the background, before finally setting it down and logging on to her computer to search for images of Greece. She might not recognise the people, but she was certain she was right about the location.

She was immediately inundated with photos of endless blue water and picturesque homes, and she sat back and held the photo up again, imagining it was in colour, knowing without a doubt that it was an island somewhere in Greece. She'd travelled there once, on her summer holidays before going to university. The last summer she'd shared with her brother.

Ella let the photo fall to her desk and stood, stretching as she went over to the little fridge behind the counter near the rear of the gallery. She'd opened a bottle of champagne barely an hour earlier with a client to celebrate their new purchase, and although she'd only had a sip at the time, she was ready for a glass now.

It had been a long day, made even longer by her having to pamper a temperamental artist the moment she'd walked through the door that morning, not to mention stroke the ego of a client who insisted on having a fuss made of him every time he set foot in the gallery. The little box of clues was certainly doing a great job of distracting her from her high-stress day, and after she'd poured herself a glass, Ella sat back at her desk and stared down at the sheet of music and the photo again.

She didn't know what she'd expected, but it certainly hadn't been clues that told her nothing at all. If it had been a letter, or perhaps even an heirloom, a birth certificate with names perhaps, or something explaining what or whom she was supposed to look for to discover her grandmother's past, she'd have understood the purpose of the box more. But these clues meant nothing to her, and she doubted they'd mean anything to anyone else in her family either.

Except for Harrison. Maybe her brother would have understood the piece of music; he was the only one in the family who could even read sheet music as far as she knew. To her, it may as well have been a foreign language, nothing more than a meticulous arrangement of marks on a page.

Ella finished her drink, enjoying the way the bubbles tickled her throat, before carefully packing the clues into the box and placing it in her bag. She left her glass on her desk and rose, turning off the lights as she walked, her heels clicking over the polished concrete floor of the gallery. She loved this time of night; alone, each piece of art illuminated by its own carefully positioned light, the building silent except for the sound of her footsteps. It reminded her of being the first to arrive for swim training as a teenager, that moment before anyone jumped in the pool, the silence matched only by the perfect, motionless water before it was marred by ripples.

It was the painting closest to the door that stopped her tonight though. Ella lifted her hand and carefully touched the edge of the canvas, her eyes flitting over the 'sold' sticker to the side as she admired the bold brushstrokes and lush colours. The artist was new to the gallery, someone she'd discovered herself and brought into the fold only weeks earlier. And now, with her first painting sold within days of arriving, Ella had single-handedly ensured the career of the young woman whose name was modestly signed in the bottom corner.

It reminded her of the scribbled words she'd read only moments earlier, and as she turned off the last light and locked the door, she wondered if she'd ever find out who this *B* was, and just how the note had come to be left in a little box bearing her grandmother's name. Did that initial stand for one of the people in the photo, or had it been written *for* one of them, signed by a friend or family member? And how was she ever supposed to make head or tail of the clues she'd been given without the help of someone who knew more? What could the photo possibly have in common with a sheet of music?

She sighed, touching her palm to her bag as she walked, feeling the shape of the little box there before going over to activate the security alarms. Perhaps her aunt would know. They were meeting for dinner in less than an hour, and she could only imagine the way her aunt's eyes would light up at the first mention of Ella's grandmother's potentially scandalous past.

Ella laughed. One thing was for sure: her aunt would have the exact opposite reaction to her mother, which was precisely why she was going to tell her first.

CHAPTER 2

Ella walked through the door of Soho's Barrafina restaurant and immediately saw that her aunt was already there, busily chatting to one of the chefs as she watched them cook from the high, bar-style chairs.

'Kate,' Ella said as her aunt rose to hug her. Kate gave real hugs—the kind of embrace that told a person you cared about them rather than the air kisses and back flutters that Ella was used to from anyone else in her life. It only made her adore her aunt all the more.

'Ella, you look beautiful, as always,' Kate said as they sat. Her eyes danced over her features as if she needed to map her niece's face out after too long apart. In reality, it had only been a few weeks. 'How's life? Busy at the gallery?'

'The gallery is amazing,' she said with a sigh. 'Amazing, but exhausting. I feel like one day is just rolling into the next at the moment, but I can't complain.'

'Are you painting?' Kate's eyebrows were drawn together in an almost comical way, she was so serious in her line of questioning.

Ella laughed. 'You do realise you ask me that every time you see me, and my answer has never once changed.'

Her aunt's face didn't change either. 'I keep asking because I hope that one day you'll surprise me.'

Ella was grateful when the server came past to ask them what they'd like to drink. They both ordered wine, but from the arch of Kate's still-raised eyebrows, she could tell that their conversation wasn't over yet.

'Isn't it enough that I surround myself with art every day?' Ella asked.

'Is it?' Kate sighed. 'It sounds to me like you're trying to convince yourself.'

'I have a great life,' Ella said, toying with her handbag, which she'd sat down with and which was still on her lap. 'I love my work, I love my *life*, I just—'

Their drinks arrived and Kate held hers up, waiting for Ella to clink hers against it. 'I love that you love your life, darling.'

They both took a sip before placing their glasses down.

'But?' Ella asked, laughing. 'I can hear the silent *but*! Come on, just say it.'

Kate grinned and raised her perfectly groomed brows again, shrugging as if she'd been caught out. '*But*, I can't forget the talented young artist who had every intention of defying her parents' wishes and forging her own path in the world.'

Ella took another sip of her wine. 'That was before.'

They sat in silence for a long moment, Kate's hand covering hers. 'I know, Ella. I know.' She cleared her throat, the air heavy whenever anyone talked about her brother, or how everything had changed since his passing. 'Anyway, tell me what happened today. At the lawyer's office? I was here thirty minutes early because I couldn't wait to hear all about it!'

Ella opened her bag and smiled up at her aunt. 'You know Mum told me not to go, don't you? That it would be a waste of time?'

'I can almost hear your mother saying those exact words,' Kate scoffed. 'Of course she said that. But thank *goodness* you didn't listen.'

Ella took out the box and passed it to Kate. 'I was given this box.'

'A box? What is it for? Is there something inside?'

She nodded and gestured to the tiny wooden box. 'Open it.'

Kate looked up at her again before tentatively lifting the lid, as if she expected something terrible to be inside. Ella watched as she carefully removed the sheet of music, taking her time to study it before placing it down and taking out the photograph. Her aunt looked perplexed.

'What is all this? Why was it given to you? I'm not quite sure I understand.'

'They're apparently clues, from my grandmother, your mother, I think. If it's all to be believed, of course.'

'Clues, you say? I thought it was going to be something left to my mother's estate. But this?' Kate shook her head. 'Well, this is certainly an unexpected turn of events.'

'Would you believe it if I told you that your mother was adopted as a baby? That she was born at a home for unmarried mothers?'

The server came to take their order then, and Ella scanned the menu and ordered a selection of food for them to share before turning her attention back to her aunt. She could see that Kate was fascinated with the box, still turning it over in her hands and not able to take her eyes from it. Ella usually ordered for the two of them when they went out, so she knew Kate wouldn't mind her taking the lead.

'Tell me everything, Ella. I want to know exactly what happened today. Don't leave anything out.'

She leaned closer to her aunt, reaching to trace her fingertips over the photo. Something about the woman and the girl looking back kept drawing her eye, kept making her want to study the picture all the more to see if there was something she was supposed to recognise, some clue that would tell her more.

'I wasn't sure what to expect when I arrived for the meeting today, but I wasn't the only one there. There were other women, most of them similar in age to me, and we were all ushered into an office.'

'And they were all there on behalf of their grandmothers? Just like you?'

Ella nodded. 'We were all there for the same reason. There was a lawyer, the one who sent the letter to Grandma's estate, and he told us that he'd represented a woman named Hope, many years ago. She apparently ran a home for unmarried mothers and their babies, and these little boxes were found there recently, by her niece. She explained that she was initially of two minds about what to do with them, because the boxes had been hidden for so long, but she felt uncomfortable discovering them and not trying to find the women they were intended for.'

'Wait.' Kate took a large sip of wine, her hand held in the air to pause the conversation. 'You're telling me that your grandma, my *mother*, was born in this home? That I wasn't biologically related to my grandparents? And that this box was left for my mother when she was adopted? That it's been hidden all this time?'

Ella nodded again. 'It certainly appears that way. They were hidden beneath floorboards in a place called Hope's House, discovered only because the home was to be demolished. It's a miracle they were found at all.'

Kate's jaw fell open and Ella grimaced. 'I take it you didn't know she was adopted.'

'Didn't know!' Kate spluttered. 'Ella, this is absurd. The fact that we've only just found this out, that these things were left behind, I don't know what to say. You think it's all true? That it's not some kind of, I don't know, and please don't tell me I sound like your mother, but it couldn't be fabricated, could it? This couldn't be part of some elaborate scam to draw us in? These things happen a lot these days, you know.'

Ella indicated to the server that they needed more wine, smiling as they nodded in reply. 'Honestly, I asked myself the very same question, but I am inclined to believe it. All they asked of me was to show identification and to sign for the box. The niece, Mia, she seemed very genuine. All she wanted was to give these little boxes to their rightful owners, and the lawyer's office was very impressive. In fact, I've had dealings with a lawyer there before, through the gallery, so I can't see how this could be anything other than legitimate.'

She watched as Kate picked the box up again and turned it over in her hands, as if she expected to find something else hidden, perhaps a secret compartment. She'd done the same thing herself on her way to the restaurant, almost convinced there was more to it than just the two items she'd found inside. 'So this little box has been hidden for years? Decades even? At this house? Just waiting for someone to discover it?'

'Hope's House,' Ella said. 'And yes, it sounds as if this Hope asked some of the mothers to leave behind something for their child that could be given to them one day, and she attached these little name tags to each box. What her niece didn't know was whether other boxes had been given out over the years as women came searching for answers. Whether perhaps these particular boxes were kept hidden for some reason, or if it was simply a case of these women not knowing they were adopted. Perhaps this Hope was intending to give them out, but died before she had the chance? I suppose we'll never know.'

'You think this Hope asked them to do this, to put these little boxes together, so the adopted children could find their biological families one day?'

Ella shrugged. 'Perhaps. Or maybe it was just so that they had something that belonged to their mothers. Maybe they weren't ever supposed to find their birth mothers, that it was more of a keepsake to send to them? All I know is that this woman, Hope, clearly put a lot of thought into what she did. Each box had a handwritten name tag, and the way it was knotted together with string, I don't know, there just seemed to be so much care taken with each one. It was quite something to see them all.'

'How many were there?'

'Seven,' Ella said. 'But there were only six women there. They hadn't been able to make contact with the family of the seventh, or if they had, she hadn't turned up.'

Their food began to arrive then, and Ella gently tucked the photo back inside the box, taking care to fold the music back down to its intended size, before putting it into her handbag. Kate's hand closed over hers as she zipped it up, their eyes meeting for a long moment.

'Your grandma would have loved this, Ella. She would have taken to these little clues with gusto and not stopped until she'd found out what they meant. I can almost see the glint in her eye.'

Ella smiled as she thought of her grandma—it had only been months since she'd died, and it hadn't been easy on any of them. But in the end, her passing had been easier than seeing her suffer. Her cancer had been so aggressive that she'd only had months to live after her diagnosis, taking her last breath with Ella's mother at her bedside.

'So you think we should try to figure out what they mean? You think we should do this for her?' Ella asked.

Kate nodded. 'I do. And I also think that we should keep this between us for now.'

'In other words, you don't want my mother to dampen our spirits and put an end to our investigation?'

'Ella, that's *exactly* what I think. You know me all too well.'

They both laughed, heads dipped together. *And you know my mother too well.* Ella held up her drink, feeling guilty for enjoying Kate's company so much more than she did her mum's these days. Kate had almost become more friend than aunt. 'To finding out who my great-grandparents were.'

'Cheers to that,' Kate said, as they clinked their glasses together before turning their attention to the food in front of them.

Ella lifted her fork to try the monkfish, but she hesitated when Kate suddenly set her own fork down and stared at her.

'What if this niece of Hope's knows more than she's let on? Maybe she has records that we could ask her to show us. Perhaps she has more clues?'

Ella thought for a moment. Mia, the niece she'd met earlier in the day, had seemed very genuine in her intentions, and if anyone could help them to piece the clues together, perhaps it was her. But wouldn't she have said if there was more to tell?

'You're right. I'll contact the lawyer in the morning and see if they'll put me in touch with her. It's certainly worth a shot.'

Kate bumped her shoulder against Ella's. 'It's most definitely worth a shot. Who knows? She could be in possession of a lot more information than she's let on.'

Ella put some of the octopus on her plate, savouring each mouthful of the delicious food. But her mind was a million miles away, trying to work out exactly how she was going to get Mia to reveal more to her about this mysterious Hope. She wanted to know more about Hope's House, and how one woman had single-handedly helped so many pregnant mothers and their babies.

*

Ella sat up in bed, curling her toes into the thick duvet as she leaned back into her pillows. The box was open on her lap, the sheet of music placed beside her as she looked at the photo. She held it so close to her eyes that it almost touched her nose, as if she might magically be able to recognise the people staring back at her if she just looked hard enough.

But if she was honest, it was the scenery that kept drawing her back. *Imagine what it would be like to paint this.* She couldn't stop the thoughts, could almost imagine herself picking up a paintbrush and recreating the beauty that was so uniquely Greek, her skin flushed from the heat, her fingers stained with paint as she worked under the bright golden sun.

What would it even feel like? It had been years since she'd painted. The day after Harrison passed away, she'd packed up her work-in-progress and stored her easel in the attic at her parents' house. That part of her had died along with her brother, and even though she'd thought about it constantly since, even though sometimes she ached to paint in a way that she could hardly describe, she'd never once wavered in the decision she'd made. But tonight, after Kate had asked, she'd started to wonder: *what if?* Would it be so bad to find that part of herself again? Why couldn't she have a career at the same time as fostering her dream? Did she have to be the perfect daughter with the perfect career that her parents approved of for the rest of her life? Or could she somehow forge a path more authentic to her own needs and desires?

She glanced at her phone, wanting to call her mum but knowing it was the wrong thing to do. Once, her mother would have been the first person she'd have called with news or to talk through how she was feeling. It would have been her mum who'd laugh with her, who'd ask her what piece she was working on, who'd tell her that her creative side was as important as her practical one. But she hadn't just lost her brother on the eve of her first day at university; she'd lost her mum too. Suddenly the warm, glass-half-full woman who'd raised her had turned into someone she barely recognised, and no matter how many years passed, she never glimpsed that mum again. Not once. Their house was a shrine to Harrison, a place of sadness, clinging to a past that had gone forever, no matter how much they all wished they could change what had happened.

Ella placed the clues on her bedside table and turned off the lamp, wriggling down under the covers and closing her eyes. But when she shut them, all she could see was herself with a paintbrush in hand, staring out at a pure blue ocean that was reflected on the canvas in front of her.

I want to be an artist again. They were words she only ever whispered in the dark of night, because she'd made a career dealing in art, not creating it, and she couldn't see how those two parts of herself could ever truly coexist. Not now.

CHAPTER 3

Konstantinidis Family Estate, Athens, Greece, 1967

'Darling, are you certain you don't want to join me?'

Alexandra looked up when her mother spoke. She was standing in the doorway of her bedroom, dressed in riding breeches, tall black leather boots and a white sleeveless shirt, looking as if she were dressed for a photo shoot. Her dark hair was swept back off her face and knotted at the nape of her neck.

Alexandra shook her head, absently touching her own dark locks that matched her mother's. Only hers were loose, falling halfway down her back in a tumble of untamed waves. 'You know I don't love riding like you do, Mama. Maybe another day.'

Her mother walked across the room and sat down on the bed beside her as she lay stretched out. Alexandra let her take the book from her hands and curled her feet up beneath her as her mama smiled at her.

'You're reading Jane Austen?'

Alexandra nodded, her cheeks colouring slightly. Her father thought her reading was a waste of time, but she loved nothing more than curling up with a book. 'I am.' She knew how much her reading impressed her mother though, especially when she was reading in English. She might not have been gracious in her acceptance of horse-riding lessons over the past few years, but she'd certainly embraced her English tutor.

'Are you certain you can't set aside your novel for an hour to ride with your mama? It's such a beautiful day, and I believe the Queen might be joining me.'

Alexandra glanced at her book, about to open her mouth when her mother touched her fingers lightly to her cheek and smiled at her, before pressing a kiss where her fingertips had been. 'Darling, enjoy your book. I should know better than to ask. How about you just promise to tell me your thoughts on the dashing Mr Darcy over dinner tonight.'

'You've read *Pride and Prejudice*?'

Her mother rose and laughed, placing the book carefully back into her daughter's hands. 'Of course I have. Only I was a little older than twelve when I was given a copy.' She smiled. 'Your grandmother would never have let me read romance at your age. She was always terribly concerned about my impressionable young mind.'

Alexandra smiled and watched her mother walk back across the room, pausing at the door. Their eyes met, and her mother gave her a look that only she could give, one that told her just how fond she was of her daughter, her only child.

'I love you, Alexandra.'

'I love you too,' she replied, wondering for a fleeting second whether she should change her mind. But it was so hot, and she didn't like horses nearly as much as her mother did.

She opened her book again and began to read, but when she heard laughter outside after a few minutes, she stood and went to her window. Below, a car had pulled up on the gravel driveway and she watched as her mother walked towards it. As if sensing her daughter was watching, she glanced up at the house, shielding her eyes from the bright sunshine. Alexandra lifted her hand in a wave and her mother blew her a kiss, before disappearing into the car.

Alexandra sighed and went back to her bed, curling into the pillows and finding her place on the page. Her mama was right; they could talk about it over dinner, and tomorrow if she asked her to go riding, Alexandra would say yes. There were worse things than riding horses for the afternoon, and she did always love having her mother's undivided attention.

*

Alexandra lifted her head, blinking as she glanced towards the window. The light had faded, and she stretched and glanced over at her clock, wondering how late it was. She placed her feet on the ground, glancing at her book on her bedside table, the spine splayed open on the last page she'd read. She must have put it there before she fell asleep.

She grinned, remembering what her mother had said about dinner, and quickly checked her appearance in the floor-length mirror in the corner of her room, smoothing her hands over the wrinkles in her dress. She brushed her hair and tied it back, smiling at her reflection before she walked quickly down the hall, listening out for her mother as she stepped down the stairs.

The house was quiet, but Alexandra made her way to the kitchen first, expecting her mother to be there overseeing dinner. Their cook looked up and smiled, and Alexandra gave a little wave, disappointed to see her mother wasn't there. She looked in the dining room and the front sitting room, but there was still no sign of her. She was usually a creature of habit, having a pre-dinner drink as she checked to make certain that everything for the evening was to her liking.

She could hear voices coming from her father's office, and she hesitated before going to his open door, wondering if perhaps her mother would be there, but also not wanting to disturb him if she wasn't. Alexandra was always cautious about entering the one space in the house that was his alone—even their maid had to ask for permission before cleaning in there.

'Alexandra? Is there something you need?'

She smiled politely at her father, going to him when he gestured for her to come closer. She smiled at the other man seated in the office, their conversation ceasing now that she was there. Her papa was usually pleased to see her, so long as she didn't make a nuisance of herself, and so long as she didn't ask anything of him. He seemed to prefer her to be seen and not heard.

'I was looking for Mama,' she said. 'Have you seen her?'

Her father kissed the top of her head. 'She's out riding, I suspect.'

'But she left hours ago,' Alexandra said. 'Papa, she—'

He turned from her and began speaking to the other man again, making it clear she'd been dismissed. *She would never stay out riding this long.* That's what she'd been about to say to her father. Instead, she lowered her head and left the room, deciding to go and look upstairs just in case Mama was in her quarters getting changed. Her father would most likely only notice her mother's absence when he sat down to dinner and found himself at an empty table.

Alexandra's fingers had only just closed around the handrail of the stairs when there was a bold knock at the door. She startled, frozen to the spot as another knock sounded out within seconds of the first. No one came to open it, and so Alexandra moved towards the door, reaching for the handle and pulling it open, something she'd hardly ever done before. There was almost always someone in the house to do tasks like that.

'Miss Konstantinidis?'

She swallowed as the two men in uniform stared back at her, seeming surprised by her appearance. She looked at the police car behind them, then back at their faces, at the way their eyes softened, the way they looked at her, as if they felt sorry for her. A knot curled deep in her stomach. Something was wrong. She should never have answered the door.

'Is it my mother?' *Is this why she isn't home yet? Have they come to tell me why?*

'Is your father home?' the officer asked gently. 'We need—'

'Please, tell me,' she whispered, holding more tightly to the door as her legs began to quiver, threatening to give way beneath her. 'Is it my mother? Has something happened—'

The words died in her throat as the officer who'd spoken took a step closer to her and reached to touch her arm, his palm awkward against the fabric of her dress. She saw then that his eyes were glistening with tears, and she knew. She knew in that moment that whatever it was, whatever news they'd come to deliver, had the potential to break her heart.

Her father appeared beside her then, but she held her ground instead of withering away behind him. She needed to hear what they'd come to say.

'We're deeply sorry for your loss, Mr Konstantinidis,' one of the men said. 'We're afraid to inform you that your wife suffered fatal injuries as a result of…'

'Loss?' Alexandra cried. He'd said *loss*. Did that mean she wasn't coming home? She blinked away tears that had formed almost instantly, the dampness caught on her lashes, struggling to digest what the officer was trying to tell her father. 'Has my, I mean, is my mother—'

'My wife has died? You've come to tell me that my wife is no longer with us?'

'Yes, sir. We understand that she died after falling from her horse.'

Alexandra shut her eyes then as her world began to spin; as she could no longer hear what he was saying; as her legs gave way beneath her; as she fell to the floor.

Why didn't I say yes? Why didn't I go with her? Why didn't I get up when she came for me? Why wasn't I there with her?

As arms circled her, as her father's raised voice filled her ears, she squeezed her eyes shut and began to scream; as tears streamed down her cheeks, as her heart ached for her beautiful mother whom she would never see again.

Her papa barely saw her, hardly had time to greet her in the mornings, but her mother, her mother had been her everything. Her mother was a bright light in a room full of stuffy old men, a woman who knew exactly what she wanted from life and wasn't afraid to demand it for herself or her daughter. Her mother had made life worth living.

Mama, I can't survive without you. I can't.

CHAPTER 4

One Month Later

Alexandra sat at the table, her hands folded in her lap as she stared at the food in front of her. A tall glass of milk sat to one side and thick pieces of bread covered in honey to the other, but she couldn't bring herself to touch anything. She'd barely eaten since her mother had passed away, her stomach twisting and turning and making it almost impossible to swallow whenever she tried. She'd noticed that morning that her dress was hanging off her frame, as if she were a coat hanger instead of a body.

A hand touched her shoulder then, and she looked up to find their maid, Thalia, staring down at her, her face creased with worry. She'd worked in their household since Alexandra was a little girl, and Alexandra often caught her wiping away her own tears, clearly grieving for the woman of the house. It at least made Alexandra feel as if someone cared, as if someone else other than her missed the presence of her mother.

'Alexandra, you must eat,' she whispered, bending low beside her. 'Please. For me?'

Alexandra glanced at her father, his newspaper raised high so that he couldn't see her, ignoring the fact that his daughter was desperately waiting for him to turn his attention to her. He'd get up from the table and leave for the day without even noticing that his only child couldn't bring herself to touch her food, just as he'd done every other day. It seemed as if he'd forgotten about their loss the moment her mother was in the ground, his life continuing on as normal, his daughter's emotions an inconvenience that he largely did his best to ignore. She hadn't even seen him shed a tear, not even when they lowered her coffin into the ground. She wondered why he was so distant, why he wasn't grieving in the way she expected. She remembered her mother saying once that he'd never recovered from losing a son, who'd been stillborn, when Alexandra had been barely two years old.

Alexandra shook her head, but Thalia merely sighed and reached for a piece of the bread, holding it for her with a look on her face that said she wasn't taking no for an answer, as she might have when Alexandra was a small child. She opened her mouth and obliged, not wanting to be difficult, forcing the bread around inside her mouth as she attempted to chew it. But her eyes found their way to the empty seat to her left, where her mother had always sat, as they did every morning. Breakfasts with her mama had been lively, the pair of them always talking and laughing, and then laughing even more when her father would rise and glare at them as if to say, *you two can't even stay quiet long enough for me to drink my morning coffee* as he threw his paper onto the table.

She tried to swallow the mouthful, and as if sensing her discomfort Thalia passed her the glass of milk and pressed a kiss to her head. She only left when Alexandra took a sip, removing her hand from her shoulder and reminding her that she was alone all over again.

Look at me, Papa. Please. Talk to me. Anything but this endless silence. Why can't you see me? Why don't you miss Mama as I do? Why have we not spoken of her since she left us?

As if hearing her pleading thoughts, her father lowered his newspaper, folding it down and placing it on the table. She watched as he drained the last of his coffee, his teaspoon of morning fruit sweets already consumed, before he fixed his gaze on her. He stared a long time, as if he were deep in thought, before letting out a long sigh.

'Alexandra, I think it would be best if you went to live with your aunt in London.'

Alexandra's face grew heated, her jaw dropping open in disbelief as she blinked back at her father. He wanted her to go and live in another country? He wanted her to leave Greece?

'Papa, you cannot mean that!'

He sighed, as if his twelve-year-old daughter was arguing with him over curfew or what she was allowed to wear on an outing with friends, not a decision that would send her to another country. To *London*!

'I have decided. It's what's best for you, Alexandra, and I won't hear any more about it.'

She fisted her hands beneath the table, her body trembling with anger. How could he be so cruel? So cold? How could he not sense how much she needed him?

'But Mama is here. I wouldn't be able to visit her.' She wanted her voice to be loud and strong, but instead it stalled in her throat and came out thick with emotion, barely a whisper. She wanted to sound like a young lady, so that he'd listen to her, but instead she sounded like a child. 'Papa, please. Please don't do this to me. Please reconsider.'

He stood and looked down at her, and she saw something in his eyes that she wished she could unsee. Did she remind him too much of his late wife? Did he not want her now that her mother was gone? Was she merely a hindrance now that he was the only parent? Because he looked away, as if he couldn't bear the sight of her, the moment their eyes met.

'Alexandra, your mother is gone. Her grave is nothing more than a place in the ground.'

'But Papa, my place is here, in Greece. My *home* is here.' *My heart is here.*

The cold stare he gave her told her that he didn't care for her pleading. Once his mind was made up, he never changed it. Her mama had always said that he was as stubborn as an ox, and for the first time Alexandra was seeing just how cruel and unmoving he could be.

Tears began to stream down her cheeks, and she bit down hard on her lip to stop from saying anything she might later regret. *I hate you. I wish it was you who'd died, not her.* That was what she wanted to scream at him, but even in her pain, she knew better. She wouldn't let herself say what she truly thought, no matter how badly the words strove to erupt from inside of her.

'I've said all I have to say on the matter. Now go and get dressed. The royal family is coming to visit today to pay their respects, and I want you downstairs and ready to greet them when they arrive.'

Her father left and Alexandra crumpled forwards, her breath coming in fast pants as she fought against the thought of leaving her mother, of all the things she would never see or do in her beloved Athens again. Of everything she would be forced to abandon. Because she knew that once her father sent her to London, she would most likely never come home. She would never walk the halls of her beautiful home, never look out of the windows to the endless grounds that she'd grown up admiring, or walk to the place where her mother had been buried. She would never visit the palace and see the princesses or go for lunch with the Queen, as she'd often done with her mother. He was telling her that he didn't want her to return, that he was passing her like an unwanted belonging to her mother's sister.

She lifted her head and reached for her glass of milk, hurling it across the room as she screamed. But it was worthless; she could cry all she liked, but her father would never change his mind, and now all she'd done was create a mess for poor Thalia to clean.

*

Alexandra watched as her father paced back and forth, waiting for King Theodore and his family to arrive. She'd been sitting waiting patiently for at least two hours now, toying with the fabric of her skirt and trying desperately to think of a way to convince her father to let her stay. But she knew in her heart that she could plead her case all she wanted; once he made up his mind, there was never any going back. *Unless of course I plead my case to the royal family. Papa would never forgive me, but he'd also never disobey them if they determined that I should stay.*

Finally there was a knock at the door, and Alexandra startled, her back rigid as she sat stiffly in the chair. Her father had stopped pacing. It wasn't the King but a messenger who entered the room, dressed formally and with a look of distress on his face. She'd grown up knowing the royal family intimately—her mother had been one of the Queen's closest friends when they were children and their friendship had continued into adulthood. Her father had become one of the King's advisers—so she knew that if they were still coming, they wouldn't have sent someone else in their place.

'Sir, I bring news from King Theodore.'

Alexandra leaned forwards, ears pricked as she waited to hear. She half expected to be told to leave the room for whatever announcement was about to be shared, but instead the messenger cleared his throat and continued on. Her father seemed too preoccupied to even remember she was there.

'What news?' her father demanded. 'Where are they?'

'The King and his family have gone, sir. The family has left on the royal plane.'

'They've fled the country?' he gasped. 'You're telling me the King has left Greece, without my being informed beforehand?'

'Yes, sir. However he has sent word that his extended family and closest advisers may wish to leave Greece as well, as they don't know how tumultuous the situation could become. He has arranged a private plane to transport you, should you wish to go.' The man paused. 'He asked me to convey how fond he and the Queen are of you both. They want to ensure that you're kept safe throughout whatever unfolds in their absence.'

The King had left Greece? Had he abdicated? Why else would the royal family leave in such a way? Could she and her father really be in danger from the people? Questions bubbled in her throat but she sat quietly, knowing that if she dared to make so much as a noise she'd be banished from the room. It was her mother who'd kept her informed of important news, so she knew nothing of the politics of what was being discussed.

Her father began to pace again, his face pale, devoid of the usual deep tan that coloured his cheeks. It made her heart race. Something terrible must have happened. Her breath caught, as it had the day the police had brought news of her mother. She wished she knew more.

'How long do we have before we have to leave?' he asked. 'Please tell me exactly what the King said. I must know his precise words.'

'The recommendation is that you leave by nightfall. The King was emphatic in his desire for you and your daughter to leave before anyone becomes aware that the royal family has gone. It won't take long for the news to spread, and it may be safer for you to leave Greece, albeit temporarily.'

The messenger nodded and left then, and as she looked up at her father, waiting for him to explain what was going on, she was instead left alone in the room. Her heart was pounding as she sat, in silence, waiting for him to return, but when he never did, she eventually stood and made her way up to her room alone. Her mother would have been the one to explain to her, to soothe her worries and tell her what one should prioritise when leaving in a hurry.

Alexandra thought of her mother's beautiful horses, left behind and no doubt wondering where their doting mistress was. She thought of the graveside she'd never sit beside again, the smell of her mother's perfume as she passed by her bedroom. If she'd thought that she had a chance of staying behind before, she most certainly didn't have one now, not after this sudden turn of events. She was leaving, whether she wanted to or not.

She ran upstairs, light-footed, to her mother's dressing room and took the bottle of her perfume, still sitting there from when she'd last used it, then hurried to her own bedroom. Thalia would be up soon, she was certain of it, but in the meantime she began to take things from her wardrobe and place them on the bed, in preparation for her cases being brought to her room. She folded dresses and collected some personal items, but when she saw her copy of *Pride and Prejudice*, still sitting beside her bed from that day she'd last read it, the day that had changed everything, she picked it up and began to rip out the pages. She furiously tore them up, crying before throwing them all to the floor, like white petals fallen from a flower.

She would never read again. That was to be her punishment, for choosing her stupid book over spending one last day with her mother. She could have basked in her smiles and praise; she could have watched as her mother cantered effortlessly over jumps in the arena, making horse riding seem like the most beautiful sport there was. She could have been there when she fell, might have been able to do something to save her life, could have at least held her in her arms. But instead, she'd chosen to stay at home and bury her nose in a book.

Alexandra curled into a ball on her bed, lying on top of the clothes she'd just folded, her cheeks wet with tears as she tightly shut her eyes, as her body heaved and shuddered, her breath almost impossible to catch.

Losing her mother was one thing, but leaving Greece behind too? Everything she'd ever known and loved was being taken from her, her life changing in a way that she could never have imagined. Who was she without her family or her country?

Mama, how could you leave me? Why couldn't it have been him, instead of you?

CHAPTER 5

Present Day

Ella stood back, her arms crossed as she studied the canvas to make sure the position was perfect. They were showcasing one of their most popular artists from New York, and she wanted everything to be perfect for the Friday-night event. Some of her best customers would be coming into London to see the work, and she was hopeful that there would be sold stickers on every piece by the end of the night.

'Ella?'

Her assistant, Becky, touched her arm and she smiled, having been lost in her own world. She was always like that when she was studying a piece of art—it was as if nothing else around her even existed.

'Your mother is here to see you.'

'My mother?' Ella nodded but took a moment before turning, still staring at the canvas before giving her art hanger a thumbs up. 'Thank you. It's perfect.' Ella looked at Becky, who was still hovering.

When she turned round, she saw her mother sitting stiffly in one of the oversize leather chairs they had near her desk. Ella walked over to her, her heels clicking and echoing through the gallery. It wasn't that she minded her calling in, it was just unexpected.

'Mum! What brings you here?'

'I was hoping you might be free for coffee. Or I can always sit here until you're ready to take a lunch break?'

Ella hugged her mum when she stood, making sure to hold on long enough that her mother knew how pleased she was to see her.

'Is everything okay?'

She studied her face, pleased to see her nod.

'Of course. Why wouldn't it be?'

'You just don't often pop in like this, that's all,' Ella said. 'But coffee sounds fabulous. Let me get my coat. I certainly won't have you sitting here until my lunch break!' What she didn't tell her mother was that she rarely ever took one—she was more likely to send Becky out to buy something for her, so that she could eat without leaving the gallery.

Ella went to her desk and took her coat from the back of her chair. 'I'll be out for half an hour. Call me if you need me.'

'We can survive without you for thirty minutes, El,' Becky said with a roll of her eyes.

Ella knew they could, of course she did, but if anything went wrong, if a canvas was hung incorrectly or a client arrived looking for her, that was on her.

'Let's just walk down to Everyman Espresso,' she said. 'We can get takeout and go for a walk, or—'

Her mum looked at her sky-high heels and Ella laughed.

'Trust me, I can walk for miles in these.'

They walked slowly, her mum looking like she wanted to say something, but every time she opened her mouth she'd close it again and look away. Ella decided to take the lead—anything to put an end to the uncomfortable silence.

'How's Dad?'

'He's good. Busy at work, you know how he is.'

She did. Every year her dad mentioned retiring, but she expected he'd still be working until he was eighty. Work gave him something to occupy his mind, and she knew that without it, he'd struggle, even though she'd love to see him relax more.

'I had dinner with Kate last night,' Ella said. She felt guilty— when was the last time she'd asked her mum to come into town for dinner? Ella knew she needed to make more of an effort, but sometimes what she needed was Kate's non-judgemental, easy-going company. With her mum, it always seemed to take more of an effort, almost like she had to be a different version of herself.

'I spoke to her this morning, actually,' her mum said slowly, as if she wasn't sure about divulging the information.

'You did?' So she already knew they'd had dinner. Perhaps that was what the impromptu visit was about.

'She said you had a lovely time.'

'Mum, please—'

'Ella, I love it that you're close to Kate, please don't worry. She always treated you kids like you were her own, and that's how I wanted it to be.' Her mum touched her arm as they stopped outside the coffee shop. 'I can see guilt written all over your face, but you have nothing to feel guilty about, and besides, she's always been great company. I can understand why you like spending time with her.'

Ella let go of the breath she hadn't even realised she'd been holding. 'Thanks.'

They walked inside and Ella ordered two coffees and paid at the counter, before joining her mother at a table.

'So if it's not about dinner last night, why did you decide to call by today?'

'She told me about the box.'

Ella slowly nodded. 'O-*kay*.' She exhaled. What happened to Kate telling her to keep it a secret from her mum? They'd agreed barely sixteen hours earlier! 'Sorry, I should have brought it to show you. When we get back to the gallery I can—'

Her mum held up her hand. 'Ella, I don't need to see it. I'm here to tell you not to waste time on it.'

'Waste time?' Ella frowned. 'What do you even mean by that? Don't you want to find out about Grandma?'

'You need to focus on work, Ella. You don't have time to worry about silly clues from the past that may or may not have a connection to your grandmother. It probably doesn't mean anything anyway.'

Ella bristled. 'Mum, first of all, I have time in my life to do things other than work. And second, what do you mean by all that? I think it's fairly clear that the box was left for Grandma. It had her name on the tag, for starters! Of course it means something.'

Her mother shrugged and reached for the sugar, toying with the paper edge of the sachet. 'Ella, I just don't want you to be distracted. You've worked very hard to get where you are with your career, and this could consume you, trying to figure out what it all means.'

'Distracted?' Ella repeated, her face heating. She knew what her mother was trying to say: she didn't want her daughter distracted like Harrison had been. The coroner had said that he'd most likely been distracted when he'd taken the corner too fast and crashed into the power line, and ever since then, her mother had been hyper-focused on making certain that no one else in their family could be distracted by *anything*. 'Mum, I'm not him.' She bit her tongue, not wanting to hurt her mother, but also wanting her to know that she needed to live her own life without fear. 'This is not that kind of distraction.'

'Ella, all I'm saying is that you want to stay focused on what you're doing. It's like when you wanted to be an artist, but in the end you made the right decision, the *sensible* decision. You put your energy into building a wonderful career, and look where you are now! You're such a success, and we couldn't be prouder.' She paused. 'I'm asking you to let it go.'

Their coffees arrived and gave Ella time to consider her answer. She'd ordered takeout cups, thinking they'd sip them as they slowly walked back, but now she could see that they'd be sitting and drinking instead.

'Mum, what if I still want to be an artist?' She lowered her voice. 'What if I question every day whether my success has been worth the sacrifice?'

'Worth it?' Her mother looked shocked. 'Sweetheart, you've achieved everything you ever dreamed of!'

No, Mum, I've achieved everything you *ever dreamed of.*

Ella took a sip of her coffee and promptly burnt the tip of her tongue. There was no use in having this conversation. They'd had it a hundred times already and if she was honest with herself, it was the reason she chose to meet her aunt for dinner over her mum, because she got to be herself, to be open about how she was feeling and what was happening in her life. To not have to censor herself.

'Aren't you just a little bit curious to find out about your mother's family? To find out who her birth mother was? Wasn't it a shock to you to find out that she was adopted? *If* she was adopted?'

She sighed, and Ella saw for perhaps the first time just how tired her mother looked—the lines around her eyes were etched deep now, and her gaze was weary. 'Sometimes we need to just leave the past in the past, that's all I'm saying. What good is there in uncovering secrets that might be better left that way?'

Ella immediately thought of Harrison when her mum spoke of the past, knowing that he was probably on her mother's mind as well.

'Mum, you know I think about him every day,' she said, reaching out to touch her mother's hand. Her fingers closed around her mum's, but she could feel her trying to pull away, as if she wasn't comfortable being touched. 'Please, look at me.'

Her mother slowly lifted her gaze.

'I miss him too. Every single day of every single month of every year, I miss him too.' Ella blinked away tears, knowing it made her mum uncomfortable talking about him. 'But I can't be scared to live my life because of him. I can't always try to be so careful, so conservative, that I stop doing the things I want to do.' She swallowed. 'I can't live my life for the both of us.' *Like following my dreams. Like travelling. Like taking risks.* 'I see Dad, doing the same job all these years, clocking in and clocking out, and—'

Her mum pulled her hand away. 'Don't speak about your father like that.'

Ella nodded. 'I'm just trying to open up to you, Mum. I don't mean Dad any disrespect, you know how much I love him.' *I just don't want to be him. I don't want to wake up in forty years' time and realise that my life has disappeared and I never got to do the things I wanted to do.*

'I thought you loved your job?'

'I do,' she said, sighing. 'Of course I do. Sometimes. Actually, I enjoy it a lot of the time.' There was no point in having this conversation, not anymore, not again. Her mother never understood. 'But going back to the box…'

Her mother pursed her lips before taking a sip of coffee.

'Would you at least like to come back to the gallery to take a look? You must be just a little curious about what was left behind?'

She smiled. 'It's this incredible little wooden box, and the clues were folded up inside.'

'Sometimes I wonder if you're Kate's daughter,' her mum muttered. 'The two of you, on and on about this box. If you must know more, then at least try not to let it consume you. But I, for one, want no part of it. I'd prefer you forget it even exists.'

Ella tried not to groan. Perhaps it was her mum who should be investigating the clues. At least then she wouldn't put all her time into worrying about her daughter. But one thing was for sure: there was no way she was walking away from this. It was too important to just discard, especially something that had been kept secret for so many years. She could no more forget about the tiny box than fly to the moon—it would be impossible.

*

Ella was back at her desk, fiddling with a pen and staring at the photo. There was something about it that she kept going back to, and now she'd positioned it beside her laptop, so that it was facing her. She found herself googling Greece again, scrolling endlessly through images until she was lost in a sea of sparkling blue water that made her yearn to actually see it with her own eyes.

It had been years since she'd had a proper holiday. She'd been about to book a trip away when the pandemic had hit and disrupted everyone's lives, including hers, and since then she'd thrown herself into work, trying to build the gallery up to what it had been before all the restrictions. Thankfully their sales had stayed high, with investors happy to partake in online auctions when they couldn't view easily in person, but now they were welcoming all their clients back through the door. It had been amazing, and she'd felt like she'd been on a high for months now, but she was also beginning to realise that there was no way she could operate at that level for much longer. Not without burning out or starting to see her health decline.

A holiday in Greece might fix that…

Her finger hovered over her mouse as she looked at the latest image. It was a link to a house for rent on an island she wasn't familiar with, but it certainly looked similar to the photo. Ella picked it up and held it beside her screen, looking back and forth between the two. She couldn't be entirely certain, especially with the image in black and white, but there was something inside of her, a little voice in her head, trying to convince her that they matched. Or perhaps that was her own voice simply wishing it to be true. They looked familiar to her, and it was then she realised why: she recognised the location from the *Mamma Mia* movie.

Ella set the photo down and decided to click on the image on her screen, which depicted a small selection of homes that were available on the island of Skopelos in the Aegean Sea. One in particular appealed to her—a very small, stucco-type home that was set at the top of a flight of steps, with a view out to the ocean. This one had doors that opened out and little planter boxes of pretty pink flowers adorning the windows, but it was the image of an easel positioned in the little courtyard, overlooking the vast expanse of water, that made her pause.

What if I went there? What if I escaped my life for a week? Two weeks? She gulped. *A month?*

She hadn't taken leave in years, and there was nothing to stop her organising time off, but when she looked up and glanced around the gallery, she knew how difficult that would be for everyone else. She *was* the gallery. Ella had taken over every part of its day-to-day management, the handling of all the artists, all their important clients… She focused on her screen again and decided to look at the dates the house was available, trying to force work from her mind. She could almost taste the salt in the air, the delicious seafood, the late afternoons sipping rosé as she stared at the images on her screen.

Ella opened her diary and glanced through it. There was nothing there that she couldn't delegate to someone else if she had to, other than the exhibition this coming Friday, and she'd still be on email if her clients needed her or there was an emergency. But...

She looked at the photo on her desk again, and then at the house on her screen.

Just do it. For once in my life, why can't I do something just for me? Why can't I make a decision without the guilt?

Ella swallowed, her mouth dry as she looked at the images from Skopelos, of the island that was seemingly calling her name, before quickly shutting her laptop. There was no way she could do something like that. *What on earth was I even thinking?*

She shook her head as if trying to shake out thoughts of Greece, before opening her laptop again and clicking on a new search window. What she needed to do was something useful, like investigating Hope's House and trying to find out the link to her family there.

There were some hits that weren't related to what she was looking for, and so she added more information to her search. And it was on the third page that she found what she was looking for.

HOUSE FOR UNMARRIED WOMEN AND BABIES SET
TO CLOSE AFTER DEATH OF FOUNDER AND LIFETIME
WOMEN'S ADVOCATE HOPE BERENSON

Ella looked up, checking there was no one who needed assistance in the gallery before clicking on the article, her curiosity piqued. She leaned forwards to read the words on her screen.

Hope Berenson, founder of the aptly named Hope's House, dedicated her life to helping unmarried women and their babies. She passed away peacefully over the weekend, surrounded by those closest to her, who often called her an angel to the unwed and a woman with the type of compassion and dedication to others that is rarely seen. Berenson didn't have children of her own, despite dedicating her life to unwanted children, but will be remembered fondly by many in the community. She left her estate to the London Women's Refuge Centre, instructing them to sell her property to fund their new refuge centre. They received an undisclosed sum for the sale of her property, in addition to a large, unexpected donation from the housing developer.

The beneficiary of her estate wanted to pay tribute to Hope's generosity, which has allowed them to continue their work helping women in the community, and has afforded them the opportunity to establish a new centre to assist young mothers with infants. This would not have been possible without Berenson's generous bequest.

At the end of the article there was a photo of the house, and Ella enlarged it so she could see it more clearly. It was an elegant two-storey brick home with a gold sign hanging at the gate stating HOPE'S HOUSE, and a red front door flanked by pots of flowers. A home that might otherwise have been for a large family; a house that no one would otherwise notice on a street full of similar properties. But to think of how many women this Hope must have helped, how many must have gone to her for assistance in their most desperate hour of need... Ella scrolled down farther, wishing she'd had the chance to meet this woman.

But she was quickly distracted by the comments section of the article. There were plenty, most referencing what a wonderful woman Hope must have been. The last one made Ella pause.

I remember this place from when I was a teenager. My best friend was sent there to give birth to her baby, back when an excuse was made up about daughters going abroad when in fact they were pregnant. It was well known that some wealthy families were drawn to Hope for her absolute discretion, and although I know for a fact that she would never turn any girl away who landed on her doorstep, many wealthy parents paid handsomely to send their daughters there. I guess many of the children born at Hope's House never even knew they were adopted, it was all shrouded in so much secrecy due to the era.

Ella reread the last two sentences as she thought about her own grandmother. Could it have been that she was from a wealthy family, and they'd sent her great-grandmother there to give birth, under the pretence of her going abroad? Was that how she'd ended up there? Or had she been penniless and thrown out of her home, and found herself on the doorstep of Hope's House because it was the only place she could go?

And perhaps the boxes had been left by the young mothers who'd least wanted to be there? The ones who were reluctant to leave their babies, the ones who desperately wanted to keep their infants? Or maybe it was simply wishful thinking on her behalf.

She closed her browser and clicked on her emails instead, deciding to follow through with what her aunt had suggested. If Hope's niece Mia could shed more light on the past, then wasn't it worth at the very least trying to make contact with her?

Ella found the email from the lawyer that she'd received only the week before, confirming her appointment, and quickly typed a message requesting Mia's contact details. It was certainly worth a shot. After that, she closed her laptop and put it in her bag, packing up for the day and deciding to go home, pour herself a glass of wine and watch Netflix. She was exhausted.

CHAPTER 6

Athens, 1967

Alexandra knew she shouldn't have left the house alone, but her father was preoccupied and she'd fled without anyone knowing she'd gone. The child within her wanted to run away and hide, to let her father leave the country without her. But the young adult that she was blossoming into knew that was a fantasy; not only would her father not leave Athens without his only daughter, but also it could be too dangerous for her to stay. If the King had already left and wanted his family and closest advisers to leave too, then the situation must be more precarious than anyone was telling her.

The sun was high in the sky as she hurried across the grass, sweat curling around her neck as she looked up at the stable block that stretched in front of her. She took a moment to catch her breath, watching to see if anyone was there before walking slowly towards the sprawling wooden building, trying to commit the image to memory. Everything about it was immaculate, from the crisp white and grey paintwork to the planter boxes full of flowers flanking the entrance—all things her mother had insisted on when they'd purchased the property. But it was the chestnut nose of a horse peeking over the closest loose box to her that stalled her heart.

Her mother's beloved Apollo. She'd had him since he was a foal, had regaled her with stories of him since Alexandra was a little girl, and of the fact that her friend the Queen had been the one to gift him to her. He was the horse her mother had once competed on, back when *she* was the queen of the showjumping ring, when she'd first caught Alexandra's father's eye, and also the same horse she'd been quietly enjoying an afternoon out riding on when the accident had happened. He was the horse her mama had loved almost as much as she'd loved her daughter. The stable was full of beautiful equines, but it was Apollo who'd held the special place in her mother's heart, and now in Alexandra's, even after what had happened. Because how could she not love an animal that her mother had adored? It didn't matter to Alexandra that he'd been a gift from the royal family; what mattered to her was that her mother had loved him.

She walked slowly forwards, wondering if she was going to feel any hatred towards him for the part he'd played in her mother's death, but all she felt was the most overwhelming sense of love for him. Alexandra approached him and held out her hand, watching as he breathed on her before nuzzling her palm and rubbing his top lip over her skin.

'I should have brought you a sugar cube,' she whispered, moving her hand to gently stroke his muzzle.

She leaned forwards against the loose box door, her forehead against the wood as emotion threatened to choke her, as Apollo nuzzled her hair, as if sensing that something was wrong. As a child, she'd spent hours trailing around after her mother at the stables, had ridden the striking chestnut before her legs were even long enough to reach the stirrups, been part of her mother's world, just the two of them. But as she'd grown older, her interest in horses had waned until she no longer wanted to ride or visit the stables each day or even each week. Now it was one of her biggest regrets.

'Alexandra?'

A voice from behind made her quickly wipe her eyes and stand straight. Her mother had insisted that everyone call them by their first names here. She might have grown up an heiress, but her mama had never allowed anyone to treat her as if she were different. Her mother liked to say that she was nothing more than a commoner, despite her wealth, even when she married Alexandra's father who, due to his work, became even closer to the royal family and their inner circle. But while she didn't believe she was any more important than anyone else, her mother had always drawn people in with her beauty and magnetism, meaning she was always treated as if she *were* someone special.

'Nico,' Alexandra said, when she finally turned.

He was holding his hat to his chest, his eyes full of tears as he stared back at her. He'd been their groom for her entire life.

'Alexandra, I'm so sorry,' he said.

'Thank you, Nico.' Her words were barely a whisper, her breath shuddering from her body.

'You're not here to ride?' He glanced down at her skirt and sandals.

'I came to see Apollo.' *Before we leave.* She almost let the last words slip out. 'I…'

He nodded and stepped forward, deftly opening the loose box door and slipping inside. 'Come in,' he said.

Alexandra hesitated before deciding to do as he'd asked, stepping inside the stall and finding herself in the small space with the enormous horse. It took a moment for her heart to stop racing, but Apollo just stood and calmly blinked at her, his big brown eyes so kind and trusting.

'He's missed your mother's affection,' Nico said in a low voice. 'He is always looking, as if expecting her to walk around the corner at any moment to saddle him up or feed him apples.'

I'm missing her affection too.

Fresh tears filled Alexandra's eyes and she leaned into Apollo, her cheek to his silky-soft neck, inhaling the smell that her mother had loved so much. She'd once declared that she'd bottle the sweet aroma of horse if she could.

Nico's hand touched her shoulder then. 'Alexandra, your father asked for him to be sold.'

She lifted her hand to Apollo once more. Part of her expected her father to have asked for him to be destroyed after the accident.

'Nico, would you like to have him as your own?' she asked as she slowly turned, using the backs of her fingers to wipe her eyes. 'There is no one my mother would have trusted him more with than you, and my father doesn't care about the money, only about getting rid of him.' He'd understood once, according to her mother, showing great interest in her horses during their courtship, but he'd certainly never shown any affection towards them during Alexandra's lifetime, not that she could recall anyway.

Nico looked past her at the horse. 'I didn't sell him, in case you wanted him for yourself. I knew your father would be furious if he found out he was still here, but I wanted to wait until I'd seen you.'

'He would be wasted on me,' she said. 'Please, he's yours.'

Nico nodded. 'It would be my honour.'

'Alexandra!'

The call was sharp, frantic even.

'Alexandra!'

Nico looked at her and she bravely lifted her palm to touch his cheek. 'Thank you,' she whispered, before stepping out of the stables and seeing Thalia running towards her, her skirts gathered up as she hurried across the grass.

'There you are! Come quickly, your father is looking for you. It's time to go.'

Alexandra looked back one last time, committing the stables and the towering trees, the green field and sprawling outdoor arena to memory, before letting Thalia take her hand and rushing back with her towards home.

Her only regret was that she hadn't been able to visit her mother's grave before they left. But she knew in her heart that her mother would have wanted her last goodbye to be for Apollo.

CHAPTER 7

Present Day

Ella stood at the door to the gallery, shielding her eyes from the sun.

'I hope you'll have more to tell me about your family mystery next time I'm in. It's mad to think you have such a big family secret that no one's known about until now.'

'I know, right? It's more fiction than real life, and to think my grandmother went her entire life without knowing.' Ella sighed. 'It's kind of sad.'

Daisy gave her a hug. 'You know, I think I might be able to help you with the musical clue.'

Ella let her go and leaned against the door. 'You do?'

'I have a friend who plays the violin in the London Symphony Orchestra. I actually have tickets for this Friday night, but I can't go. Would you like them?'

Ella's eyebrows shot up. 'You're offering me your tickets?' It had been years since she'd been to a live performance.

'I am absolutely offering you tickets. Will you wait for a bit to see him afterwards? His name is Gabriel. I'll tell him to keep an eye out for you. He owes me a favour, so perhaps he can look over the sheet of music for you? I'll email you the tickets.'

'You'd really do that for me?'

'Ella, hon, I'd do anything for you! You've just earned me enough money to pay my rent for an entire year! You changed my life the day you decided to take a chance on me, so this is the least I can do.'

She was about to tell her that she'd well and truly earnt the money herself without having to repay her, but Daisy was already running down the road as if she were late for a train, her head of dark, tight curls bouncing around her.

Gabriel, eh? Well, it would be very interesting to see what his thoughts were on the sheet of music she currently had in her possession, and whether he could help her to figure out just how old it might be.

*

It was Friday night before Ella knew it. The Barbican Centre where the orchestra was playing was wonderfully atmospheric, and she only wished she had someone to share the experience with her. Kate had intended on coming, but had to cancel at the last minute when she'd come down with a bad cold.

The lighting at the centre always made it stand out from miles away, which made approaching it at night all the more special. She queued outside for a short time before making her way into the foyer, and Ella marvelled at the architecture the moment she was inside. But it was when she went to take her seat that she was truly in awe. The theatre was substantial, and it had the most beautiful gold hue inside with all the lights on.

She didn't have long to admire the interior though before the lights dimmed, and then the audience fell so quiet she could have heard a pin drop. Ella closed her eyes when the orchestra began, the sound almost soft at first before slowly building to a crescendo that reminded her why she loved live music. There was nothing quite like the orchestra.

But as much as she tried to concentrate on the music itself, her mind began to wander and she couldn't stop thinking about her grandmother's birth parents. Had one of them sat like this and listened to the other play? Was that what the note was about? Or had they both been musicians, writing little messages on each other's sheets? And had her grandmother even known any of this? Had she played an instrument in her younger years, or felt a connection to music without knowing why? Ella was burning with so many unanswered questions, and it only made her angry all over again that her mother was so uninterested in finding out the answers.

Everyone began to clap then, and Ella brought herself back to the present, not wanting to miss any of the concert. She squinted as she tried to make out each musician on stage, looking at the violinists to see if she could guess who Gabriel might be. She should have googled him before coming to make it easier to find him afterwards, but she hadn't thought to ask for his last name.

Ella waited outside after the concert, surprised by the coolness of the wind. She'd been in such a hurry to get to the concert that she'd forgotten to bring her jacket, and she shivered absently as she looked at the crowd slowly dissolving around her. Part of her wondered if she shouldn't waste Gabriel's time; he'd just spent hours on stage performing and quite likely just as long rehearsing beforehand. Surely the last thing he wanted was to pretend he was interested in her little clues. She moved closer to one of the outdoor tables, running her fingers across the top of it and deciding it was probably safer to stay there, closer to the building.

'Ella?'

A deep voice pulled her from her thoughts. When she turned, she found a man standing a few metres from her, his black suit jacket slung casually over one shoulder, his white shirt open.

'Gabe?' She burst out laughing. 'You're *Gabriel*?'

His smile widened and brought his face to life, his dark eyes dancing across hers as he stepped towards her, kissing her cheek.

'Isabella Rose,' he said, shaking his head. 'What a surprise.'

'How did I not—' Her hand went to her mouth. 'I can't believe it didn't click. After all these years, I can't believe it's you.'

'How long has it been? Ten years? Twelve?'

Now she was the one shaking her head. 'Honestly, I'm not sure. It's been a long time, that's all I know.' Gabe had been her crush all through school, a friend until they'd kissed behind the science block, the day before he'd left to take up a scholarship at a music school in the Netherlands. She'd sobbed into her pillow for weeks after he left, and then never heard of him again. In fact, until today, she hadn't so much as thought of him in years.

'I have to say, you're far from who I expected to meet tonight when Daisy asked me for a favour.'

'Ditto,' she replied.

'Do you want the truth?'

She nervously wrapped her arms around herself, finding his smile impossible not to return. 'Go on then.'

'I figured the woman I was meeting would be older,' he said. '*Much* older.'

'Let me guess, she told you I was looking for help researching my family history, and you immediately thought I'd be some old spinster.'

'Well,' he said with a grin, 'I hadn't given any thought to the spinster part, specifically, but definitely old. You're at least two decades younger than I thought you'd be.'

They both stood for a moment, Ella trying to ignore quite how beautiful his face was, and Gabe staring back at her. His eyes were as dark as cocoa, his jawline grazed with stubble, and those full lips of his seemed permanently tipped upwards into a smile. He'd been a good-looking kid, but he'd grown into a gorgeous man. Why had she never thought to look him up?

A small group of people emerged from the building behind him then, catching both of their attention. They were all dressed similarly to Gabriel—the men in black dinner jackets and the women in long black dresses—and one of them whistled.

'Where are all the instruments?' she thought out loud, surprised to see all the musicians without them.

'They let us store everything here for the night. It's very secure, so we don't have to worry about them.'

'Gabe! Come on!' they called out.

'I'll catch you up!' he called back.

'Please, I don't want to keep you from your friends. This can wait until another time,' Ella said. 'You were so kind agreeing to meet me, and it's been so good seeing you after all these years, but—'

He cocked his head slightly to the side, as if trying to decide whether to say something or not. 'Do you want to join us for a drink? I mean, I'd love to catch up. It has been a while.'

'Oh, I couldn't.' *Could she?*

He took the jacket from his shoulder and slung it around her instead, rubbing her arms gently before gesturing for her to follow. 'Come on, you look cold, and I'm well overdue a drink. It's been a very long night. What do you say?'

Ella was never lost for words. She was also usually very hard to impress. In fact, at that moment, the feminist within wanted to reject the jacket around her shoulders and return it to sender. But the fact that this man, whom she hadn't seen since he was a teenager, had noticed that she was cold and given her his jacket without thought, and was now leading the way for her to join him for the evening, was also one of the sweetest things a man had ever done for her. And why the hell couldn't a man give a woman his jacket? It was incredibly romantic, or at least right now it seemed that way to her.

'I hope I haven't overstepped?' he said, perhaps wondering why she was frozen and gaping at him. 'If you don't want to come…'

'I am most definitely okay, and I'd love to come,' she said quickly, matching her stride to his. 'Tell me, how do you know Daisy?' *And why didn't I ask her myself when she offered me the tickets? Please don't be an ex-lover of hers. Please.*

'We met when I was abroad, many, many years ago, when she was an art student and I was away on my scholarship studies,' he said, giving Ella a quick smile as he glanced across at her. 'We were both Londoners in the Netherlands, and we had a similar group of friends.'

'Well, you've both clearly done very well. Daisy is smashing it, and although I know nothing about music, what you did on stage back there was pretty impressive. I was blown away.'

'Blown away, huh?' He laughed, and she watched as his head tipped back a little. God, he was gorgeous. 'Well, I'm happy to hear you enjoyed it so much. We put our hearts and souls into every performance.'

Ella snuggled deeper into his jacket, feeling in a way that wearing an item of his clothing was far too intimate, but also liking it.

'Where are we going?' she asked, as the small group of musicians disappeared up ahead.

'Wait and see. You'll either love it or hate it.'

'Really,' she said, shaking her head. 'Why would I hate it?'

'Because it's full of musicians and arty types, which means the drinks are cheap to keep us all coming back. The downside is that the interior is as low budget as the cocktail menu.'

Ella stopped when he gestured for her to walk ahead of him towards a nondescript door. She looked back, feeling immediately out of her depth at the same time as her stomach filled with butterflies of anticipation.

'You're not really selling it to me.'

He leaned towards her, his arm brushing hers as he opened the door, his words spoken directly into her ear.

'What I forgot to mention is that the company is excellent. It most definitely makes up for all the other parts.'

She took a deep breath and moved past him. If she'd been braver, she'd have told him that she was already enjoying the company. But the moment she walked through the door into the bar, she promptly forgot what she'd been thinking and looked around her in awe. The most hilarious part was that half the people were dressed in black evening wear and the rest were like an intense blend of misfits wearing an eclectic mix of clothing. It was the most diverse, interesting bunch of people she'd ever set eyes on in one space.

When she felt a hand touch her back she spun round, seeing the question mark on Gabriel's face.

'One drink?'

She shrugged. 'Why not?'

CHAPTER 8

'So tell me what you've been doing with yourself since I last saw you,' Gabriel said when he returned with their drinks. 'Daisy mentioned you were an art dealer.'

Ella happily took the gin and tonic, sipping from the little straw as they moved side by side to a spot at the bar that had just been vacated.

'Well,' Ella replied as she sat down. 'I went to university, graduated, took a job at an art gallery…' She laughed. 'I don't know what else to say.'

'And now you represent Daisy? I'm guessing you discover new artists as part of your job?'

'Yes and yes, although they're not all as wildly talented and successful as she is,' Ella said, as she glanced around the room. 'Let's just say that we broke our own record for a new artist with her first few sales.'

Gabriel let out a low whistle. 'At least one of us is making serious money then. I'll be sure to make her pay for dinner next time we catch up.'

They both laughed and sipped their drinks again.

'Speaking of our mutual friend, she told me you were left some clues to do with your family. She said something about you needing help deciphering a piece of music? That I might be able to help?'

Ella leaned in closer as the noise around them amplified. 'Yes! To cut a long story short, it turns out that my grandma was adopted, and one of the clues was a sheet of music that—'

'Gabe! Who's your friend?'

He gave her an apologetic look as a young man, in a white shirt unbuttoned far too low and with a pint of beer in hand, slung his arm over Gabriel's shoulders.

'Arch, this is Ella,' he said. 'She's stopped in to have a drink with us.'

'You were in the audience tonight?'

'I most certainly was. I loved it.'

'Good! That's great to hear.'

Thankfully Arch was quickly distracted by someone else, and Gabriel leaned in to apologise. 'He's our youngest member. Great on the cello, but not so talented at pacing his drinks. It's also his first season, so he's rather needy when it comes to praise.'

Ella laughed and shook her head as she watched the younger man, reminding herself to tell him just how much she'd enjoyed the cello.

'It must be an amazing feeling, playing for a crowd like that, surrounded by so many other musicians,' she said. 'A dream come true, I'm sure.'

'It is,' he said, sipping his drink as he looked at her. 'The hard part is coming down from the high of a performance. It's impossible to sleep afterwards, which is why so many of us go out to decompress. Although the older members seem so much better at compartmentalising it as work. I see them pack up and leave as if it's just a regular job, and maybe after years of performing, it does become like that.'

'Maybe. I'm like that after a big day at work though,' Ella said, fiddling with the little straw in her glass. 'I can be so exhausted, but if I went to bed, I'd just lie there for hours, unable to fall asleep, my head spinning with everything that happened during the day.'

'Gabe!' A couple came over then and Gabriel raised his eyebrows at her as he grinned. She wasn't sure what he was trying to tell her, but she almost immediately realised that they were about to be drawn into the fun.

'Ladies, this is Ella,' he introduced.

'Where did you find this one?' one of the women teased, before leaning in and giving her a quick hug and a kiss on the cheek. 'I'm Ruby, and this is Emma.'

'Lovely to meet you both,' Ella said. 'I hope I'm not intruding on your evening by being here.'

'Intruding?' Ruby asked. 'Not a chance, the more the merrier. Did you see the performance tonight?'

'I did. It was truly spectacular. I can't wait to come again.'

Someone else came over then and the intense musical conversation went way over Ella's head. She had no idea what half the words they were saying even meant, so she took the chance to gesture to their drinks when Gabriel looked over at her. She was surprised that there were so many performers in their thirties, although she guessed the younger ones all stuck together.

'Sorry,' he mouthed.

Ella just grinned. 'Another?' she mouthed back, holding up her glass.

He nodded and she left him to get another gin and tonic for them both. As she waited at the bar, she looked around and noticed how relaxed everyone seemed. She wondered who the others in the crowd were; whether most of them were in fact musicians, or whether there was a blend of customers. It certainly had a very creative kind of vibe.

She was just turning around with the drinks when a hand touched her shoulder. Ella spun round completely and found herself staring into a wall of chest. She looked up and into Gabriel's eyes.

'Hi,' he said.

'Hi,' she replied.

Her hands were full, with a drink in each, and she held one up to Gabe.

His shirt was unbuttoned lower than before, his tie completely discarded now and his jacket nowhere to be seen. He took a step closer to her, before ducking his head a little lower, and she found she hadn't been quite so attracted to a man in… She smiled to herself. *As long as I can remember.*

'Finally, we get a moment alone,' he said, taking a sip and grinning at her over his glass.

'I meant it before, I hope I'm not—'

He held up his hand. 'Don't say it, because you are absolutely not interrupting. I honestly can't believe it, that after all these years…'

She laughed. 'I know. And can I be honest and say that I hadn't thought about you, about those years of my life, for such a long time.'

'Me neither, but it's certainly been a pleasant surprise seeing you again and remembering.'

'When you first left, I wondered how different our lives would become, whether we'd ever cross paths again.'

'So did life turn out the way you thought it would?'

Ella shrugged. 'Maybe. I honestly…' She pushed away thoughts of her brother and how much her life had changed since then, not wanting to tell Gabe yet. 'I honestly don't know what I expected from my life back then. I mean, we were so young, what did we know about what we wanted from life?'

She realised the moment she spoke that Gabe was doing exactly what he thought he'd be doing, that he'd followed his dream.

'Except for you, of course. *You* knew precisely who you were and what you wanted to be.'

He was giving her the strangest look, and she laughed. 'Why are you looking at me like that?'

'I don't know why I'm even telling you this, after all these years, but—'

She put one hand on her hip as she sipped her drink through the little straw.

'I've never forgotten that kiss, Ella. All those months I waited to kiss you, and I finally gathered up the courage on my last day at school.' He shook his head. 'I spent so long wishing I'd been brave enough earlier, and then when I left, all I wanted was to come back to see you.'

Ella blushed. She'd never known he'd even liked her until that day. 'Are you remembering the part where we awkwardly bumped teeth, or...'

'I'm remembering the part where I should have been braver, so I could have had weeks' worth of kissing you, instead of one stolen moment.'

She swallowed as he looked pointedly at her mouth, before lifting his gaze. Ella nodded, almost dropping her drink when his lips unexpectedly met hers in a soft, toe-tingling kiss. She could have stood like that forever, but it wasn't to be as more people filled the bar and one jostled her as he passed, almost knocking her clean off her feet.

Gabriel was quick to save her, looping one arm around her waist and tugging her to him, the other hand reaching out to take her drink for her, which had just sloshed over her shoe.

'I don't think I'll forget that one either,' he whispered against her skin.

Ella blushed, unable to help the instant heat in her cheeks, but she didn't pull away.

'Come on, there are a few people I'd love you to meet.' He stopped and glanced down at her, putting the glass back in her hand. 'If you don't mind?'

'I don't mind at all,' she replied, taking a big sip of her drink for courage, and wondering just how it was that her evening had turned out so differently to how she'd expected.

Gabriel's fingers stroked her arm and she tucked in close to him as they navigated the crowd. It was becoming noisy and mildly raucous as it filled with even more people, but Ella didn't care. She was used to such sedate gatherings these days, and she'd barely socialised outside of work all year, which was making the entire evening even more interesting for her. And that was *without* considering the rather unexpected kiss. There was truly nowhere else she'd rather be.

She stole a glance at Gabriel's side profile, taking in the strong, square jaw. He was handsome in a classical way, his features masculine, and the way he held himself even more so, filled with a confidence that she thought might perhaps come from his ease on stage. It wasn't arrogance so much as a quiet sense of being comfortable in his own skin, which was even more appealing than his looks, and it was what she'd liked most about him as a teenager too. He'd never seemed to care what anyone else thought, not to mention that he'd been confident enough to spend his final year of school abroad.

Ella hadn't thought about Gabe in a very long time, but she was certainly thinking about him now. She sighed as his hand slipped from her waist, catching her palm instead and sending a shiver of anticipation through her body as he tugged her along. She'd have been lying if she didn't admit to having fallen just a little bit in lust with him all over again, especially when he sat down and gestured for her to join him. His thigh brushed hers and he casually slung his arm around her shoulders, gracing her with a smile before laughing at something one of his friends had said.

She had no idea how they'd managed to cross paths again, but she did know that the little box of clues was to be thanked for that. Without them, she would never have decided to go to the concert, and she would never have ended up sitting with this gorgeous, talented man's arm around her.

*

'I think it's time for us to say goodnight.' Gabe winked at her as he stood up from his chair at the bar and held out his hand.

Ella blinked and looked around, surprised to see there was only a handful of people left. She'd noticed most of his colleagues leave some time ago—they'd all called out their goodbyes and clapped Gabriel on the back on their way past—but she hadn't realised that the entire place had almost emptied out. It was most definitely time to leave.

'Tonight turned out nothing like I imagined it would,' she confessed, as she watched him put on his jacket. It fitted him like a glove, and she couldn't stop her eyes dancing over the front of his shirt as it went taut with his movement.

'Well, that makes two of us.'

They stood for a moment, awkward for the first time all night, before he ducked his head slightly and smiled down at her. For a brief moment she thought he was going to kiss her again.

'Would it be strange to ask for your number?'

Ella blushed. It had been a long time since her cheeks had flushed red, years in fact, but somehow Gabriel had turned her into a teenager again. 'It would be strange if you didn't.'

They both laughed, and Ella clapped her hand over her mouth, mortified at her terrible attempt at flirting.

'I'm sorry, I'm very out of practice.'

'Me too. You're forgetting I was the one thinking it was strange to ask for the number of a girl I like.'

A girl he liked? She cleared her throat and took his phone when he passed it to her, deciding not to say anything else in case she further embarrassed herself. Perhaps he'd meant to say *a girl he used to like.* They'd talked all evening, remembering things about the past that they'd both long forgotten—until now—and yet now that it was time to part ways, she'd never felt so awkward around another human being. It was just like being sixteen with him again.

Ella tapped her name and number into his phone before passing it back to him.

'It's been great seeing you again tonight, Ella.'

She nodded. 'Same here.'

They stood for another long moment, although this time it didn't seem so awkward.

'I'll walk you out.'

Ella moved slightly in front of him, keeping her head down as she walked out of the door onto the pavement. There was a car waiting at the kerb, and when Gabriel gestured towards it, she bristled for a second, thinking he was expecting her to go home with him. She liked him, but she certainly wasn't there yet, and she didn't want to think he'd misread her intention.

'I—' she started.

'I ordered you an Uber,' he interrupted, clearly realising that she was uncomfortable. 'You don't mind, do you?'

'No, I don't mind at all.' She was relieved when he stood back and indicated that she should get in, wishing she hadn't doubted him.

'Thanks for a great night.'

Gabriel slipped his hands into his pockets as he watched her, and she gave him one last, long look before shaking her head and opening the car door. Talk about a night full of surprises.

She looked out of the window as the car rolled forwards, holding her hand up in a wave as he began to walk in the opposite direction. Ella only hoped that he hadn't used all his spare money on her Uber, but if he had, it only made her think once again what a gentleman he was. *So much for chivalry being dead.* Gabriel had clearly been raised by someone who'd taught him the importance of looking after a woman, and if she ever met that person, she'd be sure to show her appreciation.

*

It wasn't until Ella fell into her flat twenty minutes later and locked the door behind her that she realised she'd forgotten all about showing Gabe the sheet of music that she'd had tucked in her bag. She laughed as she kicked off her shoes and padded across the wood floor to her bedroom, wondering how something that had consumed her for the past two weeks could so easily be forgotten. Although he had been rather distracting.

She touched her bag, unzipping it to check that she hadn't somehow dropped the music by mistake, and as she did so her phone buzzed. Ella took it out and glanced at the messages, seeing she'd missed one from Kate and also one from Daisy, who was wanting to see how it had gone with Gabriel. She quickly texted her back.

You could have warned me how gorgeous he was! I'm still recovering! And it's such a small world, because we actually went to school together. I pined over him when I was sixteen and he left London to pursue his dreams!

She flopped down onto her bed, phone still in hand, and clicked on the new email that had just come through. Mia. Oh, *that* Mia!

Ella quickly scanned the message, hardly able to believe that she'd heard back so quickly, or at all.

Hello Ella,

Thanks for reaching out. I don't know if I can help you, but if you'd like to meet for a coffee or lunch one day, I'd be more than happy to answer any questions you might have about my aunt. It's all such a mystery, these little boxes. I still can't stop thinking about them, and how fortunate it was that I found them at all.

Mia

Ella reread the email, more slowly this time. She'd had a few drinks, and she wouldn't normally respond to emails when she was tipsy, but she knew that if she didn't reply to Mia immediately, she'd only lie awake and think about it all night.

Her mind began to spin with all the questions she had to ask her, but she had to remind herself that Mia knew nothing about her grandmother, or at least that's what she'd said at the lawyer's office. But if she could better understand how her grandmother had ended up being born there, or if there were any records at all that could be of help to her, maybe it would take her one step closer to finding out the truth about her family's past.

CHAPTER 9

Ella stretched, sunlight rousing her awake. She squeezed her eyes more tightly shut, regretting not pulling the blinds before going to bed. It took her a moment to recalibrate and figure out what day it was. *Saturday*. She didn't have to open the gallery today, although she'd head in there on her way out for coffee just to check that everything was running smoothly.

Mia.

She sat bolt upright when she remembered that Mia had emailed, fumbling for her phone to see whether she'd replied again. Ella had messaged back immediately asking if she were free for coffee that morning, and she didn't want to miss her if she'd said yes. Her head was a little fuzzy from the gin she'd consumed the night before, so she was happy to stay sitting in bed, covers pulled to her waist, smiling to herself when she saw there was another reply.

Sure, let's meet today at 11am.

Ella grinned, about to get out of bed and attempt to make herself presentable, when another message appeared, this one a text. Gabriel?

Didn't you have a sheet of music you wanted to show me? G

She stared down at her phone, seeing Gabriel's smile in her mind as she replied. It really had been a great night, the best she'd had in a long time.

Can't believe I never showed it to you.

She waited, tucking back down under her covers as she saw the little bubbles on the screen that told her he was typing straight back. They'd been having such a great time, it had completely slipped her mind to show him the night before.

Do you have time this afternoon to show me? I'll be at rehearsals, but we take a break at 3pm?

Ella smiled at her phone.

Sure. I'll bring coffee. Espresso? Flat white?

The little bubbles appeared and then disappeared, and Ella waited a moment before deciding she really did need to get in the shower. If she was seeing Gabriel, she was definitely washing her hair and putting some time into getting ready. She abandoned her phone and was just stripping out of her pyjamas when her phone pinged again.

Double shot espresso. The next one's on me.

Followed by:

Just wait outside the rear door and I'll come out and meet you.

A shiver of anticipation ran through Ella as she dropped her phone to the bed again and hurried to the shower. She very much liked that he was already thinking of the next time they'd have coffee together.

Dating hadn't been on her radar for months. She'd been too busy with work, and although she'd dabbled in the apps, she'd felt uncomfortable meeting someone that way. Not to mention that the pandemic had completely ruined any chance of meeting someone organically. But spending time with Gabe, meeting someone who had the ability to make her heart race, was telling her that perhaps her all work, no play attitude was in need of tweaking. And maybe half her problem was that she found it hard to trust someone new. But Gabe wasn't new, he was someone she already felt she could at least halfway trust, and perhaps that was exactly what she'd been looking for.

*

Ella was early. She'd already stopped in at the gallery and made sure everything was under control, before walking down to the café where she'd arranged to meet Mia. It was a fifteen-minute walk but she'd enjoyed the fresh air, and now she was already finishing off her muffin and latte as Mia walked through the door. Ella quickly brushed her fingers on the napkin and rose to wave.

'Hi, Ella,' Mia said as she sat down.

'Thank you so much for offering to meet me. I hope you didn't have to change your plans?'

'Not at all. Do you want another coffee?'

Ella shook her head. 'No, but let me get yours.'

They chatted for a few minutes about the weather and what to drink before Ella went up to the counter and ordered. When she returned, Mia was absently touching the sugars on the table, her fingers moving gently over the edges of each packet as if she were deep in thought. She looked different to when Ella had first met her—her hair was loose about her shoulders, and she was dressed down in jeans and trainers, the complete opposite to how she'd been dressed the other day in a silk shirt and smart shoes. She definitely appeared much more relaxed.

'I have so many questions, I don't even know where to begin.'

Mia smiled up at her. 'I have so many questions too. I know how you feel.'

'You do?'

'I was also left a box. Well, the box had my aunt's name on it, and because she had no children, I was the one to claim it.'

Ella's eyes widened. 'Have you made head or tail of it? Of what was left for her?' Mia shook her head. 'No, but this one was different to the others. This one had been opened, presumably by my aunt, but then put with the others beneath the floorboards. It was obvious the string had already been pulled, and it wasn't as dusty as the others.' She laughed nervously. 'Would you believe, my box had nothing in it. It was my greatest fear, when I had you all summoned by her lawyer, that there might be nothing in all the others either, so I was actually relieved to hear from you.'

If Ella's curiosity had been piqued before, now she was downright hooked.

'There was nothing? Not even one clue?'

'Not a thing,' Mia said. 'But it only makes me even more fascinated by your box.'

'Would you like to take a look? Just in case the clues left inside mean something to you?' She reached into her bag and took out the little box, carefully passing it to Mia. 'They honestly mean nothing to me, no matter how much I stare at them.'

Ella watched as Mia studied both items, before putting them back down. 'When I found the boxes, I had this overwhelming feeling that they had to be reunited with the person on the tag, or at the very least a descendant of that person.' She hesitated. 'I actually found a list of names on her desk, names that all matched up with the boxes left behind. It made me more determined than ever to honour her life's work, or at least try to.'

'You think she'd made a list of the women she had to contact? That she intended sending the boxes to their rightful owners before she passed away?'

'That's what I'd like to believe.' Mia folded her hands on the table, and Ella could see how much it all meant to her. 'If there was more that I could tell you, I would. Part of me wonders if the boxes were ever supposed to be discovered at all, or if these were the ones that weren't to be shared, as if my aunt had hidden them for good reason. But I couldn't let them all be destroyed with the house. If I had, I would have always wondered if they contained something important, some part of someone's heritage that was supposed to be uncovered.'

Ella reached across the table and touched Mia's hand, seeing the tears shining in her eyes. She could see what a difficult decision it must have been for her to make.

'You did the right thing. You gave granddaughters like me the opportunity to find out about our family's past. Each recipient can make their own decision, and that's what's important, Mia. You gave us the choice.'

'You truly think so? You don't think I've disrespected my aunt by taking the things she'd hidden?'

Ella shook her head. 'No, I don't think that. I think that you've done something very special.'

'My aunt, she dedicated her life to helping women, but I know very little about why. She must have helped hundreds of pregnant girls over the years, and delivered equally as many babies. If there's one thing I'm certain of, it's that the women she took into her care would have been abandoned by their families if not for her.'

'And yet there were only seven boxes hidden?' Ella said. 'Despite all those babies she delivered?'

'Eight, actually. If you count the one bearing her own name. But I suppose that doesn't count, given it was empty. The writing on it is different and the box doesn't match the others either.'

'Perhaps someone once made her a little keepsake box to say thank you, and it inspired her to create all the other ones? Perhaps that is the link. Maybe that's why there was nothing inside it, and she just kept it as a memento? To remind herself why she was doing all this.'

Mia nodded as her coffee arrived. 'Perhaps. But none of this is helping you, is it? I wish there was more I could do, some way I could help you to figure out what your clues mean.'

'You've done more than enough,' Ella said. 'In fact, you've made me even more determined to find out what this all means.'

'Is your grandmother still alive?'

'No,' Ella replied. 'I loved her so much. She helped me through a very difficult time, and the more I think about all this, the more I want to understand her past. It feels like something I can do for her, even though she's not here anymore. Does that sound silly?'

'No,' Mia said, smiling over her coffee cup. 'It sounds beautiful, and it's also similar to what another granddaughter recently told me.'

Ella felt her eyebrows lift in surprise. 'One of the other women, from the day we received the boxes?'

Mia nodded. 'Her name is Claudia. She recently sent me a letter to say that following her clues completely changed her life, and that she's found family that she never even knew existed.'

'Was her family in London?' Ella asked, barely able to contain her curiosity.

'Would you believe she ended up in Cuba?' Mia said. 'I still smile thinking about what she wrote to me. It's made all my anxiety over my decision worth it.'

They both sat back as Mia sipped her coffee, the clues still sitting on the table in front of them as Ella wondered how she was going to decipher them and whether, just like Claudia, the key to understanding them might be abroad.

*

Ella usually either worked or thought about work over the weekend. She wasn't quite certain when she'd become a workaholic, but after having a fun Saturday flitting between seeing Mia and then picking up coffee to deliver to Gabriel, she was starting to see that perhaps other people actually spent their weekends doing more pleasurable things.

She stood for a moment outside the Barbican Centre, taking the time to appreciate what a beautiful building it was before walking to what she hoped was the correct door. She'd studied art as well as history at university, and she was beginning to see that she'd been rushing through life so fast she was barely stopping to appreciate architecture and landmarks in the way she should.

'Ella!'

Ella looked up and realised she was precariously close to tipping over the tray she was carrying. Gabriel was walking towards her in faded blue jeans, a white T-shirt and scuffed boots, the complete opposite of his appearance the night before, but somehow he looked even better. How was it that some men could improve with age? It was certainly the case with Gabe.

'Hey!' She righted the tray and held out his coffee. 'I come bearing caffeine!'

He grinned and lifted the cup, taking a sip and making a sound like it was the best thing he'd tasted all day.

'I wish we hadn't stayed out so late last night. It's made today brutal.'

She winced. 'Sorry. You can blame me for that.'

They stood for a moment, and she cleared her throat, surprised by how nervous she felt.

'Does it feel like work when you're rehearsing? I mean, when you love what you do so much, does it still feel like a job?'

They fell into step beside each other, slowly wandering, coffees in hand.

'Some days it does. It can be a real grind, just like any other job. But when it all comes together, when everything just falls into place, then no. It feels like magic then.'

Ella watched the way his eyes lit up, the way he was so passionate about his work. Some days her work set her on fire and ignited something within her that reminded her why she was so good at her job, why she loved what she did so much. But other days she wondered if she'd always feel that way, if she was simply channelling her love of creating art into other artists' work. And whether she could feasibly keep that up long term. Or not.

'I only have ten minutes before I have to get back in there, so if you'd like to show me the—'

'Yes! Of course.' She gave him her coffee to hold and then took the box from her bag and removed the sheet of music. They swapped items and she watched him as he looked over the sheet, taking his time to study it.

'How old do you think it is?'

'Honestly, I have no idea. I was hoping you might be able to help me with that.'

'Hmm,' Gabriel said, his eyebrows pulling down into a frown. 'What is it?'

'I don't immediately have any thoughts, but it's a complex piece of music. Whoever was playing this was a serious musician, someone extremely capable.'

'Well, that's more than I knew before I showed it to you, so thank you.'

Gabriel took another sip of his coffee, still studying the paper. 'Could I borrow this? To show some of the others inside? You never know whether someone might recognise the piece specifically, or even recognise the note or the sign off.'

She hesitated, feeling oddly connected to the clue she'd been carrying around for the past few days. He must have noticed, because he immediately took a step closer to her and gave her an earnest kind of look. He even reached out and touched her wrist with his thumb.

'I promise I'll guard it with my life. I know how important it is to you. And I'll make a copy so I can give you back the original.'

'Of course, it's silly when it means nothing to me at this point anyway.' She glanced at his hand, at the way he'd so casually touched her.

'It doesn't mean nothing to you, Ella, it was left to your grandmother at her birth. That means something, even if you haven't worked out the connection yet, so I promise I'll look after it.'

She nodded. 'Yes, you're right. It does mean something. It means more than I probably want to admit. It's just frustrating not understanding how it's linked to her.'

'How about I take you out to dinner tomorrow night, so I can return it to you?'

'Dinner?' She tried not to smile too hard.

'Dinner,' he confirmed, as he started to walk backwards. 'I have to get back, but it was great seeing you. Thanks for the coffee.' He stopped again and grinned. 'It's been really good seeing you again, Ella.'

She couldn't help but grin back at him. 'It's been good seeing you again too.'

Ella stood and watched him go; the gorgeous man who'd surprised her in the most pleasant of ways, and whom she'd just agreed to go out for dinner with. She groaned as she walked back the way she'd come, still clutching her coffee, knowing that now she was going to wonder for the rest of the weekend whether he'd actually asked her out on a date, or whether it was just a convenient way to give her back the sheet of music. Or perhaps it was simply because they were old friends who hadn't seen each other in years…

Thirty minutes later, Ella found herself standing in an art supplies shop. They were about to close, and she couldn't decide whether she was being ridiculous or whether she should just buy all the things she needed. The girl behind the counter was looking less than impressed, and kept making a show of looking at her watch, which wasn't helping. Ella went to the paints, her hand hovering as she studied them.

What harm is there in buying supplies? I don't even have to use them if I don't want to.

She looked at her own watch and saw that it was almost five o'clock now. *Just do it.*

Ella marched over to the front of the store and collected a basket, instinctively filling it with the paint and brushes she needed. She paid for it all and left the store lugging two large paper bags, not sure whether she'd gone mad. She hadn't so much as picked up a paintbrush in years; the feel of the brush against her fingers was foreign to her now, whereas once it had been as familiar to her as eating or breathing. But she was convinced it would all come back to her, a muscle that simply needing flexing.

When she was back at her flat she left her purchases on the table and went into her bedroom, opening her wardrobe and standing on tiptoe to take down the box she'd placed on a shelf in there when she'd moved in a few years earlier. It was nondescript, and no one else would have bothered to look inside, but when she'd filled it, it had been with the possessions that meant more to her than anything in the world.

She sat cross-legged with the box on the ground, slowly opening the lid and staring down at it. On top was a photo, and tears filled her eyes as she lifted it out. It was her and Harrison, her big brother, with his arm around her as they sat on the beach. She remembered the holiday: it was only about a year before he died, and she could almost hear his deep belly laugh, feel the weight of his arm as he slung it around her shoulders, as they'd tried to keep from laughing long enough for the photo to be taken.

Ella dabbed at her eyes with her knuckles and took out the tubes of paint and some of her old favourite brushes from the shoebox. They were so dry they resembled the little stiff branches of a tree, but when she held them in her hands, she knew that if she were to clean her brushes and dip them in paint, if she were to start painting then and there, a blank canvas in front of her, it would all come back to her as if she'd never stopped.

At the bottom she took out a postcard and slowly lifted it, placing her other hand over her mouth. The picture on the front was of Italy, and when she turned the card over, she could have recited the words without looking, even though it had been years since she'd last read them.

It's amazing, Ellie, you'd love it here. Promise me you'll take a gap year and travel with me! Don't listen to Mum and Dad, they have no idea what they're talking about. H.

Ella slowly put everything away, the memories too painful to remember for very long, but it did make her wonder what someone else would think if they were given this box, if what was inside would paint a picture of who she was. Of where she'd come from and what had happened to her. Would a stranger be able to find her from a collection of art supplies, a photo and a postcard?

She very much doubted it. But it did make her realise the importance of the clues she'd been given, of what they might have meant to her great-grandmother. Of what they might mean to her and the rest of her family if she could only discover why they'd been left behind, or what they were supposed to be pointing her towards.

Her brother had died in Italy. The car he'd been driving had somehow swerved off the road and collided with a power line, killing him instantly. So instead of joining her big brother on his travels and taking a gap year, painting her way through Tuscany, she'd ended up packing her things away forever, too numb to be creative, and following the path her parents had been pushing her towards for so long. Harrison had understood her; he'd seen her for who she truly was, knew that creating art had been like breathing for her. But that was all another lifetime ago.

She carefully placed the lid back on the box and stood on tiptoe again to return it to the shelf. *But what if it wasn't another lifetime ago? What if, instead of running from the past, I embraced it? Only in Greece, not Italy?*

Harrison, what would you do?

CHAPTER 10

London, 1967

'My darling Alexandra. It's so wonderful to see you again.'

They'd only just arrived in London, the night air cooler than she was used to, the fog seeming to cling to them as they stood outside the house, but her aunt's embrace was the exact opposite of the weather. She held her tightly in her arms, and Alexandra clung to her, no longer used to such affection after five weeks without her mother, relishing the warmth of her hold. Her father hadn't so much as brushed against her or patted her arm this past month, let alone thought to hold her as she grieved.

'Nicholas, it's good to see you again,' her aunt said briskly as she finally let go of Alexandra and ushered them both inside. 'I only wish it were under better circumstances.'

Alexandra stood back a moment, waiting for her father to go first and then following after him, watching the way he manoeuvred past her mother's sister so that he didn't have to touch her. She wondered where her cousins were, but then heard a noise upstairs and guessed they were probably on their way down to join them. But it was her uncle who surprised her, appearing from another room and embracing her in much the same way as her aunt had. Her father hardly seemed to notice the exchange.

'Alexandra, look at you! Last time I saw you, you were barely as tall as my hip. What a beautiful young woman you've become.' Only her aunt had come to her mother's funeral, which meant it had been some time since she'd seen her uncle.

She blushed when he held her at arm's length, before bellowing out to his children to come down. When they did, she found herself feeling shy all over again, looking down at her shoes as they poured into the room. As an only child, she was always fascinated with larger families, had always imagined being part of one, but it was also sometimes overwhelming when she was surrounded by others.

'You remember your cousins, Alexandra?' her aunt said, coming to stand beside her, her hand warm on her arm as she faced her children.

She smiled at the youngest, Thomas, who was grinning up at her, his hands clasped together as he rocked back and forth on his shiny little black leather shoes. Her closest cousin in age, Belle, smiled, but it was her other boy cousin, William, who made her laugh as he gave her a wink.

'Alex, it's good to see you again.'

Her aunt sighed beside her and gave him a withering look. 'Alex*andra*,' she said. 'Her name is Alexandra.'

He shrugged and gave her a grin that made her smile in return. 'Actually, Alex is fine,' she said, surprised when her voice came out so clear. No one had ever called her Alex before, but when William had said it, she liked it. It made her feel different, and now that she was in London, perhaps different was what she needed.

Her father was talking to her uncle now, and her aunt swept her and her cousins into the dining room, which had been set and was already beginning to fill with plates of food.

'I hope everything is to your liking, Alexandra. I know it will all seem very different to what you're used to in Greece, and I so much want you to feel at home here.' She paused. 'Perhaps I can get your cook to send over some of your favourite recipes for us to try?'

'I'm—'

'No need to treat her as a child, Elizabeth,' her father said as he joined them. 'Alexandra is grateful to be given refuge here, considering our most unfortunate circumstances. She doesn't need to be pampered and will eat whatever is put in front of her.'

Everyone fell silent then, an uncomfortable hush spreading across the room.

'Your daughter has just lost her mother, Nicholas,' her aunt said pointedly, after a particularly long pause. 'I should hope that those are the circumstances that you're referring to. And I, for one, believe that some familiar home comforts are the least I can offer to make my niece feel welcome. It's what any thoughtful host would do, regardless.'

Alexandra picked nervously at her nails, seeing how red her father's face had become. She knew how easy it was to anger him, and her aunt certainly wasn't trying to avoid it. She hadn't realised that Elizabeth disliked her father quite so much; or perhaps she was only showing her dislike now that her sister had passed away. Perhaps she no longer had to pretend.

'Of course,' he said, taking his seat at the table and giving Alexandra a look she wasn't certain how to react to, as if perhaps her aunt's displeasure was somehow her fault. 'But one cannot ignore the fact that we had to leave our home in an unexpected hurry. I shall be grieving my country during our absence, as it's not simply a wife I've lost, but my home. Not to mention the state of the Greek monarchy right now.'

Alexandra hadn't been told much, but she had listened to every whisper and conversation that she could lend her ear to, which meant she'd quickly gleaned what she needed to before they'd arrived. It seemed that the royal family was also heading for London, albeit not immediately, and she'd heard her father speaking to another of the King's advisers who'd also left with his family. But it certainly didn't appear that they would all be away from Greece for an extended period; only long enough for the situation to be handled. From the whispers she'd heard, these things never lasted long, a year or so perhaps, but no longer, and her father was to remain in the King's employ.

'Alexandra, we're so pleased to have you here with us,' her uncle said, raising his glass and indicating for everyone else to do the same. It was only then she noticed that their wine glasses were already full, although when she picked hers up and took a small sip, she realised hers was grape juice.

Her cousins smiled at her from across the table, quiet as mice even though last time she'd seen them, a few years previously, they'd been as raucous as could be. Although perhaps that was the difference between visiting the family with her mother, compared to this visit with her father. Or else her aunt had insisted they be on their best behaviour for this one occasion.

She only wished that dinner could be over as quickly as possible, because then it would be time for her father to leave, and perhaps she would be able to breathe again. She was fast realising that being in her father's company was more stifling than a Greek summer.

*

Alexandra stepped closer to the window and gently moved the thick velvet curtain aside. When her father had stood to leave, giving her a cursory pat on the shoulder as he muttered goodbye to her, her aunt had stormed after him as if she'd waited all night to give him a very forthright piece of her mind. Which had left Alexandra in the dining room with her cousins, who were slowly starting to talk and joke with one another in the way she remembered, their voices no longer hushed now that there were no adults near.

'What are they saying?' Belle asked, coming to stand beside her.

'I think your mother is giving him a telling-off,' Alexandra whispered, leaning so close to the glass she almost had her ear pressed against it. She could see her aunt standing with her hands on her hips, illuminated under the outside light, and her father trying to back away from her. 'She seems very cross with him.'

'Come with me,' Belle said, taking her hand. 'It'll be much easier to hear if we hide behind the front door.'

Alexandra scurried along with her cousin, still holding her hand as they pressed themselves against the short bit of wall beside the front door, which had conveniently been left ajar. Belle smiled at her, and Alexandra found herself smiling back, one of the first smiles she remembered since *that* day.

'You're treating her as if she's a possession you no longer want, Nicholas. She's your daughter, in case you've forgotten!' her aunt roared. 'Not to mention that she's a young girl grieving for her mother. She needs her father.'

'She most certainly doesn't need me,' her father blustered in reply. 'She's far better here with you.'

There was silence for a moment, and Belle patted her hand. 'Alex, we can be like sisters while you're here. You know you'll always be made to feel welcome here, don't you? We're all so happy to have you, and you'll have the room beside mine.'

'Thank you,' Alexandra whispered in reply, swallowing away her tears but so thankful for the kindness being extended to her.

She wished she could tell Belle just how much it meant to her, but the words simply wouldn't come.

Belle leaned in close to her again as if she were about to speak, but the argument thundering back to life outside again made them both freeze to the spot.

'And where exactly do you plan to go, Nicholas? To Rome, with the royal family? Or are you going to be travelling abroad as a bachelor?'

He cleared his throat, and that seemed to anger her aunt, because her voice increased in volume. Alexandra knew that he should be referred to as a widower, not a bachelor, which made it abundantly obvious that her aunt was trying to anger her father.

'Where are you going, Nicholas? If I'm to take your daughter in, don't you think I at least need to know where her father intends on residing? Where we can find you if the need arises.'

'I shall be visiting the King in a professional capacity, and then travelling to the South of France, but I see no reason why you could possibly need to know my whereabouts.'

Belle tightened her hold on Alexandra's hand then, at the same moment as Alexandra squeezed her eyes shut, wishing she hadn't heard her father's cruel words. He was discarding his daughter, and he was using their temporary exile, and his new life as an unmarried man, to enjoy the South of France for the rest of the summer. There was no hiding that he was happy to be without her. She doubted he'd even considered taking her with him.

'What happened to the charismatic, loving man who my sister married all those years ago?'

There was a long pause, and Alexandra could almost hear the silent pain that rested between them. She'd heard the stories of how her father had courted her mother, how impressed he'd been with the beautiful woman who'd been in command of horses that would test the abilities of the most capable of men. But she'd also heard whispers that her mother had been too good for him, that he'd used her connections to the royal family for his own personal gain, that he'd taken command of her mother's fortune the moment her parents had passed away. And she knew too that if her father had married for love, he couldn't have carried on so easily after her mother's death, as much as she wished it were different.

'I shall check in on Alexandra periodically, and I shall ensure she has funds enough to—'

'We don't want your money, Nicholas! You know perfectly well that's not what this conversation is about, and if you don't, then you're more fool than I thought.'

'You're acting as if my family hasn't just had to flee Greece!' her father declared. 'The King was forced to stage a coup against the government, and—'

'My husband has ensured that I've stayed very much up to date with what is happening in your country,' Elizabeth said calmly, which seemed to infuriate her father even more. 'I'm terribly sorry that the monarchy isn't receiving the respect it deserves, but Nicholas, in case you've forgotten, you're not the King—you are one of his advisers. And in case you've also forgotten, you had already decided well before this unfortunate turn of events that you were going to send your daughter to me. Please don't pretend otherwise, for it would only be insulting to both me and Alexandra.'

Belle pulled her away then, as her mother's furious footsteps echoed towards them, the conversation clearly over, but they didn't move quickly enough. Her cousin kept moving, but Alexandra stopped and waited to be discovered, not wanting to show defiance on her first night in her aunt's home. She'd been eavesdropping, and she wasn't going to pretend otherwise.

But if she'd been about to tell her off for listening, the tears shining in Alexandra's eyes must have stopped her, for her aunt merely opened her arms and she fled into them, needing her affection more now than ever before. Elizabeth's hold was firm, as if she never wanted to let her go.

'My darling girl,' her aunt said, stepping back just enough so that she could gently wipe Alexandra's tears from her cheeks. 'I intend on loving you as if you are my own child, do you hear me? You will find only love and kindness in our home. I just wish you hadn't had to hear any of that.'

Alexandra nodded, and her aunt tucked her fingers beneath her chin and lifted her face so that they were looking into each other's eyes.

'Your mother meant the world to me, second only to my own children. Your father might not be grieving her in the same way that you are, but I want you to know that *I* am. I feel her loss as keenly as if one of my limbs had been ripped from my body, and that means you can come to me whenever you need to cry or talk about her. I will always be here for you, my love, *always*. You'll never be alone again.'

Alexandra nodded again, as a fat tear escaped and slipped down her cheek. She had never not loved her aunt, but now she truly saw her as her mother's sister, as the only woman who could ever come close to replacing her mother in her life. As someone grieving her mother as deeply as she was herself.

Her aunt took another step back, but not before taking Alexandra's hand.

'Do you play the violin?'

Alexandra shook her head.

'The piano?'

She shook her head again, embarrassed that she had learnt neither. She had always enjoyed music, but she'd received singing lessons instead of taking up an instrument.

'Then come with me. Perhaps learning to play something will help to settle your mind. I know it always helps me. Or would you rather read?'

'No, thank you,' she said quickly. 'I would much prefer to learn to play an instrument.'

'While you're here, my darling, you will find life perhaps simpler than it was for you in Greece.' Her aunt's smile was kind, her gaze warm. 'I suspect you'll come to like finding yourself here, without being part of such an exclusive social circle. In fact, your mother and I often spoke of it, of you spending time here as a young adult without the pressures of being in Greece.'

'You did?' Why had her mother never said anything to her? It would have made coming to London so much easier if she'd known it was part of her mother's plan for her future.

'We were always exchanging letters, and it was one of the things she wrote of most. Giving you a year or two in London, away from Athens, although I dare say she'd have liked to come with you.'

Alexandra followed her aunt upstairs, unable to stop herself from comparing this kind, warm woman to her mother. They were so similar, both in looks and demeanour, and she began to wonder why she'd ever thought to resist the opportunity to move into her home. She would never stop missing her mother, but she couldn't help but wonder if this was where her mama would have wanted her to be in her absence. With the only other woman in the world who could love her as if she were her own.

And maybe one day she'd tell her aunt why she could no longer read; why she would forever punish herself by removing books from her life. She squeezed her eyes shut for a moment as that day came flooding back to her—most of the time she was able to push it from her mind, but other times it was like a wave crashing through her thoughts, and there was nothing she could do not to remember.

CHAPTER 11

Present Day

The restaurant was completely different to the bar they'd spent their first night at. Ella walked in and looked around, liking the light-filled space and immediately imagining the walls hung with beautiful pieces of art. She was just about to tell the maître d' that she had a booking, when Gabriel caught her eye, standing and waving to her from a table at the back. She gestured towards him and walked through the restaurant, her skin flushing when he leaned over and kissed her cheek.

'You look beautiful,' he said, smiling as they both sat down.

'Thank you. It's so nice to be out for dinner on a Sunday night.'

'Not your usual way to end the week?'

Ella laughed. 'Most definitely not. I'm usually eating takeout with my diary in front of me on a Sunday, planning out the week ahead for work.'

He looked like he was struggling not to laugh.

'I sound like a complete bore, don't I?'

'No, you sound like a woman who takes her work very seriously. There's nothing wrong with that.' Gabriel picked up the wine list, smiling at her over the top of it. 'In fact, I wouldn't expect anything less from London's most successful young art dealer.'

Ella blushed. 'Has someone been reading up on me?'

He put the list down. 'Graduated from Sotheby's Institute of Art with an MA in Art Business, made her mark on the art world by selling a Warhol for over one million pounds before she was twenty-five, and was then asked to open what has become one of Soho's, if not *London's*, most exciting new galleries showcasing work from contemporary artists in England and abroad. Does that sound about right?'

'It sounds like I should have done some reading of my own, on *you*,' she said, shaking her head and leaning back in her chair.

'I'm impressed,' he said. 'You've accomplished a lot since graduating. I only wish I'd thought to look you up before now.'

Ella was never comfortable talking about her own success, but she also knew that she should accept his praise graciously. She *had* achieved a lot; she just wasn't great at acknowledging it. 'Thank you. It's been a busy few years. But tell me more about you. I want to know everything that happened between your leaving school and now. How did you become a member of the London Symphony Orchestra?'

'How about I order the wine first? It's a long story.'

They swapped smiles, and Ella found herself wondering how, after kissing so many frogs over the past ten years, she'd managed to pick up with Gabe so effortlessly. She was going to have to send Daisy a gift basket, although the thought alone made her want to laugh. Was a gift basket appropriate thanks for the woman who'd so nonchalantly put her in Gabriel's path again? Perhaps she should think of something more extravagant.

'First of all, do you like rosé, and second, why are you smiling like that?'

Ella bit her lip for a moment to disguise her smile. 'Yes to the rosé, it's my favourite, but I have no idea what smile you're talking about.'

Gabriel just shook his head and waved the server over, ordering a bottle of wine before leaning back in his chair.

'So tell me, how does a man convince his family that being a musician is a good idea, or did they always believe in your talent? I don't think I ever met your family when we were younger.'

Gabriel blew out a breath. 'Straight to the hard questions. I feel like you're speaking from experience.'

'Let's just say that my parents squashed my plans to be an artist. Apparently it wouldn't pay the bills.' She knew she really needed to let that go, but she'd been dwelling on it a lot lately. Or perhaps she was just frustrated with herself for not being braver, or for still being scared of what her parents might think if she didn't fulfil their expectations. Surely she was too old to still be carrying that kind of baggage.

'Ahh, the old pay-the-bills guilt trip. You know, that's ironic, because you're making a living selling other people's art, and I'd say those artists are very much able to pay their bills, and then some.'

Ella groaned. 'Tell me about it. I often sit at my parents' dinner table and want to scream at them about how well my artists are doing. That when they praise me for the huge sales I make, or whatever they read about online, I'm making big money not just for the gallery, but for the artists too. At least when it comes to their new pieces. It's almost like they can't see that, or maybe they just think that being the broker rather than the talent is a safer bet.' She closed her eyes for a moment, feeling her heart begin to race. 'I'm sorry, I—'

'Don't be. I get it. Artists, musicians, we're all the same. We try to create a living from doing what we love, and to make that work, we have to be the very best in our field, otherwise we make nothing. But not everyone supports that, or knows how to accept it.'

Their wine arrived and Ella watched the light pink liquid fill her glass. When he was finished, Gabriel held up his glass and she clinked hers to it.

'To doing what we love.'

She met his gaze. 'To doing what we love.' Ella took a sip of her wine. 'So tell me—your family. How did they react when you told them you wanted to be a musician? You didn't actually answer my question before.'

'You're going to hate me for saying this, but my family have always been very supportive of what I do.' He took a sip of wine. 'I mean, don't get me wrong, I'm sure they would have liked me to go to university and take a more traditional path just for security's sake, but they sacrificed so much when I was younger to support my passion. And it helped that my grandfather was a musician too. He spent ten years with the LSO.'

'So you've followed in his footsteps? That's amazing that you're playing in the same orchestra as he was.'

'It is. In fact, when he died he left me his cello. I wasn't old enough to appreciate it then, but it's one of my most treasured possessions now.'

'That's so special. It must have made him so proud to see you so passionate about music.'

He nodded. 'It did. It was something that made us very close and helped me to feel close to him after he died too. Money was always tight, but my parents knew how much my lessons meant to me, and they never let me miss one. Now I'm old enough to reflect, I can't imagine the things they must have gone without to make that happen.'

'I love that,' Ella said, thinking of her own parents and their disapproving gaze when she'd opened up to them about the career she'd always dreamed of. 'I think so many parents try to put their own hopes and aspirations on their kids, rather than helping their child's own dreams come to fruition.'

'I wonder sometimes if parents even realise they do that,' he said. 'Sometimes I think they project themselves onto their offspring without even realising.'

Ella sat back, relaxed in his company. 'Tell me how long you play for. Is it a long season?'

'Our season has almost ended here, although we're touring at the end of summer this year,' he said. 'You know, the season ending is one of those things that I look forward to on the one hand, but on the other, I'm playing with almost a hundred other musicians every night. It's this magical feeling that just never gets old, so I don't want it to end either.'

'I wish you could see the way your eyes light up when you talk about playing,' she said, smiling across the table at him. 'What do you do when you're not working? No, let me guess, I bet you play for fun at home. Or maybe you busk. Yes! I can see you busking on the street with your little hat out for tips.'

'Oh, really? You can see me busking, eh?' He pretended to look offended, only he couldn't keep a straight face. 'I most definitely don't go from one of the most prestigious orchestras in London to the streets,' he said in a posh voice.

'Now, the clues,' he said. 'We have to remember to actually talk about your clues this time. I'd hate to have to message you tonight telling you we managed to forget about them all over again.'

Then again, she thought, *another excuse for dinner would be nice.*

'Yes, the clues,' she said, as Gabriel passed her the piece of folded paper she'd given him the previous day. 'Did you have any luck deciphering anything about it?'

She took out her bag and carefully tucked the paper inside, beside the photo she'd brought with her. Ever since she'd been given them, she'd preferred to keep them with her, not wanting to risk losing them or somehow misplacing them.

'I showed your sheet of music to a few friends after rehearsals, and I couldn't stop looking at it that night. There's something about it that makes me think I'll be able to understand it if I only stare at it just a bit longer.'

'I know the feeling. I feel like that about the photo.' She put down her wine glass. 'But? You look like you've either discovered something or you're about to give me a *but*.' Her hands went clammy and she folded them in her lap for something to do.

'Don't get too excited just yet, because I don't know how this is going to help you, but I believe your mystery person was a violinist.'

'Like you?' she gasped. 'I can't believe it. What a coincidence would that be?'

'The sheet of music is an excerpt of Pachelbel's "Canon in D".' Gabriel's mouth lifted into a smile. 'Sorry, I can see that means nothing to you. Let me find it so you can listen.'

He took his phone from his pocket and she watched as he searched for the piece and then beckoned for her to come closer. Ella moved her chair around so that she was beside him instead of across the table from him, leaning in when he pressed play, the volume low so as not to disturb the other diners.

The song was familiar to her almost immediately, although she'd never known what it was called. When she looked up, Gabriel was watching her, and she smiled at him.

'I know this,' she said. 'It's beautiful. Don't brides sometimes walk down the aisle to this?'

He nodded. 'They do. To be honest, it took me a moment, seeing this part out of context like that, but the moment I played it—'

'You played the sheet of music I gave you?' She sighed. 'Of course you did. I wish I'd been there to hear it.' *How special would that have been, seeing the sheet of music come to life on his violin.*

'It's a stunning piece when it's played well, and my guess is that it was an important piece for whomever the violinist was. Perhaps they had been practising it for a concert or an audition? Perhaps this was their one chance to prove themselves?' Gabriel laughed. 'I might be getting carried away in the story of it all, but there's something about it, the whole romance of it being left behind, I suppose. I mean, there has to be a story behind it, right?'

'So we're thinking that this piece was for something special, an audition perhaps, and this B, whoever they are, wrote a little note of encouragement on the sheet?'

Gabriel nodded. 'I think that's the only explanation. But how you ever find out who B was, I don't know. It seems like a complete needle-in-a-haystack situation if you ask me, although I'm prepared to keep showing it around. Who knows, maybe one of the older members will know more. Our principal violinist has been away due to illness, but when he's back, I want to see what his take is.'

'Thank you,' Ella said. 'Even if we find out nothing else, I'm so grateful that you've pieced together a little of the puzzle for me.'

'So, what's next?'

She sighed, taking a sip of wine. 'There is no next. I don't know what else I could do, because how would I ever find the women in the photo? I mean, the only thing I'm certain of is that it was taken on one of the Greek islands, potentially the island of Skopelos.'

He leaned forwards, his eyes on hers. 'Ella, what if you went to Greece?'

She spluttered her next sip of wine. 'You think I should travel to Greece?'

'Why not? You've just told me that you don't have any other leads, and if the only starting point is an island…' He laughed. 'Tell me you haven't already considered it?'

She sighed, knowing she needed to be truthful. 'Of course I've considered it. But I decided it was mad and impulsive and—'

'A brilliant idea?' he finished for her, reaching over and stroking her hand, his thumb against hers. 'You've told me a few things tonight. One of them is that the photograph points to Greece, and the other is that you wished you'd followed your heart and become an artist.' He paused, his eyes searching her face. 'So would it be so mad for you to take some time off work to have a holiday, and solve a mystery along the way? There are worse places to go than Greece, you know.'

That made her laugh. 'There are most *definitely* worse places to go than Greece.'

Gabriel poured them both another glass of wine as she digested his words. Would it be so mad to take some time off? She'd been telling herself for months that she needed to have a break, so that she didn't burn out, or that one day she simply might not be able to face going into the gallery. She loved it there, but it took everything from her. And she had seen that gorgeous little house for rent…

'Look, it's not every day you find out that clues left to your grandmother about her birth have surfaced. Your family could have a secret heritage that you'd never otherwise uncover, and who knows? You might have time to rediscover your passion for painting while you're there.'

She didn't tell him that she'd already been so inspired by him that she'd gone and bought supplies to start painting again.

'So I go there with the intention of looking for a beautiful Greek woman who may or may not play the violin?'

Gabriel groaned. 'Unfortunately, I think you're looking for an *old* Greek woman who may or may not play the violin. But there's a chance someone might recognise her in the photo, or remember a woman who left the island to follow her dream of becoming a musician.'

'Or an old man,' Ella mused. 'I keep thinking this sheet of music must have belonged to my great-grandmother, but what if it belonged to my grandma's father? Maybe the music belonged to a man?'

'Do you know what I think?' Gabriel asked.

She watched him expectantly, unable to drag her eyes from his as they seemed to dance under the lights in the restaurant.

'I think we should order our food before the kitchen closes. Our server has been hovering for at least an hour, and I fear that if we don't order what we want soon, the server won't be able to bring us anything.'

They both laughed, and Ella wondered all over again how she could be so relaxed with Gabe after so many years apart. His company was lively and fun, the way he smiled at her making her feel more alive, more *seen*, than she had in a very long time.

'But while we wait for our food, how about you show me the photo?' Gabriel asked, shuffling his chair closer to hers. 'I'm rather invested in the whole mystery of it now.'

Ella grinned, more than happy to oblige as she took the photo from the box and slid it the short distance across the table for Gabriel to see.

*

It had been the most enjoyable evening with Gabe. He was kind and funny and ridiculously charming, and even if they never crossed paths again, she'd had a wonderful time with him. Although deep down, she was very much hoping to see him again.

Ella was home now, although nowhere near ready for bed yet, and she made herself a cup of tea and curled up on the sofa, deciding to text her aunt.

Are you still awake?

By the time she'd taken a sip, the little bubbles appeared on her phone, telling her that Kate was texting her back.

Awake!

She smiled at her phone, imagining the way her aunt would smile to herself as she typed. She texted the same way she spoke: lots of exclamation marks and capitals. She was about to reply when her phone rang. Ella answered it immediately.

'Why are you texting me after ten on a school night?'

Ella laughed. 'Because I've just got home from dinner with the musician, and I'm too wired to sleep.'

Kate gasped. 'The gorgeous violinist? The one you reunited with? Was it a date?'

'I'm not sure. It felt like one, but then he also wanted to tell me what he'd discovered about the sheet of music.'

She filled her aunt in, hearing the excitement in her voice as she asked questions. But it took her until the end of the conversation to tell her what he'd suggested.

'Kate, he had this wild idea that I should go to Greece, to see if I could find the answer to the clues there. Do you think that's completely mad?'

There was a pause before she answered. 'I don't think it's mad at all, and let's be honest, we both know you could do with a break.' Kate laughed. 'I do think it would be a fabulous idea to take the gorgeous musician *with* you though.'

Ella didn't even pretend to be shocked. 'You know, you could always come with me if you're worried about me going on holiday alone.' She'd actually thought about asking Kate on her way home, worried that she might tire of the solitude. *If I go, that is.*

'Darling, I can't. And perhaps being alone isn't the worst thing you could experience.' Ella could practically hear her smile down the line. 'Maybe you could take time to paint again while you're there?'

She didn't tell Kate that was one of the reasons it appealed to her so much; almost as much as trying to solve their family mystery.

'But if you *do* decide you don't want to be alone, I would wholeheartedly support the idea of inviting Gabriel.'

There was no way Ella would ask Gabe. First of all, they were only just getting to know each other again. They'd had a great time together, but asking him to join her in Greece? Not a chance. And wouldn't he have suggested it if he wanted to go with her? Besides, he had his tour to prepare for.

'I'll let you know if Gabriel manages to find out anything else about the music,' Ella said, deliberately not replying about asking him. 'He's taken a copy to show some other musicians, just in case it means something to them.'

'Sounds like an excuse to see you again, if you ask me.'

'Goodnight, Kate.'

Her aunt laughed, wickedly. 'Goodnight, my darling. Sweet dreams.'

Ella hung up and found herself smiling into her cup of tea. Sometimes her aunt was just too much, but then that was one of the reasons she loved her.

But Greece? Could she actually be brave enough to step aside from work for a few weeks and book a trip away on her own?

CHAPTER 12

Two Weeks Later

Ella curled her body against Gabriel's, sliding her hand across his chest and pressing her cheek into his shoulder. She didn't want to open her eyes—wished she could stay in his bed for at least another few hours—and she groaned when he moved away from her.

'Sorry I was so late last night.'

She stretched beside him. 'I tried to wait up for you, but I was so tired I couldn't seem to keep my eyes open.'

When she sat up, she saw that the wine she'd poured the night before was still sitting on the bedside table, completely untouched. Gabriel followed her gaze and chuckled. Clearly she'd been more tired than she realised.

'Coffee?'

She ignored his question and leaned in closer to him, pressing a kiss to his warm lips, running her fingers through his hair as she smiled against his mouth. 'Good morning.'

He pulled her down on top of him, kissing her back, but she laughed and pulled away from him, escaping his grasp and heading for the bathroom. If she started along that track, she was never going to leave his apartment. 'You get the coffee, I'll get showered.' She was always in a rush in the mornings to get

to work, and he was always bleary-eyed from performing and
coming home late, but in the two weeks they'd been seeing each
other, he'd never failed to rise and have coffee with her, before
returning to bed when she left. They'd fallen into a pattern of
seeing each other every day, making the most of being together
before he went away on tour, and Ella smiled to herself as she
stepped under the warm water, thinking about Gabe. There was
something different about him, and she knew it wasn't just that
she was falling very quickly for him. It was the fact that they'd
known each other when they were younger, and it wasn't so
much that they'd picked up where they'd left off, but that she felt
comfortable with him just from having known him before. When
she finished her shower and walked out of the bathroom with her
towel around her, Gabe was leaning on the kitchen bench, a mug
of coffee in his hand. He nudged another one in her direction,
but she saw that his eyes were trained on something else.

Ella walked around him, leaning against him from behind
and resting her chin on his shoulder. 'What are you looking at?'

But the words had just fallen from her mouth when she saw
the photo sitting beside her handbag. She must have left it there
the night before.

Gabe turned and wrapped his arms around her, his lips warm
from coffee when he pressed them to her forehead. She knew what
he was thinking as she leaned into him. They'd spoken about it
a few times, but every time she'd resisted, not sure whether she
could, or even wanted to, do it.

'I know,' she said with a sigh.

'I keep thinking that you only have a month before your next
exhibition, and you said that if you didn't go soon, if you didn't
just book the trip…'

She nodded, tucking her head to his chest, snuggling deeper
into him. 'I know, but I just want to keep enjoying this, I—'

'Ella,' he said, looking down at her as she leaned back, his thumb beneath her chin as he lifted her head. 'I'm only gone for two months. We can pick this up where we left off as soon as I'm back.' He smiled. 'Nothing is going to change the way I feel about you, even with all that time apart.'

She glanced down at the photo again before looking back up at him. She'd never made a decision around a man before, but Gabriel was going away on tour at the end of the month, and right now she just wanted to soak up every second with him. But he was right: if she waited until he was gone, it would be too late—work would become chaotic, and she would have to wait until the following year to take a few weeks off. And what if it was too late? What if something else came up that meant she couldn't go then? She owed it to her grandmother to find out the truth about her past, didn't she?

'I'll be honest, I don't want you to go,' he said. 'I'd rather spend every night until I leave with you in my bed. But there's something about this that feels urgent, that—'

'Feels as if it needs to be discovered now,' she finished for him, reaching past Gabe for her coffee. She took a sip, closing her eyes for a moment as she thought about what she needed to do.

'I wish I'd discovered more for you from the sheet of music,' he said. 'I'll keep trying, but no one seems to have any clue as to who it might have belonged to.'

Ella took another sip of her coffee, a shiver running the length of her body when she saw Gabriel's laptop sitting on the sofa. She knew what she had to do.

'Do you mind if I use that?'

He followed her gaze. 'Sure.'

She left her coffee on the bench and hurried across the room, re-tucking her towel against her breasts to make sure it didn't slip. Doing this was going to make her even later for work than she was already, but it was something she needed to do now before she lost her nerve or changed her mind.

'What are you…' Gabriel came to sit beside her, his leg pressed against hers as she leaned forwards, seeing what site she had opened.

Ella knew the dates she could go; she'd gone over them a thousand times already, and it only took her seconds to select the airports. Her hands were shaking as she chose her seats and entered her credit card details by heart, but it wasn't until she reached the final confirmation button that she stalled.

Gabriel dropped a kiss to her shoulder then, and that was all it took for her to make the final click. She turned slowly and looked at him, her heart racing. She'd done it. She'd finally done it.

'I'll miss you,' he murmured.

Butterflies exploded in her stomach as she kissed him, wishing the timing had been better but knowing she'd done the right thing.

'We have six days together before I go,' she whispered. *And then three months after that until I see him again.* 'But you're right, if this thing between us has legs, being apart will only make us want to be together more.' It would just make their reunion all the sweeter.

He laughed and pulled her towards him, his mouth against her skin. 'Then we'd best make the most of it.'

CHAPTER 13

As she'd boarded her flight from London to Agios Konstantinos six days later, Ella had been filled with trepidation. She couldn't stop thinking about all the things that could go wrong, most especially with the house she'd booked. What if it was nothing like the pictures? What if she didn't feel safe there alone? Her head was filled with so many worries that had been almost impossible to ignore—they'd been building ever since she'd booked the tickets.

But now that she was actually on the ferry on her way to Skopelos, watching the world pass by and seeing the Sporades islands and the Aegean Sea with her own eyes, she was slowly starting to relax. Why had she ever doubted that this was the right place to come? What was not to love about Greece? Gabriel had been right; she'd never forgive herself if she didn't do everything within her power to discover the links hidden within the photo, the music and her own family secrets, even if it did mean missing out on time with him.

As the ferry sailed closer to Skopelos, Ella lifted her hand to shield her eyes from the sun, smiling as she looked at the beautiful Venetian-style houses, rising up from the port, with quaint balconies and terracotta roof tiles. She could see little stone-paved paths connecting the white-painted houses—they looked as if they'd all been built at the same time to create a cohesive style of architecture. She could almost imagine the scenes from *Mamma Mia* being filmed as the boat slowly came into port.

It didn't take long to disembark, and Ella found herself standing with her bags in hand, trying to figure out where to go. She watched as many of the other tourists who'd been on the ferry with her walked over to the bars and coffee shops that stretched along the harbour front, the tables and chairs facing out to the view. It was the perfect spot to people-watch, but Ella wanted to get settled into her accommodation before stopping for lunch.

The instructions from the owner of the house had been to catch a bus and then walk the short distance from the bus stop, or take a taxi if she preferred, but she decided to get the bus. It allowed her time to look around and really soak in the atmosphere and visuals on the island, rejoicing in the fact that she wasn't on a schedule. It didn't matter how long she took to get there or what time she arrived: there was no one waiting for her, and it was a nice feeling.

Skopelos, I love you already.

The moment Ella set foot in the house, dropping her bags to the cool tiled floor, she knew it had been the perfect place to rent. She walked through the house in awe of how quaint it was, from the little kitchen that took up one wall to the windows that completely framed the view out to the sparkling blue ocean. It was the complete opposite of her contemporary-style, inner-city flat, which only made her love it all the more. Outside, it had bright blue shutters adorning the windows and pink flowers creating a cascade of colour—like something from a postcard.

She went upstairs and found the primary bedroom, wanting on the one hand to flop straight down onto the bed and close her eyes, but on the other hand, wanting to go out and at least glimpse the island. Ella went to a window and opened it, breathing in the fresh sea air and dreaming about what the next two-and-a-half weeks might bring. When she'd opened all of them, she went straight downstairs and over to one of her bags, taking out her painting supplies and setting them out on the table. She looked at them all for a moment—at the blank canvas, the new brushes and the old, and the colourful tubes of paint just waiting to be started. And it was then she remembered the easel in the photograph, but when she went outside it wasn't there. She walked around the entire courtyard, but found nothing.

She went back inside and picked up her purse. It was time to soak up the island, and then find somewhere that sold art supplies so she could purchase an easel of her own. After buying something delicious to eat, she wanted to paint. Even if she didn't find the answers to what she was searching for, at the very least she was going to rediscover one of the things she missed most in her life, and for that she knew she'd always be grateful. She also knew it was one of the reasons Gabriel had wanted her to come, and it was the same reason her aunt had been so encouraging—and she had no intention of letting either of them down.

*

Ella stood, her hair gently wisping around her face in the wind as she looked out at the water. Everything about Greece was different to home. The sun as it graced her shoulders, the way the air filled her lungs, the colours, *everything*. It was the assault on her senses that she hadn't known she needed—she'd barely been in Skopelos three hours, and already she knew it was one of the best decisions she'd ever made in her life. That this was what she'd been craving, *needing*, to fill the void that had slowly begun to appear inside of her these past few months, or maybe even years. From the moment she'd arrived on the island, she'd been filled with the most overwhelming sensation of belonging, of finally taking the time to do something just for her.

And now, after walking the cobbled streets and sitting at a table beneath a canopy of perfectly manicured trees, eating beautiful food and drinking a rare-for-her glass of lunchtime wine as she sat and watched the world go by, there was only one thing left to do. She'd been truthful when she'd told herself she'd be fine alone, but there was something about eating stuffed sardines and grilled octopus, and twirling the most delicate pasta she'd ever tasted, that made her wonder what it would be like to enjoy her trip with another person. To be able to share the experience with someone else.

She held up her phone as she stood and looked out at the water, an easel under her other arm that she'd managed to procure after leaving the restaurant. Ella wasn't sure what had got into her—she was ready to blame the heat or the beauty of her surroundings—because in all her life, she'd never put her heart on the line like this before.

Putting the easel down, she looked up Gabriel's number and took a deep breath, quickly typing before she had time to change her mind. It was he who'd suggested she come, and she only wished she'd been brave enough to ask him at the time, or at least before she'd left London. Why hadn't she invited him to come with her before he went away on tour? Or had she simply presumed that if he'd been able to come, he'd have suggested it?

It's more beautiful here than I could ever have imagined.
Join me before you go?

Ella slipped her phone into her bag and picked up the wooden easel, sticking it under her arm as she walked back to the house. If he didn't come, then she would enjoy every second of her trip alone and bask in her own company with no regrets. But if he did? She swallowed, nervously listening out for a ping that would tell her he'd replied. If he did, she had a feeling that she was going to fall head over heels with more than just Skopelos, because she was already starting to wonder if the way she felt about Gabriel was different to how she'd ever felt about a man before.

CHAPTER 14

London, 1973

'I still can't believe you made me do this,' Alexandra cried, staring at her reflection in the mirror. She was trying on clothes in Biba, arguably one of the best boutiques in London, but it wasn't the beautiful clothes she was thinking about—it was her hair.

Alexandra's eyes were wide as she blinked back at herself. She'd resisted her cousin's insistence that she cut her hair into a short, blunt crop for years, but somehow at the hairdresser today she'd decided to be brave. It made her look younger, which hadn't been part of the plan, and it *did* make her look more fashionable, but she no longer had locks that cascaded over her shoulders as they'd done for most of her life. She hadn't realised how much she loved them until they'd been chopped off.

'Try this on.'

Belle had always been more daring than her, and although Alexandra loved the miniskirts and brightly coloured fashions of the day on her cousin, it was a style that had taken her much longer to embrace. They'd become like sisters over the years that Alex had been in London; just as her other two cousins had become like brothers to her. Her aunt's family had embraced her without a second thought, not once making her feel as if she didn't belong. And now here she was, almost an adult, as much a Londoner as her cousins after six years living away from Greece. Six years after losing her mother, and her world as she knew it changing forever.

Alexandra took the skirt, top and dress that Belle passed to her and stepped back inside the dressing room, knowing that she didn't really have a choice in the matter.

'You know, we're supposed to be looking for appropriate clothes for tomorrow night,' Alexandra said as she shimmied into the skirt, conscious that she didn't exactly have the waiflike Twiggy figure that it was designed for. She was slender but not skinny; another thing that made her different to her racehorse-like cousin.

'We'll find something boring for tomorrow night, to keep Mummy happy,' Belle said, as she flung the door open before Alexandra was ready, eyes wide with excitement, clapping her hands together when she saw Alexandra squeezed into the outfit she'd chosen for her. 'Oh, it's perfect!'

'It's nice,' Alexandra said, 'but I think I like the dress more. I'll try that before I decide.' The dress was short, but at least the style was slightly more forgiving.

'Let's take both. The skirt will be perfect for Saturday.'

Alexandra paused before half closing the door to the dressing room, peeking back out at Belle. 'What's this Saturday?'

'Your birthday!' Belle sighed and firmly pushed the door shut. 'Did you forget you were turning eighteen? Now we can all go out and have the time of our lives. At last.'

Alexandra leaned back against the wall, groaning. Not only did they have very different fashion sense, but they also disagreed on what constituted the perfect night out. She would rather have a special dinner out at The Ivy or Wiltons, maybe even a picture, and then go home. She didn't need the kind of raging social life that her cousin seemed to desire.

'I thought the tickets to the orchestra were for my birthday?'

'They were my parents' gift to you. Saturday is *my* gift.'

She'd been looking forward to seeing the London Luminary Ensemble play for weeks. Music was her big love, and had been ever since her aunt had introduced her to the violin, and although they weren't the biggest orchestra in London, they were fast becoming one of the most prestigious.

'How does it look? The minidress is the height of fashion now, Alex. It's exactly what you need to be seen in.'

Alexandra wasn't sure who exactly would be seeing her, but she begrudgingly put it on and faked a smile when Belle squealed with excitement.

There's no chance I'm leaving this store without everything I've just tried on.

Later that day, after Belle had dragged her to Soho to go to every boutique on Carnaby Street, they finally arrived home. They were both carrying enough bags to make their arms ache, and Alexandra was grateful to flop down into a chair, kicking off her shoes and rubbing at her swollen feet. Belle certainly had stamina when it came to shopping, that was for sure.

'Girls, you're back!'

Her aunt Elizabeth glided into the room, her hair pinned into an elegant, bouffant bun that she'd taken to wearing for the past five years. Her elegance often reminded Alexandra of her mother, the way they held themselves, the way they moved, and of course the way they looked. Sometimes she worried that she'd started to lose the image of her mother in her mind, and had replaced her with Elizabeth, after all these years.

Elizabeth was holding something in her hand, and she came to sit beside Alexandra. It appeared it was an envelope, and she kept it in her hand as she spoke.

'I see the shopping trip was successful,' her aunt said with a knowing smile. It was no secret that Belle did enough shopping for both her cousin and mother combined—both of whom preferred the solitude of home, if given the chance, whereas Belle loved to be out and about. 'Your father is going to have a fit, as usual. Did you charge everything?'

Belle smiled. 'He won't mind at all. I'll break the news to him over dinner.'

'Speaking of fathers,' her aunt said, shuffling a little closer. 'This arrived for you today. I wanted to give it to you as soon as you arrived home. I thought it might be from yours.'

'Oh.' Alexandra reached out a hand for the cream envelope, her heart picking up its beat as she slid her fingernail beneath the seal. Her father had barely acknowledged her existence these past few years—she imagined he was still gallivanting in the South of France, entertaining himself with women half her mother's age. The few things she'd overheard from her aunt and uncle hadn't exactly painted him in the best light, and most days she was grateful to be estranged from him.

Alexandra's eyes quickly traced over the words, furiously blinking away tears when she realised who the card was from. Trust her to get her hopes up and end up disappointed by him.

'What does he say?' Belle asked.

Alexandra cleared her throat and looked directly into her aunt's eyes, knowing that she would understand, given that she had never tried to hide her dislike of her brother-in-law. 'It's actually from the royal family,' she said. 'Wishing me a happy birthday.' She cleared her throat, knowing it had most likely been sent by the Queen, who'd faithfully written to her every birthday, as well as on the anniversary of her mother's passing. 'It was very kind of them to send me best wishes, although it appears the same cannot be said about my father. Truth be told, he probably doesn't even know what date my birthday is.'

Elizabeth took her hand and held it gently for a long moment. Her aunt didn't need to say anything—her eyes said it all.

'I've been hoping for weeks that he might send you something special,' Elizabeth confessed. 'But in case he didn't, I wanted to give you these. I hope they will make you forget all about your father's absence.'

Alexandra watched as her aunt took a small velvet box from her pocket, holding it out to her. *For me?*

'But it's not my birthday until Saturday,' Alexandra whispered, taking the box and looking up in wonder at her aunt. 'And I don't expect anything from you, certainly nothing extravagant.' Her aunt and uncle had kept her all this time, had refused to receive money from her father and been beyond generous when it came to both her education and care, so she certainly didn't want them making a fuss on her birthday.

'We have another present to give you on Saturday, but I like to think of this as a little something from me,' Elizabeth said, her voice lowering an octave, 'and from your mother. I'm sure she would have wanted you to have them. As do I.'

Alexandra opened the box and gasped when she saw two diamonds twinkling back at her—the most beautiful, elegant earrings she'd ever set eyes upon, and easily a carat each in size.

'They're too much.' Alexandra's eyes filled with tears again, but happy ones this time as she touched her fingertips to one of them.

'They belonged to your grandmother,' her aunt said, leaning over to carefully take one out and gently pushing it through the single hole in Alexandra's earlobe. 'Your mother and I always argued over who was to have them, but our mother chose to give them to me on my wedding day, with the explicit promise that they were to remain in our family forever. I was the first to marry, and that was how she chose between us.'

Alexandra turned her head so her aunt could place the other one in her right lobe, before standing to look in the large, gilded mirror above the fireplace. 'They're beautiful,' she said, turning ever so slightly one way and then the other, and watching as each earring caught the light. 'But Belle, surely you want—'

'Belle has plenty of other pieces of family jewellery she can inherit from me,' her aunt said firmly, interrupting her. 'These are for you, Alexandra. I lent them to your mother on her wedding day, so they have a connection to her that is special beyond words, and now they belong to you. There is no one I want to have them more than you.'

'Thank you,' she said, throwing her arms around her aunt. 'For everything, not just these. Thank you for everything you've done for me.'

'You're more than welcome,' Elizabeth said, but Alexandra could see how much her words meant to her, for tears were filling her aunt's eyes now too. They both dabbed at their cheeks then, smiling through their tears. 'And who knows? Perhaps your father will surprise us all by sending you something on Saturday too.'

Alexandra resisted the urge to roll her eyes. It seemed that pigs would sooner fly than her papa remember his only daughter on her eighteenth birthday. He could have remarried or had more children for all she knew, it had been that long since he'd bothered to contact her, although she was fairly certain her uncle made sure to keep abreast of her father's whereabouts. Something as significant as marriage would most likely have been news that was reported back to him.

'Perhaps,' she said politely, holding her tongue on everything else she'd have liked to say about him. She was going to ask her aunt about her mother's jewellery collection, but decided not to—she had so many pieces that were family heirlooms and items that had been gifted to them by the royal family over the years. She'd wondered for some time where her jewellery might be, or what would have happened to the possessions in their home back in Athens after so long. 'These are truly the most beautiful gift that anyone has ever given me. Thank you.'

'Now, let's talk about tomorrow night,' Elizabeth said with a big grin. 'I cannot wait to take you all. The opera would have been my first choice, but the orchestra will be just as magical. I was thinking we could have a glass of champagne here first, before we go.'

'That sounds perfect,' Alexandra said. 'Thank you, both of you.' She looked from her aunt to her cousin. 'I know I probably don't say it enough, but I'm so grateful for everything you both do for me.'

Belle jumped to her feet then and linked her arm through hers. 'Come on, let's go upstairs and plan out our outfits for the weekend.' They picked up some of the shopping bags and headed for the stairs, Belle dragging her along at speed to her bedroom.

'Did I mention we're meeting William on Saturday night?' Belle asked as she flopped onto her bed. 'He said he'll take us out with some of his university friends, would you believe it? I think we're going to have the best night of our lives! It's going to be amazing.'

Alexandra lay down beside her, staring up at the ceiling, suddenly much more interested in the plans Belle had made for them. She adored Will, and she'd always wanted to meet his friends from the Royal Academy of Music. Next year she was going to be attending university too, although Belle had convinced her to take a gap year with her this year so they could figure out what they truly wanted to do. Alexandra's great love was music, and

Will had tried to twist her arm countless times to consider the academy, but in truth she wasn't certain whether he was only being kind to her when he said such things. The application process was rigorous, and she had no idea whether she was even talented enough to audition.

Belle's fingers closed around hers then, gently squeezing, and she squeezed them back. Not a day passed that she didn't think how fortunate she was. What had happened to her as a girl had been a tragedy beyond words, but the love and kindness she'd been shown since was nothing short of a fairy tale. Her father be damned.

*

Alexandra stood in her floor-length silk gown in the foyer of the Royal Festival Hall, her bag clutched under her arm as she indulged in looking around at all the people dressed in their finery. It certainly was quite something to attend an evening out like this, and although Belle looked less than enthused, her other cousin, Will, looked positively thrilled. There was a feeling of anticipation among the crowd that only ever came with seeing a live performance. It was just a shame her younger cousin was away at boarding school and hadn't been able to join them.

He came closer and took her arm, leaning in close to her as he spoke. 'You look beautiful, Alex,' Will said. 'Although I'd grow your hair out again if I were you. Every girl in London was jealous of your dark, glossy curls.'

Belle punched him in the arm from the other side. 'I heard that!' she huffed. 'Alex looks amazing, and besides, you wouldn't know anything. We're trying to keep up with the latest fashions, in case you hadn't noticed.'

Alexandra only sighed. She had to admit that she agreed with him about her haircut, and she couldn't be angry with Will even if she hadn't shared his view. He treated her like a sister—well, in all fairness he probably treated her more good-naturedly than he treated his own sister. Regardless, she loved him all the more for it. They had a very close relationship and she loved that he was always truthful with her.

'How are your studies coming along?' she asked, as they began to walk with the crowd to take their seats.

'Amazing,' he said, running a hand through his slightly too-long hair. 'Truly amazing. It's like a dream come true.'

Will's cello was his most prized possession, and she loved the thought of him playing every day and immersing himself in something he loved. Her aunt and uncle would have supported him in anything he wanted to do—they were like that with all three of their children and with her too.

'One of my friends, someone who has already graduated, actually, is playing here tonight. Can you imagine? Playing to a crowd of this size?' He let out a whistle. 'He's the youngest cellist ever to join the London Luminary Ensemble. We're all ridiculously jealous.'

'We?' Alexandra asked.

'My academy friends. If I'm perfectly honest, we're all equal parts jealous and thrilled for him.'

Alexandra looked around at the people taking their seats as Will leaned over to speak to his sister, the theatre quickly filling to capacity with women in elegant dresses and men in dinner jackets. There was nothing about the entire experience that she didn't love. She settled into her chair with Will on one side and Belle on the other, her aunt and uncle filing in after them. She watched as they bent their heads together to study the programme, so different to how her father had been with her mother. It still took her by surprise sometimes, the way they were so comfortable with each other without any formality. 'You said your friend plays the cello?' she asked.

'Yes, just like me,' Will said. 'But he also plays the piano like you've never heard before. He's the most talented musician I know, the way he can switch between instruments, but the cello is his true love.'

She wondered how young this friend must be as the lights began to dim, the crowd slowly growing silent around her, an excited murmur humming between them. Alexandra glanced first at Will and then at Belle before it went completely dark, noticing the difference between the pair of them. She and Will could have been twins, the way they both wished to live and breathe music, whereas Belle had simply seen it as a chore when they'd had lessons as younger teenagers, and no matter how much she'd practised, Belle had still managed to make a sound on the flute that made the rest of the family wish to block their ears. Belle was restless and went from one thing to another, whereas Alexandra and Will had discovered what they loved at a young age. She imagined that her adventurous cousin would probably choose not to enrol at university when the year ended, and instead decide to travel the world.

Her mind emptied of all thoughts then, as a sound so magical filled the air that it sent goosepimples across Alexandra's skin, her entire body alive as the orchestra came to life, as bows touched strings and filled the theatre with the most exquisite sound she had ever heard.

Afterwards, as they stood in the foyer and waited while her aunt and uncle talked with acquaintances they'd spotted, Will unexpectedly grabbed her hand and whispered in her ear. 'Come with me. Let's see if we can say a quick hello.'

'To your friend?' Alexandra asked. 'But—'

She looked behind at Belle, who hurried to catch up with them when she saw that Will was steering her away. 'Not without me,' she said. 'I want to meet this famous young musician too. How old is he? How do you even know him?'

Will shrugged. 'Young enough to be a big deal, and I know him because he graduated from the academy and we have some mutual friends.'

They walked around to another door and went back into the theatre, making their way closer to the stage without anyone stopping them. She half expected an usher to tell them to leave, given that everyone else had already vacated their seats.

'I told him we were coming tonight, and he said he'd try to sneak back out onto the stage to say hello at the end of the performance.'

Alexandra was quickly distracted as Belle chatted to her and she looked around, thinking how different the theatre looked without anyone in the seats, so empty and void of the life that had so recently filled it. There was a shuffle on stage then that caught her attention, and she looked up to see someone coming towards them, a sole figure in the large expanse before them.

'Bernard!' Will called out. 'That was amazing. What a performance!'

Bernard had his hand up to shield his eyes from the bright lights, but even as he squinted, Alexandra could see how handsome he was. From their seats it had been difficult to make out the individual musicians, and perhaps he'd been positioned near the back, but there was something about him that made her want to edge closer. He was wearing a crisp white shirt and a dinner jacket, his dark hair brushed slightly to the side, and he was tall, with long legs that made her wonder how short she'd be beside him.

'Now that is one handsome man,' Belle whispered. 'Why didn't Will tell us how good-looking his new friends were? I'd have insisted on meeting them sooner!'

Alexandra only nodded, edging closer to Will so that their shoulders were almost touching, and keeping her eyes on the stage. Bernard had dropped to his haunches as he spoke to Will, close enough for them to talk, but too far away, and with the stage far too high, for him to jump down. She found herself wishing that he would though, or find a way to come down to speak to them properly.

'See you tomorrow night?' Will called out.

'See you then.' Bernard waved and took a step back, and Alexandra didn't know if she was imagining his eyes pausing as they met hers or not. But she did see that he waited a moment before turning, and she couldn't take her eyes off him.

'He's coming out tomorrow night with us?' Belle asked. 'For Alex's birthday?'

But it was Alexandra who Will looked at, giving her a grin that told her he'd seen just how long she'd stared after his friend. She would thank him later for his discretion, because if Belle knew, she wouldn't stop talking about it.

'Yes, Belle, he is. Along with a handful of my other friends, so you'd better be on your best behaviour. Don't forget I'm doing you a favour by letting you come.' He smiled. 'Actually, I'm doing it for Alex. It might just be the best birthday she's ever had.'

Alexandra fanned her face with the evening's programme she was still holding as she tried to avoid Will's gaze. Suddenly, Saturday evening seemed a whole lot more appealing than the quiet night she'd previously been wishing for all these weeks.

As they walked back out to the foyer, Alexandra found herself lost in her own thoughts, thinking about what she would wear.

Perhaps the minidress would be fun after all. It was fashionable but not a complete departure from what she would usually wear, and she'd get Belle to help her with her hair to make sure it looked sleek and styled.

She doubted Will's friend Bernard would even notice her, especially with him most likely being a few years older than her, not to mention such a talented musician, but a girl could only hope.

'Alex?'

Alexandra looked up, blinking at Will as she realised she had no idea what they were talking about.

'She's daydreaming about the orchestra, I suspect,' Belle said with a sigh. 'Honestly, sometimes I wonder if you and I are even related.'

As they caught up to her aunt and uncle, William extended his arm and Alexandra happily took it, dropping her head to his shoulder. There was kind, and then there was Will; he'd been her constant since she'd arrived to live with the family. Quick to make her laugh, the first to tease her if he could see she needed cheering up, and the person who'd patiently sat with her for hours when she'd first begun trying to decipher sheet music. She also suspected that he might be trying to hide something from those around him, although she'd never ask him. It was one of those things she expected would always remain unspoken between them.

'How did you enjoy the evening, Alexandra?' her aunt asked as they all strolled together from the Royal Festival Hall out into the night air.

'It was magical,' she said truthfully. 'I couldn't think of a more beautiful way to spend an evening if I tried. It will truly be a birthday I'll never forget.'

Her aunt and uncle beamed at her, and she tucked closer to her cousin. Sometimes she dreamed of what it would be like to perform to a crowd like that, to live a life of music, but most times she was simply content with being a spectator. Although tonight had made her start to wonder all over again.

CHAPTER 15

Alexandra had never been in such a place, and certainly not at this time of night, not without her aunt or uncle. She looked up at the gold Café de Paris lettering above the door, her arm linked firmly through Belle's, not wanting to become lost in the crowd. Smoke clung to the air and there were people everywhere, many of them facing the cabaret performance on the stage, with others drinking and talking in groups. It was like nothing she'd ever seen before, and she immediately loved it.

Will walked ahead of them, and they hurried in their higher-than-usual heels to keep up with him, stopping only when they saw him wave and make his way to a table. There were five young men about the same age as him, and two of them had girlfriends who looked both her and Belle up and down.

'Will! Good of you to join us!'

'I see you've brought some lovely young women with you.'

His friends all called out and grinned, clearly having already consumed a few drinks.

'My sister and my cousin,' he said grimly. 'So hands off. It's Alexandra's birthday, so you'd all better be on your best behaviour.'

Alexandra was disappointed that Bernard wasn't there. She'd thought about him all day after meeting him the night before, hopeful that she might get to meet the talented young musician properly, but clearly it wasn't meant to be.

'Ladies, what are you drinking?'

'Champagne, of course,' Belle said. 'It's a celebration, after all.'

'Did I miss the introductions?'

A deep man's voice raised over the loud music on stage made Alexandra turn. Her heart practically skipped a beat as she found herself face to face with Bernard.

'Belle,' her cousin said, inching forward past Alexandra and extending her hand.

'Your sister?' Bernard asked Will with a grin.

'Yes, my sister, how could you tell?' Will groaned. 'And don't tell me it's because we're so alike.'

'And I'm Alexandra,' she said, mustering all her courage and hoping she wasn't blushing. 'Will's cousin.'

When Bernard took her hand, all the tiny hairs on her arms stood on end. He was easily as handsome up close as he'd been on stage, and she found herself desperately hoping they could sit together.

A server came over then, which led to her cousins arguing about which champagne should be ordered, and Bernard shook his head.

'Are they always like this?' he asked her.

She grinned. 'Always. In fact, the only reason he agreed to Belle coming out with him tonight was because it's my birthday.'

Bernard smiled back at her. 'Well, then, I can see why they're arguing over which champagne to order. It's an important occasion.' He gestured for her to take a seat and she slid onto the cushion that curved around the table, pleased when he sat beside her, his leg brushing hers. 'Happy birthday, Alexandra.'

'Thank you,' she whispered.

He didn't take his eyes off her, and she glanced down at the table before looking back up at him, curious as to why he was watching her.

'Tell me, did you enjoy the performance last night?'

She sighed. 'It was absolutely magical. I can't imagine anything more incredible than mastering an instrument the way you have, and then dedicating your life to your craft.'

'You're a musician too?'

She shook her head, biting down on her bottom lip. 'I play, but I wouldn't call myself a musician.'

Bernard sat back and studied her, as if he could read her thoughts. 'Do you play every day?'

'Yes,' she answered without hesitation.

'Does it make you feel more alive than anything else in the world?'

The music on stage became louder then, and he leaned in closer to hear her answer.

'Yes.'

Bernard smiled, running a hand through his thick, dark hair. 'Then, Alexandra, you are a musician, whether you realise it or not.'

She let his words sink in as Will sat down beside Bernard. Belle didn't look the least bit shy and had sat on the opposite side of the table.

'Why didn't you tell me your cousin was a musician?'

Will laughed. 'Did she tell you that? Because whenever I tell her that she should audition for the academy, she insists she's not one.'

Alexandra rolled her eyes, embarrassed to be the centre of conversation, but also secretly thrilled that Will had praised her so openly.

'What is your instrument of choice?'

'The violin,' she said.

'Ahh, so we are both lovers of the strings.'

The champagne arrived then and Will opened it, managing to splash it over the table. She had the chance to study Bernard amid the commotion, who had taken over the pouring and was in the process of filling the glasses. Alexandra noticed his hands first—long, tapered fingers—which of course made her recall what Will had said about him also being a talented pianist. But she quickly lifted her gaze to his face, drinking in his easy smile and strong jaw, his dark, almost black eyebrows that matched his hair.

'May tonight be a birthday to remember,' he said, when he turned to her and held out a glass.

She smiled and took a sip, the bubbles tickling her nose and causing mayhem in her throat. She felt them as they reached her stomach, which was already twisted into knots.

She had little doubt that it would indeed be a birthday to remember.

'So tell me, Alexandra, how did you end up in London? I detect an accent.'

She raised her brows, leaning back into the seat as Bernard spoke to her. It was late now, although she wasn't certain quite how late, and the others had either dispersed or were up dancing still. It was just the two of them at the table, and she was sitting at a slight angle so that she could face him.

'I came here from Greece when I was twelve. It seems like a lifetime ago though, and I've tried very hard to make my accent as neutral as possible.'

'Greece?' He lifted his hand, his fingers skimming against hers where she had them resting on the chair. She looked down at his touch, a butterfly-soft shiver tracing her spine.

'My father was a close aide to the King, so we left Greece when the royal family was forced into exile.'

She studied his face to see his reaction, to see if it made him uncomfortable, but he only smiled.

'You become even more interesting by the moment, Alexandra.'

Alexandra moved her fingers slightly to see what he did, but Bernard only touched his knuckles to hers again.

'I have lived with my aunt and uncle, Will's parents, since I arrived,' she said, not sure why she was telling Bernard her secrets when she'd worked so hard to keep them hidden. 'My mother passed away, and my father decided it would be better for me to live somewhere other than with him.'

'Ahh, so that's why I like you. We have our fathers in common.'

She stared at him. 'We do?'

'My father decided it would be better for me to live somewhere other than with him too.' His fingers moved against hers again, only this time he intertwined them, his gaze fixed on their hands. 'He gave me exactly an hour to pack my things and find a new place to live when I announced I was going to be a musician.'

'Well, I suppose he was rather generous giving you an entire hour. How kind of him.'

Bernard laughed and tipped his head back, taking proper hold of her hand now. 'And all because I told him I wanted to follow my passion instead of becoming a surgeon like him. It seemed he wanted a carbon copy of himself.'

'But he must be so proud of you, now that you're in the orchestra? Does he often come to watch you?'

Bernard laughed. 'My father hasn't spoken to me since I left home, and my mother is too afraid of upsetting him to come to one of my performances.'

'I'm sorry,' she said, moving slightly closer to him.

'Don't be.' His voice was low. 'I have my orchestra family, and I know I will always have a home so long as I'm playing music and doing what I love.'

Alexandra reached up and touched Bernard's face. She wasn't certain if it was the amount of champagne she'd consumed or if it was simply a natural reaction, but she had the most overwhelming urge to brush her fingertips down his cheek. He had a hint of stubble that was rough to her skin, and she wondered what it would feel like against her cheek.

'Do I have to give you a warning about staying away from my cousin?'

Will was suddenly standing over them then, but Bernard didn't let go of her hand. Instead he smiled and lifted it, pressing a slow kiss to it.

'Permission to see your cousin again?' he asked, without taking his eyes off her.

'Yes,' she said.

'No,' Will declared.

Alexandra burst out laughing when she spoke at the exact same time as Will, who simply threw his hands up in the air.

'Now it's time to get you home before you turn into a pumpkin,' Will said, taking her other hand and tugging her away from Bernard. 'If I don't get you home by curfew, no one will be seeing her again.'

Before she left, Alexandra extracted herself from Will and leaned down to Bernard, whispering a soft kiss to his cheek. He somehow smelt like a blend of cinnamon and leather, and she knew that she would still be thinking about how that rough edge of stubble felt against her soft skin come morning.

And when he lifted her hand and kissed her in return, his lips against her knuckles as his eyes met hers, she found herself biting down hard on her lip in an attempt to hide her smile.

CHAPTER 16

Alexandra woke with Bernard on her mind. The second her eyes opened she clutched the sheets to her chest, remembering the soft touch of his lips on her skin, the warmth of his breath as he'd hovered there. It wasn't a true first kiss, but it had certainly made her eighteenth birthday memorable, and it was something she was going to think about for days, she just knew it.

She rose, going to the window and parting the thick velvet drapes so she could look outside. The sun was shining, and she watched the happenings outside, wondering what time it was. All she knew for certain was that she'd most likely slept past breakfast after her late night out. Alexandra's stomach growled as if in protest, but she was quickly distracted by a soft knock at the door. It certainly wasn't Belle, for she would have simply burst in without warning.

'Miss Alexandra?'

'Come in,' she called back, recognising the housekeeper's voice.

'Miss Belle has just risen and thought you might like to join her for a late breakfast. Your aunt had me make pancakes and bacon since it was your birthday weekend, and they're downstairs waiting for you.'

'You're so kind, that's exactly what I feel like for breakfast,' Alexandra replied. 'Tell her I'll be down as soon as I'm dressed.'

'Oh, and there's a letter waiting for you, hand-delivered by a young man this morning. While you were sleeping, would you believe?'

Alexandra froze. 'A young man?' She tried to keep her voice steady. 'And you're certain it's for me?'

'Oh, yes, a very handsome young man, and it's most definitely for you. He was sliding it under the door when I was on my way in, so he gave it to me instead and told me to make sure you got it just as soon as you were up for the day.'

Alexandra almost choked when she tried to swallow. She was trying to keep her composure, but it was impossible. She checked her buttons were all done up on her nightgown and ran down the hall, not bothering to change, taking the stairs two at a time and not caring that she sounded as loud as an elephant. It had to be from Bernard, it just had to be! But why would he be leaving a letter for her? What could he possibly have to tell her?

She looked on the hallstand but didn't see anything, so ran into the kitchen. Why hadn't she asked the housekeeper where it was! But as she rounded the corner, she saw Belle sitting at the table, an amused smile on her lips and her eyebrows arched high.

'Looking for this?' Belle waved a cream envelope in the air.

'No games, Belle. Please give it to me,' Alexandra begged.

'Why don't I read it out loud for you?'

'Belle!' Alexandra fumed, marching over to her, her heart thumping. She thought she was going to faint from the excitement. 'Please, I have to see what's inside. Give it to me.'

'Fine,' Belle huffed, holding it out. 'But I expect you to tell me what it says. I heard it's from a young gentleman. Are you keeping someone secret from me?'

Alexandra had forgotten her hunger, even as she stood beside Belle, who was licking syrup from her fingertips and sipping tea. All she could think about was the letter.

Her hands were shaking as she tore open the seal, eyes darting to read the words.

Dear A,

I know it's not fashionable to appear too eager, but I thought about you all night. Can I see you again? And don't forget that I want to hear you play that violin of yours! I'm sure you've been far too modest about your musical talents. I'll call on you at six. Perhaps we could have dinner, just the two of us?

B.

Alexandra closed her eyes and held the letter to her heart. *He thought about me. He wants to see me again.* She tried not to giggle when she reread the part about being too eager.

'Alex! Who is it from?'

'It's from Bernard.'

'Bernard?' Belle squealed. 'Gorgeous musician Bernard?'

'He wants to call on me tonight,' she whispered, holding out the letter for Belle, her voice trembling too much to read it out to her. 'He wants to take me for dinner.'

'To dinner?' Belle's eyes widened, and she snatched the letter, her lips moving silently as she read the words. 'Oh, please let me dress you! This is so exciting!'

'Do you think your mother and father will let me go unchaperoned?' She'd never asked if she was allowed to date, but surely now that she was eighteen she'd be permitted to go to dinner with a young man?

Belle waved her free hand in the air as if she wasn't to worry about it. 'He's a friend of Will's, and they'll be impressed that he's a member of the orchestra. I'll make certain they say yes, even if I have to beg them myself.'

Alexandra stared at her cousin, her eyes as wide as saucers. 'He wants to see me again. Bernard actually wants to see me again!'

'Why do you seem so surprised? Have you looked in a mirror lately, Alex? You're absolutely beautiful. Any man would fall in love with you, and you just so happen to be fabulous company.'

'Truly?' She had no idea Belle saw her that way; she'd always felt so plain beside her fashionable, confident cousin.

'Have something to eat,' Belle said, nudging the plate towards her. 'Lucy made these pancakes especially for you, and she'll be devastated if you don't have some.'

Alexandra sat and took a bite, barely listening to Belle as she ran through what sounded like a hundred different options for what she should wear to see Bernard again. But as soon as she was finished she made an excuse and raced upstairs, still clutching the letter as she went to her violin case and placed it on the bed, sitting down beside it.

Her eyes danced over the words again, committing his note to memory before folding it and slipping it inside her case, beneath her violin. It felt like the only place for it, tucked away from prying eyes but also with her most treasured possession.

Once she'd put her case away, Alexandra fell onto her bed and buried her face into her pillow, muffling an excited scream. *Bernard. I'm going on a proper date with Bernard.* She didn't even want to think about how heartbroken she'd be if her aunt and uncle said no.

Her eighteenth birthday was now officially the best birthday of her life.

CHAPTER 17

Alexandra had never been so nervous in her life. She'd been hovering upstairs for at least thirty minutes, alternating between pacing back and forth and sitting on the top step, listening out for Bernard's arrival. But when the knock at the door finally came, she wanted to run back to her room and hide. Sweat broke out across her top lip and her hands turned clammy.

'Alex, calm down, you look like you're about to be sick.' Belle sighed and came closer, staring at her face. 'You're as white as a sheet.'

'What if he doesn't like me? What if I don't know what to say to him?' She gripped Belle's hand tightly. 'I've never been on a date before, I don't know what to do!'

Belle rolled her eyes. 'You two talked for hours last night, there's nothing to worry about,' she said. 'Trust me. He likes you, and I'm almost certain that he'll be as nervous as you. It's just two people going out for dinner.'

Alexandra wasn't convinced that Bernard would be nervous— he was at least a few years older than her and probably very experienced. But Belle was right; it was just two people going out for dinner. Even if it went horribly, she would be home within a few hours.

'Don't keep the man waiting,' Belle scolded. 'I'll be right behind you, now come on.'

She squeezed her cousin's hand. 'Thank you. For everything.'

Belle just blew her a kiss. 'You're very welcome. Now go! Have the best night of your life, and then come home and tell me all about it. Not all of us have dates on a Sunday night, you know.'

Alexandra curled her fingers around the handrail then, taking her first step down the stairs. She kept her gaze down to begin with, but when she looked up she saw Bernard standing near the door, speaking with her uncle. They both turned when they saw her, and she suddenly had to focus on each step, worried that if she didn't, she'd fall all the way to the bottom.

Bernard watched her the way she'd seen her uncle look at her aunt when they thought no one was watching—his eyes danced over her, as if he simply couldn't take his gaze from her even if he wanted to. It made every little hair on her arms rise, and when she was finally standing in front of him, his smile calmed her nerves. She'd been so worried he might not like her when he saw her again, but there was no way she could misinterpret his interest now.

'It's lovely to see you again, Alexandra,' Bernard said. 'I was just telling your uncle that I've made reservations at Quo Vadis. I've come to know the owner, and he was kind enough to find a table for me at short notice.'

'Is that the Italian restaurant?' her uncle asked. 'I recall the owner was rounded up during the war with all the other Italians, and he rebuilt the place from the ground up when he returned, as it was all but destroyed.'

Alexandra looked up at Bernard, desperately hoping he would say yes. She was more interested in getting going than hearing a history lesson on the restaurant Bernard had booked.

'Alexandra?' he asked, taking her by surprise. 'I take it you'd like to go?'

She nodded, hoping she didn't appear too eager. But then she remembered Bernard's words in his letter.

'Yes,' she said. 'I'd very much like to go to dinner. I love Italian food.' She wasn't actually sure if she'd ever eaten Italian, but she knew she sounded convincing. He could have said any cuisine and she'd have been sure to sound enthusiastic.

'Well, make sure she's home by ten p.m., young man, and not a minute later.' Her uncle grinned at her. 'She's very precious to us, our Alexandra. She's the second daughter we never had.'

Tears welled in her eyes then, but she quickly blinked them away as her aunt rushed in, holding her arms wide as if she were about to greet a long-lost friend.

'Bernard! Thank goodness I got to meet you before you left. Will has told me such wonderful things about you.' Her aunt looked between them. 'Can we tempt you to stay for a pre-dinner drink, so we can hear all about your rise to fame in the orchestra?'

Alexandra looked up at Bernard, praying he would decline, and she could barely hide her relief when he politely refused.

'Perhaps next time, if I could be so bold as to presume Alexandra will want to see me again,' he said, giving her a quick wink. 'I would hate to miss our reservation.'

'Of course, of course,' her aunt murmured, before giving Alex an affectionate pat on the shoulder. 'Have a wonderful night. You two make *such* a handsome couple.'

Alexandra's cheeks heated, but if Bernard noticed her embarrassment, he certainly didn't show it.

'I'll have her back before ten, I promise,' he said, shaking her uncle's hand. 'Alexandra will be very safe with me, you have my word.'

Bernard stood back slightly to let Alexandra pass as her uncle opened the front door, his palm skimming her lower back as he gently guided her. She glanced briefly over her shoulder and saw Belle standing halfway down the stairs, her hand raised in a wave, and Alexandra gave her a quick smile before stepping out into the cool night air. She would be sure to tell Belle about every minute of the evening when she returned, the two of them curled up in bed together, heads on the pillow, as they did each time the other had something exciting to share.

There was a black cab waiting, pulled up to the kerb right outside the house, and when they reached it Bernard opened the door and waited for her to settle herself before sliding into the seat beside her. Their knees bumped, and when he looked at her, Alexandra let out a big breath she hadn't even known she was holding, which made them both laugh.

Bernard took her hand in his, resting their hands against her leg.

'It's so good to see you again,' he whispered.

Alexandra only nodded, not sure what to say. In the end, she didn't need to say anything: she simply dropped her head to his shoulder as he told the driver where to take them, and they rode in silence with their fingers intertwined. It should have been the most uncomfortable journey of her life, with not a word said to the man beside her, but to Alexandra, she simply had the strangest feeling of coming home. Beside Bernard she felt safe and content, and she only hoped that he felt the same.

Bernard hadn't embellished the fact that he knew the owner— they'd been given the quaintest table for two tucked away against the wall, and he personally waited on their table. 'Thank you, Peppino,' Bernard said, when he brought them a bottle of wine.

'On the house,' the enthusiastic Italian said, slapping Bernard on the back. 'I cried last time I went to the orchestra, this man is so talented.'

She smiled and nodded, but she was grateful when they were finally left alone. Bernard leaned forwards.

'I have something to confess.'

Alexandra smiled, although she was puzzled at what he might have to tell her.

'I brought you here because I knew he'd look after us. Otherwise it would have been a cheap steak dinner somewhere far less fancy.'

'You don't have to try to impress me, Bernard,' she said, glancing away and fiddling with the napkin on her knee. 'I would have been happy with fish and chips.'

He sighed. 'It's not every day a man gets to take a young woman like you out for dinner, Alexandra. I wanted to do something nice for you.'

Alexandra's cheeks flushed with colour and she didn't know what to say.

Bernard poured her a glass of wine and passed it to her. 'Just let me impress you this one night. After this, it will be fish and chips every time, I promise.'

She took the glass and waited for him to pour his own, before clinking them gently together, unable to stop smiling at him.

'To being extravagant, just this once,' he said with a wink.

She found herself laughing, despite her embarrassment, and nodding in agreement with him.

'Will mentioned that you play the violin,' he said. 'But that you don't want to audition for the academy?'

Alexandra nodded. 'That is all true.' She took a little sip of her wine and found it pleasant on her tongue. She hadn't tasted red wine before, but it was warm and silky in her throat, and she found she very much liked it.

'Do you perform?'

'Never!' she laughed. 'I play for hours sometimes, lost in the music, but only ever for myself.'

'You've never wanted to perform?'

She opened her mouth to say no, but then found herself telling the truth. 'I've always dreamed of performing for an audience. I can't imagine the rush of adrenaline you must feel as the curtains are raised, as everyone is waiting with bated breath for the music to begin.'

He sat back in his chair and studied her, eyes dancing over hers. 'You're nothing like I expected, Alexandra. Nothing at all.'

She met his gaze, even as her skin grew pink and her fingers nervously played along the stem of the wine glass. How was she supposed to reply to such a statement?

'What do you say about going to meet some friends of mine after dinner? I will still have you back home before ten.'

'Musician friends?' she asked.

'They're the only friends I have, if I'm being perfectly honest, but yes, musicians.'

She realised she was nodding, even though she was nervous.

'I want to hear you play the violin, Alexandra, and I want to hear you play tonight.'

Two hours later, Alexandra found herself in the living room of a beautiful home in London's Notting Hill, scarcely fifteen minutes from where she lived, tucked against the back wall and listening to some of the most beautiful music she'd ever heard. But as much as the music had captured her interest, the man next to her was making it almost impossible to focus, especially when his shoulder kept nudging hers and his fingers brushed hers every few seconds.

She breathed deeply, wondering if he'd even noticed the touch, or if he was oblivious. She liked to think that it was intentional, but she had such little experience with men that she wasn't certain what to expect.

The young man playing the violin finished, and everyone clapped politely before turning to face her and Bernard. There were just two other women in the room, and Alexandra looked down as they appeared to study her openly. She could only imagine that female musicians were a rarity in this world.

'Everyone, this is Alex,' Bernard said, before leaning down and whispering in her ear. 'Is it all right for me to call you Alex?'

She nodded, knowing that even her ears would be a deep pink now, her blush was so intense. He took her hand, threading his fingers through hers as everyone in the room smiled back at them, some calling out hello. They certainly seemed friendly, although she imagined they all hugely respected Bernard.

'Ben, could I borrow your violin for a moment?'

The man who'd been playing previously appeared unruffled and passed the violin to Bernard, who then turned to Alexandra and presented her with it, as if it were a gift.

'Play for us,' he said.

Alexandra looked slowly from the violin in his hands back to his face. 'No,' she whispered. 'Oh, no, I couldn't, not in front of all these people!'

He held it closer to her. 'Don't overthink this moment, just take it, close your eyes a second to ground yourself, and then play.'

Alexandra looked at the others gathered, saw that they were talking among themselves and appeared barely interested in what she was doing or what Bernard was saying to her.

She looked up at him, questioning him with her gaze. Bernard didn't say anything, but he did step forwards and whisper a kiss to her cheek.

'Play for yourself, Alex. Play as if you're in your room alone, wishing the world could hear you. Close your eyes if you need to, but just promise me that you open them before you reach the end.'

She eventually nodded and took the violin from him, her hands trembling as she slowly walked to the front of the room, where the previous musician had stood. Everyone had gone quiet now, and as she looked at their unfamiliar faces, her every instinct told her to flee, but she didn't. She wouldn't let herself. Instead she did as Bernard had suggested and closed her eyes, keeping them shut as she lifted the bow, the violin positioned on her collarbone as she began to play the first song that came into her mind.

And when she was finished, as everyone clapped for her, she opened her eyes and saw that Bernard was watching her intently, still clapping as he stepped forwards, his face somehow even more alive than it had been earlier. His eyes never left hers.

'That was brilliant, Alex, absolutely brilliant,' he said, holding out his hands to clasp her shoulders. 'How do you feel?'

She laughed. 'Amazing,' she said. 'I actually feel amazing.'

'Good,' he said, as he took the violin from her and gave it back to its rightful owner. 'Now come with me, there's someone I'd like you to meet.'

After thanking the young man for the loan of the instrument, she leaned into Bernard, loving the way his arm slipped so naturally around her waist, drawing her against him.

'Alexandra, this is Franz,' he said, introducing her to a man slightly older than the others. 'He is the music tutor to some of the best violinists in London, and I very much want you to meet him.'

'How do you do?' she said, extending her hand.

'My dear, are you in need of tutelage?' Franz asked. 'Or are you already studying under one of my peers?'

Alexandra couldn't wipe the smile from her face, and when Bernard's fingers brushed hers this time, she knew it was most certainly not a mistake.

CHAPTER 18

Present Day

Ella stood back and brushed her hands on her shorts. She had paint under her fingernails, on her clothes and probably streaked across her face, but she'd never been so content. She admired her work; it turned out that painting was the same as riding a horse: once you knew how, you never forgot. The moment she'd held the paintbrush in her hand again it had all come back to her, and although it wasn't her best work, she felt alive just from creating something.

She'd positioned herself in the shade beneath the pretty, flowering wisteria that grew along the wooden pergola, and even without being in the sun she was starting to get hot. Ella moved her easel farther into the shade, admiring her brushstrokes one last time before looking out at the view she'd been trying to recreate. *The blue still isn't quite vivid enough, but it's close.* She collected her brushes to wash out and vowed to return to work on the colours later in the day. She'd been painting since early morning, and, with only a coffee in her stomach, she was beginning to get hungry.

Today she was going to take her bag with her to do some shopping for supplies, which would mean she could actually nourish herself without leaving home in the morning, and hopefully find something delicious for lunch that would keep her going until the evening. She gathered her things and walked inside, going to the sink to clean her brushes and then stripping off her paint-stained clothes, before taking a shower and dressing again, this time in a simple sundress. She tied her hair in a ponytail and put on some sunscreen and light make-up, before rummaging around for her shopping bag. And that was when she saw the little box, sitting beside her bed. Ella hesitated for a moment before reaching for it and taking out the photo. She knew she'd regret not taking it with her—what if she met someone she could show it to?

Ten minutes later, she was meandering down the little cobbled stone paths, back towards the only place she knew—the waterfront area where she'd come off the boat the day before. She knew there must be so much more to explore on the island, and as soon as she'd had something to eat, she planned on walking some of it.

She found herself in a quaint restaurant surrounded by some other tourists, and when the server came over to her table, she smiled and prayed that he spoke English.

'I need help with the menu,' she said, hopefully.

'Can I help you order?' he asked, in thickly accented English.

'Thank you,' she said. 'I want a glass of wine and some fabulous food. Could you order for me?'

He grinned. 'I can. I will order you my favourites.'

Ella handed him the menu. 'Perfect. Oh, but before you go.'

He hesitated and leaned forwards slightly.

'Could I show you this photograph?' she asked, taking it from her bag and holding it up to him. 'I wondered if you might recognise the women in it?' She'd already shown the woman who owned the art store and stopped a few people in the street, but so far no one had been able to help her.

He gave her a curious look before taking it, but quickly shook his head. 'No, I don't recognise them, but it looks like Skopelos.'

She nodded and thanked him, leaving the photo on the table so she could look at it some more, as if she still might somehow untangle the mystery on her own just from staring at it. She agreed with him; it was unmistakably Skopelos, of that she was absolutely certain. But within minutes she felt a gentle tap on her shoulder, and she turned to see the server standing there again, but this time with an older man.

'This is Tobias, he owns the restaurant,' the server said. 'Could he see the photo?'

Ella picked up the photo and passed it to Tobias, who said something in Greek she couldn't understand. But when he sat down heavily in the chair opposite her and crossed himself, she knew that there was something about the photograph that must have been familiar to him.

He muttered something else, before looking up at her and pointing at the older woman in the picture.

'What's he saying?' she asked the server, who lowered himself beside her.

'He says that he knows the identity of this woman.'

Ella's heart skipped a beat. 'He does?'

They had an exchange in Greek before Tobias passed the photo back to her, pointing at the older of the two females in the photograph.

'He says that this woman spent many holidays here with her daughter, before the fall of the monarchy. She was known to all the restaurant owners, and they all loved her, even though many of them voted to overthrow the King.'

Ella frowned. 'I'm sorry, what does this woman have to do with the King being overthrown?' She recalled reading about the exiled Greek royal family many years ago, something about them residing in London still after all these years, but her knowledge wasn't expansive.

'The family was closely connected to the royal family. My grandfather remembered her from when she was a girl, holidaying with the King's wife, when she was just a girl too, and her husband became a trusted adviser to the monarchy before its demise.'

'And you're certain this is her?' she asked, her heart beginning to race. Surely the woman connected to her family wasn't linked to royalty; what a scandal it would have been for an upper-class woman like that to give birth to a child who wasn't her husband's!

'He wants to know why you have this photo. Why you are asking questions about her.'

The older man leaned forwards across the table towards her, seeming to search her eyes. She was taken aback for a moment, still shocked that he'd recognised the women.

'Please, tell him that this photo was left for my grandmother. Tell him that I believe the woman in this photo is my great-grandmother.' She paused, taking a breath. 'It's why I'm here, in Greece. I'm looking for answers.'

Her server slowly stood, as did Tobias, but he leaned forwards, both of his gnarled hands planted on the table.

'Go down to the market today, it's only a five-minute walk from here, and I can draw you a map,' he said. 'The woman selling fruit may be able to tell you more.'

'Thank you,' she said, standing and reaching out to the older man, grasping his hands. 'Thank you so much.'

He patted her hand affectionately before disappearing back into the kitchen.

'I think he's going to send you out some amazing food now. I hope you're hungry.'

Ella sat back, her gaze drawn once more to the photo. Had she finally found the link to the woman and the girl she'd been staring at for so many weeks? Could this be the start of her journey into her family's past?

She didn't have long to study the photograph though before a crisp glass of white wine was placed on her table, followed by the most incredible array of grilled sardines, octopus, stuffed aubergines, olives and bread that she'd ever seen. Ella thanked her server repeatedly, before wondering how on earth she would even roll herself down to the market after such a feast.

Ella walked slowly to the market after lunch, her bag over her shoulder and a stomach so full she thought she might burst. With so many small plates of food being sent out from the kitchen, she'd wondered if it would ever stop, so she was certainly grateful for the walk.

The market wasn't hard to find, and she wandered along the rows of stalls, looking at the biggest display of olives she'd ever seen, as well as vegetables, breads and even fresh seafood, but it was when she reached the fruit stall that she paused. Despite knowing who she was looking for, she still wasn't quite sure what she was going to say. She reached for the photograph in her pocket and took it out, holding it against her chest as she approached the woman behind the stand.

'Excuse me,' she said, smiling at a woman who was probably no older than her. 'I was told you might be able to recognise the women in this photograph?' She hesitated.

The woman nodded, taking the photograph from her. 'It will be my grandmother you're looking for. Give me a moment.'

Ella stood and looked over the produce, nervously waiting for her to return. She didn't have a copy of the photograph, and she wished she hadn't handed it over without explaining its importance. Other people milled around and looked at the fruit, some picking up peaches and apricots to inspect them, and Ella decided to select some pieces herself while she was waiting, loving the look of the fresh figs.

When she looked up, she saw that there were now three women on the other side of the stall watching her—presumably three generations of the same family. Suddenly she forgot all about the figs.

'This is her?' asked one of them, pointing at Ella.

The younger woman nodded before returning to her customers, and Ella set down the fruit she'd chosen.

'I was told you might know the woman and the girl in the photograph?'

The grandmother lifted her hand and gestured for Ella to go with them, and she followed them a few steps away to the shade of a doorway.

'This is my grandmother, and she would like to know why you are asking.'

Ella took a deep breath, looking between the two women. 'I believe that this lady,' she said, pointing at the photograph that was now in the gnarled hands of the older woman, 'is my great-grandmother. This photo was left by the woman who gave birth to my grandmother.'

She waited for her words to be translated, surprised when the old lady took her hand and squeezed it.

'She wants you to know that the woman in the photograph is Maria Konstantinidis.'

'I was told she may have holidayed here with her family,' Ella said. 'That this girl was her daughter.'

'They did holiday here, often. But Maria died tragically many, many years ago, when her daughter was only a girl.'

Ella couldn't hide her surprise. 'I don't understand. So this photo was taken just before her death?' She was confused—how could this woman have died such a long time ago? Could it all be some sort of mistake? If she'd passed away soon after the photo was taken, which she must have if her daughter was still a girl, then how did her own grandmother fit into the story?

'It was a terrible tragedy,' the older woman said, suddenly speaking in heavily accented English. 'Her daughter's name was Alexandra, but her father fled Greece when the royal family was forced into exile. He worked closely with the King, and he and some others connected to the family all left.'

'Did you ever hear what happened to her daughter? To Alexandra?' she asked, pointing at the girl in the picture. 'What happened to her after she left Greece?'

This time both the women smiled, but it was the younger of the two who replied this time.

'Alexandra Konstantinidis was gone for many years, but she returned as a young woman when she married. Alexandra came home.'

Ella took the photograph when it was passed back to her. 'To Greece?'

'To the islands,' the older woman said. 'She lives in Alonissos to this day, in a house that was originally gifted to her mother by the royal family. It was no secret that she was one of the Queen's closest friends and confidantes before her death.'

'Alonissos?' Ella repeated, not familiar with the name. 'Is it far?'

'Twenty minutes by ferry,' the youngest woman from the stand said, making Ella turn as she approached, a bag of nectarines in her hand that she was holding out to her. 'The ferry runs three times a day, and you can't miss her house. It's the largest on the island.'

Ella looked among the three women, before taking the bag of fruit and tucking the photograph back into her bag.

'Thank you,' she said. 'Thank you so much for the fruit and for all the information. It truly means so much to me.'

'I hope you find what you're searching for,' the youngest woman said. 'You look like her, you know. There's almost something about you that reminds me of the Konstantinidis women.'

Ella didn't know what to say, but she smiled and turned away, forgetting all about the other food she'd planned to purchase to fill her fridge with, and hurrying back the way she'd come.

Alexandra Konstantinidis. But what could the link to this woman possibly be, and could she just island-hop and turn up at her house with a photograph and nothing else? But then if this woman was the link to her family's secret past, surely the fact that she had this photograph in her possession would mean something to this Alexandra? Although if the link was to this girl's mother, then perhaps it would be as much of a mystery to her too.

Ella took out her phone to see if Gabriel had replied, but there was still nothing from him, so she slid it back into her bag, refusing to feel deflated. They'd made a plan to pick up where they'd left off after her trip and his tour, and he was busy preparing for the biggest opportunity of his professional career. She needed to focus on why she'd chosen to come to Greece in the first place. She had a name to go on now, which meant she might actually be able to uncover at least part of the mystery while she was in Greece. But as far as her looking like the woman and her daughter in the photo… she touched her hair, running her fingers through it. She might have the dark hair, but to actually be a relative of this Alexandra Konstantinidis? There was no way she resembled the woman and the girl in the photo.

Or did she?

*

Gabriel? 'Gabriel!'

She hurried along the waterfront and took off her sunglasses to be absolutely certain she wasn't seeing things. But from the smile on his face and the way he opened one arm to her, the other holding his bag, she knew without a doubt that it was him. She'd slowed to watch the ferry come in and disembark its passengers on her way back to the house, wondering which ferry service might travel to Alonissos, which was how she'd seen him in the first place.

'I can't believe you came!' she called out as she neared him.

'A beautiful girl asks me to visit her in the Greek islands? How could I say no?'

Ella ran into his arms and looped hers around his neck, hugging him before leaning back a little. He kissed her without hesitation, his lips as soft and warm as the sunshine beating down on them. She lifted her hand and touched her palm to his cheek, hardly able to believe he was there. Only moments earlier she'd felt disappointed, wondering if perhaps he didn't feel the same way about her as she did him, and yet here he was in the flesh.

'I have so much to tell you! I've made great progress on the photo, but—' Gabriel's grin stopped her mid-sentence. 'Why are you smiling at me like that?'

'Because I think I've discovered who your mysterious "B" is.'

Ella planted her hands on her hips. 'I don't believe you.'

'I didn't come all this way just to have a holiday,' he said, slinging an arm around her shoulders. 'I've spent the past few days asking everybody I know if they recognised the note, and this morning, I finally found someone who could solve at least part of the puzzle.'

CHAPTER 19

'So are you going to keep me in suspense?'

Ella and Gabriel walked side by side along the water, heading back to the house. She couldn't stop stealing glances at him, finding it hard to believe that he was actually there. So much for thinking she'd gone too far by asking him to join her—why had she even thought to doubt that he wanted to be with her as much as she him?

'Do you remember I told you that our principal violinist had been away due to illness?'

She nodded. 'Yes, and you were going to ask him to look over the music when he returned.'

Gabriel grinned. 'You see, he's older than many of the other musicians. I think he might be in his early sixties.' He paused. 'Do you have the sheet of music with you?'

'Only the photo. I left the music back at the house.'

'Well, he believes that the B stands for a very famous cellist from the 1970s and 1980s named Bernard Goldman. He was a member of the London Luminary Ensemble, before moving to the London Symphony Orchestra for more than two decades. He then went on to tutor talented young cellists after his retirement, and he put me in touch with an old friend of his, who confirmed that this was indeed Bernard's writing.'

Ella stopped walking, holding her hand up to shield her eyes from the sun as she stared at Gabriel. 'You're serious? You believe that's who this B is? That he was a famous cellist named Bernard?'

'I do. He recognised both his handwriting and his use of the initial B to sign off his message. He said that Bernard used to write notes on the sheet music of all his pupils, especially if they were preparing for an important audition or concert, and he contacted an old friend who still had a sheet he'd saved that had a personal note in the corner.' Gabriel grinned. 'I cross-checked the writing side by side and it was clearly a match.'

Ella knew her jaw was hanging open. 'I can't believe it. I honestly can't believe that you managed to find the link.'

'Neither can I, but it has to be him, don't you think? It would be too much of a coincidence to not be him.'

'And did this person know anything else about him? Where he lived, or about his family, or—'

'No. He said the last time he saw him was at a party for his retirement, at least ten years ago, in London,' Gabriel said. 'The only thing he could tell me was that all of his pupils loved him, that he had a very quiet, encouraging manner, and that when he played no one could take their eyes off him.'

Ella started to laugh. How was it that she'd gone from knowing nothing to suddenly having two solid leads all within a few short hours?

'I felt like I'd found a needle in a haystack. Can you believe it?'

She shook her head. 'About as much as I can believe that I'm only a few islands away from the woman in the photo.'

Gabriel's eyes widened. 'You've worked out who she is?'

She linked her arm in his as they began to walk again, dropping her head to his shoulder. 'I have. Or at least, I think so, if the locals I've spoken to are right.'

'I can't believe it's all falling into place, Ella. This is incredible. Coming here was absolutely the right thing for you to do.'

She smiled and hugged him even tighter against her. 'Trust me, I can't believe it either.'

The minute they arrived back at the house she intended on googling this family to find out everything there was to know about the Konstantinidis women, and now she was going to have to look up Bernard Goldman too. She had no idea how the two were linked, but she was determined to try to find out.

It turned out that googling wasn't the *first* thing that Ella did when she got back to the house. She looked up from where she was sitting an hour or so later, in bed with the sheets pooled around her waist, pillows propped up behind her and her phone in her hand. Gabriel was half asleep beside her, his hand over her leg as she scrolled through page after page about the Greek monarchy and its ultimate demise.

'Anything interesting?' he asked as he yawned and rolled closer to her.

'Well, other than the fact that the royal family and those closest to them were forced to leave Greece, and that the monarchy was eventually abolished entirely,' she said, as Gabriel's fingers trailed up and down her arm. 'Oh, this is what I've been looking for.'

Gabriel sat up and leaned over her shoulder to see the screen.

'"The wife of Nicholas Konstantinidis, one of the King's most trusted aides, was killed in a tragic horse-riding accident yesterday afternoon, and was discovered by her long-time groom when she failed to return. Maria Konstantinidis was once a champion show jumper who defied all odds to beat countless male competitors and famously declared that she wouldn't give up the sport for anyone, not even her husband, although she did retire from competing after the birth of her first and only child",' she read out. '"She leaves behind a twelve-year-old daughter, Alexandra, who was not believed to be with her mother at the time of the fatal accident. Previously the pair had been seen at the stables together, but it is thought that Miss Konstantinidis was not a competitive rider".'

Gabriel pulled away from her for a moment, and when she glanced over she saw that he was reaching for the photograph she'd left beside the bed.

'Is this her?' he asked. 'The older of the two?'

She clicked on the picture on her screen and held it beside the photograph. 'I think it is,' she said. 'I mean, in this one she's all dressed up, compared to this very relaxed one on holiday, but I think it's the same woman.' Ella stared into the eyes of mother and daughter, sad now as she looked at them, knowing the tragedy that had occurred. But if the older of the two women had died, then how was her grandmother related to either of them? It was as if her mystery had deepened—she certainly didn't feel any closer to solving it, despite their discoveries.

Gabriel leaned forwards and studied them. 'It's definitely her. We'd have to search for a photo of the daughter, but—'

Ella clicked on the next photo and showed it to him. It was, without a doubt, mother and daughter.

'I don't even know them, yet I feel so sad to know she didn't live to see her daughter grow up.' Ella put the photo down and started to scroll through more hits on the Konstantinidis family, wanting to know as much as she could about them. 'Why don't you look up this Bernard, the musician, and see what you can discover about him. I want to know everything we can find out about both of them.'

Gabriel knocked her phone from her hand and caught her arms, pinning them above her head as he pushed her down.

'You know what?'

'What?' she asked, biting down on her bottom lip to keep from laughing.

'I can think of better things to do.'

'Really?' she protested, laughing when he dipped his head to kiss her collarbone, trailing kisses up her neck.

His hold on her wrists loosened but she kept them on the pillow, content to be the recipient of his featherlight touch.

'Did I tell you I'm only here for three nights?' he murmured. 'Then I have to get back to London to catch a plane. I think the research can wait.'

Ella sighed as she wrapped her arms around him. She had no intention of resisting, not if she only had him for a few short days. The clues weren't going anywhere.

*

Ella stepped out of the bathroom with a towel wrapped around her, her hair wet about her shoulders. Gabriel had disappeared to make them coffee, but rather than bringing a steaming mug upstairs for her, he seemed to have gone missing.

She padded through the house, heading downstairs, but instead of finding him in the kitchen, she discovered that he was outside, looking at her painting.

'What do you think?' she asked, surprised by how shy she felt at him seeing her work.

Gabriel turned, his eyes bright. 'It's amazing. I can't tell you how happy this makes me, to know that you've been creating something so incredible while you've been here.' He smiled. 'Does it feel as good as you thought it would, painting again?'

She went to stand beside him, staring at the art she'd created. 'It was as if I'd held it back for so long, that when I finally picked up a brush again, I couldn't stop.'

'It's beautiful, Ella. Absolutely beautiful.'

'Thank you.'

They stood for a moment longer, both staring at the painting.

'I have you to thank for this,' she said at last. 'For telling me to come here, for encouraging me to follow my dreams again…' She took a deep breath. 'For believing in me.'

He turned to her and placed his hands on her bare shoulders. 'Tell me you hadn't already thought about coming here long before I suggested it.'

She laughed. 'I had *thought* about it, but I would never have come, not without you prompting me.'

'Well, I hope you're planning on painting for the rest of your time here, because what you've created so far is very special,' he said. 'Will you show it at the gallery when you return?'

'The gallery?' Her reply sounded more yelp than spoken word. 'No, absolutely not. I'm a hobby painter, nothing more.'

He shook his head. 'You're too hard on yourself, Ella. You have a talent that deserves to be nurtured, and it also deserves to be shown to the world.'

She looked back at her painting again, digesting his words. If only she were brave enough to believe him.

'I think I liked it better when we were talking about my family mystery.'

He chuckled. 'Well, speaking of that, I've got another great idea.'

Ella groaned. 'What is it this time?'

He looped his arm around her and steered her past her painting and the pretty wisteria, so that they were both looking out at the water. It was the most magical blue she'd ever seen, more vivid than she could have imagined before visiting Greece herself; the kind of view you could become lost in and stare out at for hours.

'You told me that Alexandra Konstantinidis lives less than twenty minutes away by boat,' he said, moving to stand behind her, his chin on her shoulder as he looked out at the water with her. 'I think you should go there and visit her.'

Ella stayed silent, leaning back into Gabriel. He wasn't wrong; she'd had the very same thought as soon as she'd found out how close she was.

'This is your chance to solve the mystery once and for all,' he said. 'I think you'd regret it forever if you didn't try to put this final piece of the puzzle together. Who knows? She might be able to explain the link and tell you exactly how your family is connected to hers.'

'Or she might slam the door in my face and think I'm mad.'

Gabriel kissed her cheek. 'She might. But isn't it worth the risk?'

He was right, of course he was right, but the idea of turning up unannounced on the doorstep of a stranger, and telling her that she thought they might be related… She sighed and turned around in Gabriel's arms, deciding to enjoy every opportunity she had to spend with him.

Tomorrow, she'd decide. Today, she was going to enjoy every moment she had with the man who'd dropped everything to travel to Greece for just seventy-two hours to be by her side.

CHAPTER 20

London, 1973

Alexandra trailed her fingers across Bernard's bare chest, through the sprinkling of hair there, and then across to his shoulder, exploring his skin. He was propped up on one elbow, looking down at her, and when her fingers stopped he brushed a kiss across her lips. She'd never been with a man before him, and she knew that she could bask in his attention and adoration for hours, content just being tucked beside him.

She would have to go soon, to make it home in time for curfew, but all she wanted was to stay cocooned in his arms. They'd told her aunt they were going out for dinner with Bernard's friends, but instead they'd gone to his apartment, preferring to soak up every moment they could alone.

'I hear you're making incredible progress with your tuition,' he said between kisses. 'You're a star in the making.'

'I think you're exaggerating. Who did you hear that from?' She swatted at him, her cheeks flushing at his praise.

'I heard it from your tutor,' he said with a laugh, still trailing his fingers across her skin. 'So it cannot be wrong. He said he's surprised your previous teacher didn't recognise your talent, and to be honest, so am I.'

Alexandra didn't comment. Her previous teacher had been sufficient, but it had been nothing like the tutelage Bernard had arranged for her. She was seeing Franz twice per week, and he expected nothing less than perfection, constantly pushing her to try harder compositions, which had her practising for hours every day. It was the happiest she'd ever been, studying something she truly loved, although she wasn't entirely sure if the praise being given to her was warranted. There was always a little voice in her head telling her that Franz was only bothering with her as a favour to Bernard.

'One day all the orchestras around the world will be open to female musicians, and we'll be able to tour the globe together,' Bernard said as he stroked her hair. 'We could choose whichever country takes our fancy, and play in some of the most beautiful venues. I can just see us, the perfect musical pair.'

'I've always wished to see Vienna,' Alexandra confessed, her mind racing with all the places she wanted to travel to. 'It seems like one of the most romantic places in the world.'

'Then we shall set our sights on the Vienna Philharmonic Orchestra and live in an apartment overlooking the Karlsplatz square,' he said.

Alexandra groaned and lay on her back, staring up at the ceiling. 'You shouldn't put such fantasies in my head. It's unfair.'

Bernard pulled the sheets up to cover them as he rolled over on top of her, bracing himself on his elbows as he looked down at her, his arms framing her face.

'It isn't a fantasy, Alex. We will have no other responsibilities, nothing stopping us from going where we want, when we want. It's just you and me, and the world at our fingertips.' He shook his head slightly. 'I wish you'd believe me when I say that one day you could be one of the most talented violinists in London.'

He kissed her, his lips lingering as she stared up at him, knowing that he truly believed what he was telling her, whether she agreed with him or not. She lost herself looking into his eyes, knowing that even when she closed hers tonight and fell asleep, she'd still see the way he looked at her. His irises were brown flecked with green, the most unique hazel, and they somehow always seemed to dance when he gazed at her.

'B, what if I'm not as talented as you think I am?' she asked. 'What if you're like a parent who thinks their child is better than all the others, when in fact they're decidedly average?'

Bernard just laughed at her, as if it were the silliest statement in the world. 'Why is it so hard for you to believe in your talent? You are one of the most gifted violinists I've heard play, Alex. You put your heart and soul into your music, and Franz wouldn't be tutoring you if he didn't agree with me. I don't know when he last took on a new pupil, but he doesn't spend his time with violinists he doesn't see huge promise in.'

She stared up at him, reaching for his hair and running her fingers through it, before tugging him back down to her so she could kiss him again. Sometimes she believed in herself, sometimes she let herself imagine that she truly was as gifted as Bernard insisted she was, but most of the time she told herself that he was just being nice to her.

'Stop overthinking it,' Bernard whispered to her, trailing kisses down her neck and across her collarbone, at the intimate juncture where she rested her violin. 'Just believe me when I tell you that one day, you will be on stage giving the performance of your life, and no one in the audience will be able to take their eyes off you.'

'Stop,' she whispered, shaking her head, not believing him for a moment.

'I won't stop, not until you see yourself the way I see you. The way other people see you.'

His kisses became more insistent as she looped her arms around his neck to draw him even closer again.

'I have to go,' Alexandra groaned. 'You know my uncle will never let me see you again if you don't have me home by curfew.'

Bernard ignored her, and soon Alexandra had forgotten all about what time she was supposed to be home, lost to Bernard's fingertips on her skin and his lips that had found their way back to her mouth.

CHAPTER 21

The next day, Alexandra walked down the stairs, her hand skimming gently across the top of the handrail. She smiled as she remembered unsuccessfully sliding down the rail years earlier, desperately trying to beat her cousins, who were already well practised at doing so. She'd landed awkwardly at the bottom with a very loud thud, and she still recalled the way her uncle had walked out of the dining room, given her a prod, and then told her that she had best work on her landing. Her own father would have turned red in the face with anger and sent her indefinitely to her room, and it was those differences between the two men in her life that she often pondered.

'Alex?'

She hurried the last few steps down the hall and found her aunt and uncle already seated at the dinner table. They often sat down early for a pre-dinner drink, and she always loved hearing them laugh and talk about their day, but tonight they didn't seem as jovial as usual.

'Is everything all right?' she asked. 'I hope I'm not late to dinner?'

Belle wasn't there yet, but then Belle had a penchant for arriving late to almost everything.

'No, of course not. We just wanted to keep you abreast of what's happening in Greece,' her aunt said.

'Oh?' She sat across the table from them, studying their faces. She was surprised to see them exchange rather serious-looking glances, as if they were trying to decide who should tell her the news, before her uncle cleared his throat and spoke.

'Alex, there's been a quite significant development regarding the monarchy,' he said. 'Have you read any of the news about what's happening, politically speaking, in Greece?'

She sat back in her chair, pleased that whatever concerns they had were about an entire country, not her or her cousins specifically. 'No, I haven't. I can't confess to being up to date with any political news, either here or in Greece, for that matter.'

'A national referendum was held, and the support was overwhelmingly in favour of abolishing the monarchy and establishing a republic in its place,' her uncle explained. 'King Theodore is making a live address tonight on national television, broadcast all through Greece, but my dear, he's being stripped of his title. The monarchy in Greece has effectively ended.'

Alexandra digested the news, feeling mildly sorry for the King, who had by all accounts always been kind to her when she'd met him. She wondered what life would be like for his family on the heels of such news.

'So they will remain exiled in London?' she asked, still not quite sure what all this had to do with her.

'I imagine so, although he has expressed his desire to return to Greece, regardless,' her aunt said. 'It seems all he wants is to return home, no matter whether he is king or not.'

'Although he's been advised publicly that it would not be wise for him to return, at least not until quite some considerable time has passed. Many Greeks are happy the King and his family won't be coming back. There have been celebrations on the streets and in the town squares across the country.'

'I can see that this would have come as quite a shock to the family,' Alexandra said carefully, looking between her aunt and uncle, 'but you both seem worried. Do you think this will have implications for me? Is my father still an aide to him, after all this time?'

She'd often thought of returning to Athens, wondering if she could travel with her aunt and uncle to see her old home and explore the places of her childhood. To visit her mother's grave, to see if her horses were still being kept at the same stables, to gather some of the things she'd left behind in their hasty departure all those years ago, if that were even possible.

'We are both quite concerned about how this might affect your father,' her aunt said.

'My father?' She certainly wasn't going to worry about her father, not after he'd made it abundantly clear that he had no intention of worrying about her.

'I know he hasn't kept in contact with you, but we've always made a concerted effort to know where he is and how he's faring.'

'How he's *faring*?' she retorted. 'Please don't waste your time worrying about him, of all people. I'm certainly not, not after all these years.'

'But Alex, this could affect him financially, not to mention that it will potentially stop him from returning to Greece too,' her uncle said. 'We would just hate it if you were to get caught up in any of this, for him to return because he suddenly needs your, well, your assistance. I imagine, knowing his ambition, that he will be trying to do something to reinstate himself, perhaps with the new government.'

'My assistance?' she asked, perplexed. 'Whatever do you mean? How could I possibly be of assistance to him?'

'Well,' her aunt said, as she poured herself another drink. 'Once, when you were younger, he angered your mother terribly by suggesting that he would secure a good marriage for you. Or should I say, a financially lucrative one. One that would benefit him personally.'

'He thought to bargain with me, as one might a horse?' she asked, laughing. 'No thank you, I wouldn't hear of it.'

Her aunt smiled at her. 'I think your mother said something along those lines too, only her choice of words may have been slightly more colourful.'

'The last thing we want to do is worry you,' her uncle continued. 'But we also need to be prepared in case your father were to show up unexpectedly. If he asks you to leave with him, or even tries to return to Greece and wants his only child by his side, it would be up to you to decide. We'd support you in whatever decision you chose to make. But your mother was very well known and highly respected in Athens, and he may well intend on reminding everyone of that.'

'You look so like her, Alex,' her aunt murmured. 'Sometimes I have to blink and remind myself that you're not her.'

Alexandra didn't need time to consider her words. 'This is my home now,' she said firmly. 'This is the only place I feel welcomed and truly part of a family, so no matter what my father claims to need, I shall not be going anywhere with him, and I shall certainly not be used by him so that he can elevate his position in society.'

Her aunt smiled at her across the table, and her uncle stroked his moustache, but she could tell that they were trying to hide their concerns. They had done so much for her, and continued to do so, and she would never know quite how to thank them for their generosity.

'What did I miss?' Belle entered the room with a dramatic look on her face, as if she'd missed an important party. 'Why the glum faces? Has someone died?'

'The monarchy has been abolished in Greece,' Alexandra said as Belle took the seat beside her.

'Oh, that's a shame.' Belle didn't seem overly interested in the development, which only made Alex love her all the more for her indifference.

'Do you know if Will is joining us tonight?' her aunt said.

Both Alexandra and Belle shrugged.

'Well, let's start dinner. We can always set another place for him if he arrives.'

Alexandra sat back and listened as Belle and her father began to bicker good-naturedly over something, smiling at her aunt as she sipped her wine and stared back at her. It took a lot to rattle Elizabeth, but something about tonight's announcement had certainly unsettled her aunt.

When Alexandra thought of her father, it was as if someone was clenching their fist in her stomach. It almost took her breath away sometimes when she thought about him returning for her, although as the years had passed she'd stopped worrying about him doing such a thing. In the beginning she'd been fearful every time the front doorbell rang, but by the time she'd turned eighteen, she'd believed he could no longer force her to leave with him or do anything against her will. She only hoped her beliefs hadn't been naïve; for if he did return for her now, he would have to take her kicking and screaming, no matter what his intentions.

*

The next evening, Alexandra sat and watched the orchestra. Her eyes were fixed on Bernard, unable to look at anyone else as she watched him play. It was like art, the way he lost himself in the music, the way his entire body seemed to live the melody. She looked around when it was over at the other people in the audience, the way they were chatting and laughing as they moved from their seats, and she wondered if they felt as invigorated and alive as she did. Whether they'd truly experienced the intimacy of the music.

Alexandra eventually followed everyone out into the foyer, waiting near the front desk for Bernard to come and find her. She'd been fortunate tonight because he'd been able to give her a ticket—the concert hadn't been sold out and he'd pretended she was family—so she could observe and learn as much as she could. She wouldn't tell him that she'd barely noticed the violinists, because she'd been too busy looking at him.

'There you are.'

She turned and found herself in Bernard's arms, his mouth finding hers in a soft kiss. Alexandra slid her hands up the front of his shirt and tugged him forwards, looking up into his eyes.

'You were incredible,' she murmured. 'As always.'

The foyer was almost empty now, and Bernard kissed her again before catching her hand and leading him with her. 'Come on, we're going to go out for a drink since it's Saturday night.'

She loved it when they went out afterwards, and she happily stayed by his side as they left the foyer to find some of the other musicians.

'If it isn't our resident lovebirds,' one of them said, letting out a whistle. 'Young love, eh?'

She grinned up at Bernard, and he gave her a wink in return.

'Where are we going?' she asked.

'Somewhere new,' he said. 'There's a jazz band playing, and we thought we'd try to catch the last half.'

Alexandra nodded, happy to go wherever he wanted.

'You seem distracted,' Bernard said, his thumb grazing her hand.

Alexandra knew better than to pretend she was fine, for he would immediately see through it. 'I've been thinking about something my aunt and uncle mentioned last night, that's all.'

Bernard's eyebrows peaked. 'Is everything all right?'

'The Greek monarchy has officially been abolished,' she told him. 'I watched the address the King delivered to the nation, and it was very sad to see him defeated. There were actually people in the street saying awful things about him, but he was very gracious and said that if the people wanted a republic, then they were entitled to one.'

Bernard shifted slightly in front of her. 'I'm sorry to hear all that. You've never talked about your connection to the royal family, but I do recall hearing that they live in London now.'

She nodded.

'And tell me what's troubling your aunt and uncle? They are concerned about your personal implications in some way?'

She sighed. 'They're concerned that my father may return for me. That he may want us to go back to Greece to rebuild our lives there.'

Bernard laughed. 'Darling, you are a grown woman of eighteen. Your father cannot return for you as if you're a child.'

'I know, of course I know that, but my father—'

'Is a difficult man. As my father is,' Bernard said. 'But we can forge a life without the approval or support of our fathers, Alex. I promise you we can.'

She tightened her grip on his hand. 'I don't know why I worry so. I suppose something about what they said, about him maybe needing money or wanting to elevate his own position with the new government…'

Bernard lifted her hand and kissed her knuckles. 'No more worrying. I want your head filled with music, not worries. Just put it out of your mind. We can deal with your father if and when he returns.' He watched her a moment longer. 'We can't choose our family, Alexandra, but we can choose what we do with our lives. Never forget that.'

As they went to leave, Alexandra tried to do what Bernard had suggested, but it was impossible to put her father completely from her mind. She also knew that she couldn't expect her aunt and uncle to keep her forever, so if she was going to sever all ties with him, she needed to find a way to support herself financially.

Besides, it was easier for Bernard to say that they could choose their own lives; he was a man.

The jazz music was every bit as good as Bernard had promised, and she did eventually find herself forgetting all her worries as they danced and laughed and drank too much wine.

'How did you learn to dance like this?' she gasped, as Bernard caught her around the waist and pulled her against his body.

She tipped back, laughing as the music seemed to get louder and faster, almost as if it were dancing across her skin. Her face was damp with perspiration, her throat parched from song after song on the dance floor.

'I used to work at a bar that played jazz,' he said, his breath hot against her cheek as he leaned in close to speak to her. 'I had a lot of time to watch in between waiting tables.'

'I didn't know that,' she said, as the song came to an end.

'I had to support myself the moment I walked out of my home. I worked at a bar as well as tutoring young musicians— anything to pay my way through college. I wasn't going home with my tail between my legs.'

Alexandra had never had to fend for herself, but hearing the reality of what Bernard had been through was sobering, to say the least.

'Your face! Darling, it wasn't as if I was forced to live on the streets! Come on, let's get another drink.'

She let him take her hand and they pushed past the couples around them to make their way to the bar. But as Alexandra sat and looked around, waiting for Bernard to get their drinks, she saw a man that bore a striking resemblance to her father. She blinked, squinting as she looked through the smoky haze where she'd seen the man.

'You look like you've seen a ghost,' Bernard said, passing her a glass of champagne.

When she looked again, the man was gone, and she shook her head, convinced she was seeing things. Surely if her father was in London, she'd know? Or at least her aunt and uncle would, wouldn't they? They'd said they'd been keeping tabs on him, after all.

'Alexandra,' Bernard said. 'I want you to close your eyes a moment and listen to the music.'

She gave him a quizzical look but followed his instructions, closing her eyes as he stood behind her and wrapped her in his arms.

'Feel the music,' he whispered. 'It should be like a living thing, breathing around you, drawing you in.'

Alexandra blew out the breath she was holding and leaned back into him, holding on to his arms, her head dipped back to rest on his chest. She forgot everything then, as the lively music, so different to what the orchestra had played, seemed to echo through her heart.

'Now open your eyes,' he said, directly into her ear. 'And come with me.'

Her eyes flew open. 'Come where?'

She noticed some of his colleagues watching them, grinning at her, and when she looked up at Bernard he had the same mischievous smile on his face.

'Bernard?' she demanded. 'Tell me what's happening.'

'Do you trust me?'

She nodded. 'Of course.'

'Then come with me. I've organised something special for you tonight.'

Alexandra would have followed Bernard to the ends of the earth if he'd asked—trusting him wasn't the problem. The problem was wanting to know all the details of his plans, because she certainly wasn't comfortable with surprises!

His palm was firm against hers as he walked her past the tables and the dancers, right up to the stage. The band finished a song then, and she watched as the lead singer smiled down at her, appearing to give Bernard a little wave.

'You know her?' Alexandra asked, feeling an unfamiliar pang of jealousy that he knew the blonde singer on stage.

'I know a lot of people in the music world,' he said, giving her a quick kiss on the cheek. 'That's all.'

She went to open her mouth again, but he shook his head and nudged her to make her look up.

'We have a very special guest joining us on the stage tonight,' the singer said. 'Alexandra, would you like to come up and introduce yourself?'

She froze. *Alexandra? Why had the woman on stage just said her name?*

'Bernard, she said my name,' she mumbled.

'Go on,' he said.

'What do you mean?'

But before she could wait for him to reply, the singer was stepping down from the stage and holding out her hand. The lights on the stage were bright, and Alexandra felt like a deer caught in headlights as she stood, not sure what she was supposed to do.

'This is for you,' the musician holding out a violin said.

'But—'

'We're playing something a little different: "Fly Me to the Moon." I'm told you know it?' the singer said, before holding out her hand. 'I'm Gigi, by the way.'

Alexandra nodded, still numb as she shook Gigi's hand. 'How did you, I mean, what—'

'You've got your man down there to thank,' Gigi said. 'He told me that you had dreams of being a musician, and he wanted you to know what it felt like to perform live.'

'I can't believe he's done this.'

Gigi grinned. 'Ready?'

Alexandra couldn't even see Bernard through the bright lights, but she knew he would be out there watching. If he believed in her this much, then she supposed she was going to have to believe in herself, whether she felt ready for a live performance or not.

'Ready,' she said, breathing deeply as she lifted the violin.

After she'd played the first few notes, as the entire band began to join in and Gigi started singing, Alexandra could barely wipe the smile from her face. If Bernard's goal had been to make her feel more alive than she'd ever felt before, to make her fall even more in love with music, and to believe that she belonged on the stage, then he'd most definitely succeeded.

CHAPTER 22

'Alexandra!'

She'd fallen asleep in Bernard's bed. Alexandra sat up and rubbed her eyes, disorientated for a moment as she glanced around. Her violin was where she'd left it on the chair, sheets of music strewn everywhere, and Bernard was standing in the entrance to the door.

'What time is it?' she asked, as he came to sit beside her. 'And why do you look so excited?' His eyes were wide, and he couldn't stop smiling. 'Is it truly so amazing, finding me in your bed?'

Bernard leaned forwards and claimed her mouth with a kiss. 'Yes, it is truly so amazing finding you here, all rumpled from sleep, but that's not why I'm smiling.'

She caught him around the back of his neck with her hand and pulled him towards her, indulging in one more kiss.

'Alex, I have news.'

She reluctantly let him go. 'Tell me. I can see you're about to burst.'

'The orchestra is auditioning next month for new string members.' He grinned. 'And they're officially opening up to female musicians for the very first time.'

She met his gaze, her heart immediately starting to pound. 'They're not,' she whispered. 'I don't believe you.'

'Alex, this is not something I would say if it weren't true.' He smoothed a fallen strand of hair away from her face. 'You could audition.'

'No,' she gasped. 'I'm nowhere near good enough, I'm—'

'One of the most talented violinists I've ever heard play,' he interrupted. 'I only wish you could see yourself as I see you. Alex, you have as good a chance as anyone else.'

'You truly believe so?'

'I absolutely believe so. And at the very least, they will become aware of you.' His hand rested over her leg, his eyes never leaving hers. 'This is the opportunity you've been waiting for, that *we've* been waiting for.'

She swallowed, her mind suddenly racing. 'But what piece would I play? How many pieces would I be expected to perform? When—'

'Slow down,' he said with a grin. 'I'll find out everything I can tomorrow, and we can talk to the other violinists to see what they think might impress the panel.'

Alexandra flopped back into the pillows, groaning and covering her face with her hands.

'I don't even know if I could walk on stage. You have so much confidence in me, but—'

'Stop,' Bernard said. 'At some point, you have to believe in yourself. You are a musician, Alexandra, and musicians have an obligation to share their talent with the world.'

'Oh, really,' she said, laughing at the earnest expression on his face.

'Yes,' he replied, grinning back at her. 'They do. But the other obligation you have right now is going home, so your uncle doesn't send out a search party for you. He'll have my head on a spike if he finds out you've been here all night.'

'You never did tell me what time it was.'

'It's after lunch,' he said, moving out of her way when she leapt up, scooping up her papers and putting her violin in its case, before quickly dressing.

'I'll see you tonight?' she asked, smoothing the rumples from her clothes and straightening her hair in the mirror. It was starting to grow out now, so it was finally transforming from manicured bob back to the more tousled, longer style she'd always had.

Bernard came up behind her and swept her hair from her neck, placing his lips there instead. She leaned back into him, smiling as he trailed kisses across her skin.

'Look at yourself, Alexandra,' he murmured.

She opened her eyes, looking at his reflection in the mirror before slowly training her gaze on herself. Bernard's body skimmed hers from behind, and he placed his hands on her shoulders as he smiled at her.

'You are beautiful and talented,' he said. 'Even if you're not chosen this time, the orchestra opening up to women changes everything.'

She studied herself, looked at her skin, at the way she held herself. Alexandra stood a little straighter and squared her shoulders, tilting her chin upwards slightly as she tried to appear more confident.

'If this is the life you see for yourself, this is your chance,' he whispered. 'Imagine us, both in the orchestra, living our dream, together. Just the two of us.'

Alexandra found herself nodding, seeing the life that he was describing. How she'd ever met a man like Bernard, she would never know.

'I love you,' she said, the words falling from her mouth as she lifted her gaze to look instead at Bernard in the mirror.

He slowly turned her around in his arms, his hands sliding down her body and settling on her waist now.

'I love you too,' he said.

Alexandra stood on tiptoe and kissed him, smiling against his mouth as they both started to laugh. She'd thought those words a hundred times, but never been brave enough to say them, until now.

'I need to go,' she groaned, kissing him one more time.

'Then go,' he replied. 'But be ready tonight. We're going to eat dinner here and then go through some music, and I'll speak to your tutor today, let him know the good news.'

Alexandra collected her things and dashed down the stairs, hoping it wouldn't take her too long to get back home. She was supposed to be having lunch with Belle, and her cousin was already annoyed by how much time Alexandra was spending with Bernard.

I'm going to audition for the orchestra. She chewed on her bottom lip to stop herself grinning, knowing how ridiculous she must look hurrying down the street with such a big smile on her face.

When she'd first arrived in London, she'd thought it was the end of the world. But now, as much as part of her still yearned to return to Greece, she was starting to realise that she at least had one thing to thank her father for. Because if she'd never been sent to London, she'd never have met Bernard, and he was easily the most incredible thing that had ever happened to her.

*

'Don't even think you can sneak down the hall without being noticed.'

Alexandra cringed and walked back a few steps. Belle was sitting in the front room, her arms folded across her chest. She wasn't used to seeing her cousin angry.

'I'm sorry I'm so late. Just let me put my things away and we can go for lunch.'

Belle's eyebrows lifted. 'Late? Are we going to pretend that you came home at all last night?'

Alexandra knew her cheeks had turned a deep red, but she wasn't going to lie to Belle.

'Did your mother notice?' she asked.

Belle sighed and came towards her. 'If she noticed, you'd know about it.'

'So we're still having lunch?'

'We're still having lunch,' Belle replied. 'But now I expect you to come shopping with me after, as punishment for standing me up.'

Alexandra grinned. 'I'll do anything, just please don't tell anyone I wasn't here last night.'

They walked up the stairs in unison. Alexandra stifled a yawn, wishing she was heading up to her room to catch up on some sleep instead of going straight out.

'Who would have thought you'd be the one having a torrid love affair out of the two of us,' Belle said with a loud sigh. 'I would have bet my allowance on me being the naughty one.'

Alexandra rolled her eyes and turned to her cousin when they reached the top. 'It's not a torrid affair, Belle. He's kind and sweet and so knowledgeable about music—'

'You're in love with him, aren't you? You're actually in love with him!'

She wished Belle would keep her voice down, and she also hated the fact that her cheeks had turned beetroot red again.

'Maybe I am,' Alexandra finally said, clearing her throat. *I love you too.* She remembered the words he'd repeated to her, the way it had made her feel when he'd looked at her afterwards.

'What does it feel like?' Belle asked as she followed Alexandra into her bedroom. 'I'm serious, how does it feel?'

Alexandra shut the door behind them, not wanting anyone else to hear their conversation. 'It's the most incredible feeling in the world,' she confessed, as they both flopped back onto her bed, staring up at the ceiling as they lay side by side. 'I just, I can't imagine life without him, and I know that sounds ridiculous but—'

'You're in love,' Belle finished for her. 'It's not ridiculous. It's what we all dream of.'

Alexandra linked their fingers together and turned her head so that she was looking at Belle. 'Something happened today, something that I think could change everything for me.'

Belle sat up, looking down at her. 'What happened?'

Alexandra sat up too, wrapping her arms around her knees. 'I'm going to audition for the London Luminary Ensemble. I know that means we won't be able to go to university next year together if I'm chosen, but—'

Belle hugged her tightly, fiercely. 'Stop,' she said. 'I was planning on taking another gap year anyway, and if this is what you really want?' She shook her head and smiled. 'I'm so happy for you, Alex. You deserve every amazing thing that's happening for you.'

'I keep imagining us living in some gorgeous flat together, with sheets of music pinned to the walls and having friends over to practise.' She sighed. 'I know, I'm getting carried away, but it feels so good to dream.'

'Then dream you may,' Belle announced. 'But right now you're getting ready for lunch with your cousin, who, for the record, was your best friend *before* you were famous.'

They both laughed and Belle dragged Alexandra from the bed.

'Girls?' There was a knock at the door, followed by its opening just enough for her aunt to poke her head round. 'What's all the excitement about?'

'Well,' Belle said, with a conspiratorial smile, 'Alex is in love and she's going to audition for the orchestra.'

'Well, how about that?' her aunt said. 'I mean, the being in love part isn't exactly a surprise, but the orchestra? That's just splendid. You've been working very hard on your music, Alexandra. We're all so proud of you.'

'Thank you,' Alexandra replied. 'I have a long way to go, with choosing what piece to play and practising, but I'm so excited to even have the opportunity. They've never been open to considering female musicians before.' She hesitated. 'All these years, I've never thanked you for introducing me to music. I can't imagine what my life would be like without it now, so thank you, Aunt Elizabeth. It means the world to me.'

Her aunt's smile was serene, but there were tears shining in her eyes, and Alex only wished she'd thanked her sooner. 'You're very welcome. It's you who has had the talent, but it very much sounds like we should be celebrating today. May I join you both for lunch?'

Alexandra nodded to her aunt as Belle slipped away, presumably to get ready to go.

'Oh, and Alex?'

She turned and smiled, waiting for her aunt to speak again.

'Love or not, it would be nice to know you were asleep in your own bed at night. I would hate to have to restrict your time with Bernard.'

Her aunt gave her a steady look before leaving her, and Alexandra stood very still, mortified. So much for thinking that her aunt hadn't noticed her absence.

She turned and looked at her violin where she'd laid it on the bed, wishing she could take it out now and begin practising, to start work on what she might play at her audition. But most of all she wished she were in Bernard's flat, with him curled up on the bed watching her as she played for him.

CHAPTER 23

Four Months Later

Alexandra closed her eyes, her breath shallow as she tightened her fingers around her violin. She lifted her chin, rehearsing in her mind, trying not to listen to the impeccable performance of the musician ahead of her, trying not to compare herself as she prepared for what was to come.

I can't do this.

Fear rose inside of her, a line of sweat forming on her upper lip as her heart started to pound, as she thought for one fleeting moment that she should simply gather her things and run, that she should avoid the heartache of what she was about to put herself through. That she shouldn't have been there in the first place.

'Alex.'

A hand closed over her shoulder, gentle and reassuring. She opened her eyes and turned to find Bernard standing there, his thick dark hair falling over his brow, his soft brown eyes reassuring as she stared back at him; at the man who'd made all of this possible.

'This is your moment to show the world who you truly are,' he whispered, his hands light against her back as he pulled her closer, as she tucked her violin to her chest and stared back at him. 'You *deserve* to be here, Alex. You deserve everything that has brought you to this moment.'

His lips brushed hers, and when he pulled away he pressed his forehead gently to hers, carefully stroking her hair as they stood. His breath was warm against her skin, the feel of him so close reminding her of just how far she'd come, of the opportunity she'd been given, of the gift he'd given her.

'Nothing will ever be the same after today,' he murmured. 'Today is your day, my love.'

She looked up at him as he took a step back, as he reached for the hand that held her bow and gently lifted it, placing a kiss against her skin as she looked into his eyes; eyes that told her she had nothing to fear. Eyes that told her he believed in her.

'Thank you,' she whispered, swallowing past the fear in her throat, choosing in that moment to believe the words of the man who loved her.

Then her name was called, and as Bernard slipped into the background, Alexandra stood tall and took her first step onto the stage, her heels clicking as everything around her fell silent.

Bernard was right. It was time to show the world who she truly was.

It only took Alexandra seconds to walk across the stage. She stood, trying not to hold her violin too tightly, trying not to bunch her shoulders, to breathe evenly. If she was to be part of the orchestra, she would have to be confident, so focused on her music that she didn't falter beneath the bright lights or become bewildered by the crowd.

'Name?'

She tried not to squint as she looked out at the small panel of men waiting to assess her. She knew one of them was the current conductor of the orchestra, as well as the principal violinist.

'Alexandra Konstantinidis,' she said, squaring her shoulders as she spoke, and making sure her voice was loud enough to carry to them.

'Please tell us what you are playing today.'

'I will be playing Pachelbel's "Canon in D".'

There were no further questions, and Alexandra waited a moment, composing herself. It was then that a movement caught her eye, someone entering at the rear door, presumably the only other person in the theatre besides those immediately before her.

Bernard. It was impossible to see that far, the lights were too bright, but she could feel him, knew that it was him.

Play for me. That's what he'd told her. *Imagine you are playing for me and only me.*

A smile quivered across her lips as she lifted her violin and positioned it between her chin and shoulder, keeping her arms soft as she blew out the gentlest of breaths.

And then she began. Her bow danced across the strings, the music coming to life as she played with everything she had, as she smiled at Bernard in her mind and imagined that she was simply standing in his attic bedroom, with him sitting on the bed as her audience of one.

Perspiration touched her forehead and her upper lip, but Alexandra wasn't nervous. Not now. Bernard had been right when he'd told her it was her time to show the world who she was. All those years she'd wondered what it would be like to perform, and here she was, playing with all her heart.

As she played the final note, she paused, her breath shallow as she closed her eyes, wanting to absorb the feeling of being on stage, to remember it forever. She half expected someone to clap, but instead she was greeted with silence.

She lowered her instrument and took a step forwards, hoping for praise but receiving none.

'Thank you, Miss Konstantinidis.'

Alexandra nodded and walked slowly and confidently from the stage, as if she weren't terrified, as if her hands weren't trembling from the adrenaline surging through her body. Her legs felt like a newborn foal's, ready to buckle at the knees after each unsteady step.

But when she was out of sight, the next musician to audition striding past her, she collapsed against the wall.

I did it. I actually did it! If they don't think I'm good enough, then so be it, because I played with all my heart.

Alexandra knew it was the performance of her lifetime. She had played as if her very life depended upon it.

'Alex!' Bernard's excited whisper wrapped around her.

'Please tell me I was good,' she asked, as Bernard took her hand and guided her out through the back door into the fresh air.

'Good?' he asked, scooping her up and swinging her in a big circle. 'Alex, you were phenomenal! It took every inch of my willpower to stop from clapping and cheering when you finished.'

'Truly?' she asked, when he finally set her down.

'Truly,' he repeated. 'If they don't invite you to become a member, they're mad.'

Alexandra knew she had to be so much better than anyone else there to be chosen. She was a woman, for starters, which meant that she had to be better than any man. And then there was her age, although she wasn't certain if they'd take that into consideration or not. She imagined her gender was likely the one thing that could hold her back, unless she was far better than anyone else auditioning.

Bernard kissed her forehead. 'Wait there. I'll go back and get your case.'

She was about to protest and tell him she'd go back herself, but something stopped her. She actually wanted a moment to herself, to replay her audition in her mind, to remember what it had felt like to be on the stage.

Bernard was only gone a moment though, and when he returned he dropped to one knee and opened the case for her. She opened her mouth to stop him, dropped down low to her haunches to try to prevent him from opening it, but it was too late.

'What's this?' he asked, taking one of the folded pieces of paper out.

'Please don't,' she said, trying to snatch it from him.

But Bernard's arms were longer than hers and he opened it without her being able to stop him, smiling down at her as he read the note.

'I can't believe you kept this,' he said.

She blushed, hating how hot her cheeks were. 'It was the first note you ever wrote me. Of course I kept it!'

'And this?' he asked.

Alexandra didn't even bother trying to stop him this time. Bernard unfolded the sheet of music.

'The day you told me what you were going to play,' he said. 'I wrote on this.'

'You left it on the pillow beside my bed,' she murmured. 'I'd been working on the piece all night, trying to understand every part and intricacy of the composition.'

Bernard cupped her cheek against his palm, and she found herself staring at his mouth.

'My greatest fear was that you wouldn't believe in yourself,' he whispered.

'And my greatest fear is losing you.' The words slipped from her lips before she could stop them, and suddenly all she could wish for was to retract them. But Bernard didn't falter.

'There is nothing you could do, nothing that could happen, that would make that come true.'

Before she could answer he kissed her, gently, a barely-there brush of their lips. She wasn't going to ruin the moment by telling him all the things that could part them, but even his kiss was only enough to distract her, not to make her forget. She never took Bernard for granted, but she did sometimes wonder what he saw in her.

She looked away and put her violin in the case, her bow carefully tucked in its place, followed by the papers Bernard had removed. She plucked them from his hand and placed them where they belonged.

'Are you certain you don't have any other treasures tucked away in there?' he teased.

'Well, if you don't count the letters from my past lovers…'

Bernard laughed, his head tipped back as they rose and began to walk.

'You're going to be the most fabulous new member of the orchestra,' he finally said, leaning closer and putting his arm around her. 'Your family will be so proud of you.'

Alexandra sighed. It was true; her aunt and uncle, and her cousins, would be immensely proud of her. But her father was another story entirely, if he ever bothered to remember he had a daughter.

'You don't think they will?'

'The family you know will be, of course they will, but my father…'

Bernard looked down at her and she braved a smile. He was one of the few people in her life who genuinely understood what it was like for her.

'Do you think your parents will ever come to watch you perform?' she asked.

Bernard shook his head, looking away as he spoke. 'My mother would. If she could make her own decision on the matter I know she would, but when my father disowned me, he told me I'd never see either of them again, and he's been true to his word.'

Tears welled in Alexandra's eyes. 'You only have one mother. Please, Bernard, can we not at least try to see her?'

Bernard began to walk faster, his stride too long for her to match.

'Bernard!' she called. 'I'm sorry, I shouldn't have said anything.'

His smile had returned by the time she caught up, and she curled her fingers around his arm.

'I think we should celebrate,' Bernard said. 'It's not every day you get to audition for the London Luminary Ensemble.'

'Would you like to come home with me? I'm sure my aunt and uncle would be more than happy to host us.'

Bernard's smile told her that he would very much like that, and so they kept walking, the sunshine on their shoulders as they slipped into an easy stride, and an even easier conversation about the music they both loved.

'Darling, why didn't you tell us it was today!' Alexandra's aunt threw her hands in the air as her uncle poured champagne that evening. 'You never said anything this morning.'

'What a reason to celebrate,' her uncle said. 'I hear you were the catalyst for our Alexandra deciding to audition at all, so we owe you a debt of gratitude, young man.'

Alexandra found herself beaming at Bernard, barely able to take her eyes from him, and she knew her aunt had noticed. She was staring back at her with her brows arched, as if she'd just discovered a secret.

She held her glass up when the others did, and they all clinked them together in celebration. Alexandra took a sip, the bubbles tickling her nose as she swallowed.

'Tell us, what was she like on stage?' her aunt asked.

'Mesmerising,' Bernard said, his eyes never leaving hers as he spoke. 'If they don't offer her a position, they're mad.'

'I'm sure they will,' her uncle said, adding a little more champagne to each of their glasses. 'Who wouldn't love our darling Alexandra?'

She lifted her glass again to take another sip, but when she swallowed this time her stomach lurched. Alexandra placed her hand there, flat against her belly, but she suddenly had the most overwhelming sensation that she was going to be sick.

'I'm sorry, I—' Alexandra thrust her glass at Bernard and scurried from the room, her hand rising to cover her mouth as she ran.

Alexandra only just made it to the bathroom, shutting the door behind her before bending over the basin and turning the water on. She was sick once, then twice, and then again until there was absolutely nothing left inside her.

She swirled the water, trying to clean up her mess, wishing she'd made it the few steps further to the toilet. She was still feeling off-balance and unwell a few minutes later, and she lowered herself to the cool tiles on the floor, wondering for a moment if she should actually lie down.

'Alexandra?' Her name was followed by a soft knock. 'Is everything all right?'

'Yes,' she called back, hating how feeble her voice sounded.

'May I come in?'

The door opened a crack and her aunt stood there, peering in. When she saw her on the floor, she pushed the door further open and came in.

'Darling, what's wrong?'

'I think it was something I ate,' Alexandra said. 'Thank goodness it didn't happen when I was on stage.'

Her aunt touched her forehead. 'You do feel a little clammy. Shall I go and tell Bernard you're not feeling well? We can always celebrate another day.'

'No, I'll be fine,' she said, forcing herself to stand. The room seemed to spin then, and Alexandra reached for the basin to stop herself from falling straight over.

'Well, you're most definitely not fine,' her aunt muttered.

'I am,' Alexandra insisted, not about to ruin the evening with Bernard. He needed this as much as she did, a night to celebrate with her family, to feel as if he belonged, that he could be proud of who he was and the way he chose to spend his life.

'Alexandra?'

She held her hands up and did a little spin, praying she wouldn't fall over. 'I'm fine,' she insisted. 'Now can we please go and celebrate?'

Her aunt sighed, but within minutes they were both back out in the sitting room, champagne in hand as they joined the men again. Only Alexandra didn't take a sip—for even the smell of the bubbles was making her stomach turn, and she hadn't the faintest idea why.

CHAPTER 24

Present Day

Ella stepped off the boat and took out her map, trying to figure out where she was and where she had to go. On the boat, she'd managed to find a kind man who spoke a little English, and he'd clearly marked the path she needed to take—it seemed as if everyone knew the house she was looking for. Apparently she would be able to walk without needing transport, but she decided to stop for coffee first. She wasn't sure if it was because she needed the caffeine, or because she was grateful for anything that delayed her journey; either way, she didn't need much convincing to stop. She was also thinking about Gabriel and how nice it had been to have him on holiday with her—he'd left on one ferry to return to London, as she'd got on another to go to Alonissos.

She ordered her coffee and sat outside in the sunshine, taking the worn photo from the little box in her bag and staring at the woman and the girl, as she'd already done so many times since she'd been given the clues. Part of her wondered if she wasn't on a wild goose chase—what were the chances of this woman being the link to her grandmother's past? The more she'd had time to think about it, the less likely it all seemed. Ella sighed, still staring at the photo in her hands, of two minds about following through with her plans at all.

'Do you know them?'

Ella jumped and almost knocked the coffee from the server's hands, not having realised he'd come to stand beside her. 'Sorry, I was lost in thought.'

The server placed the coffee down, leaning on the chair beside her as he pointed at the picture. 'How do you know the women in the photo?'

She looked up, shielding her eyes from the sun. 'I think one of them could be my great-grandmother.'

The server made a face as if he wasn't convinced. 'Do you know who they are?'

'Yes,' she said, slowly. 'Well, I've been told who they might be, but—' *Why am I even having this conversation with a stranger?* 'Sorry, do you know them? Are they familiar to you?'

He grinned. 'I know Alexandra, we all do. She comes here every morning for her coffee.'

'She does?' Well, at least that meant she was on the right island. The information she'd gleaned over the past few days had clearly been correct.

'She takes it black with three drops of milk, and she always has a spoonful of sweets on the side.'

He smiled and pushed off from the chair, leaving her to her thoughts and her coffee. Ella was slowly getting used to the strong black coffee she'd been served in Greece since she'd arrived, but she could see why sweets or pieces of Turkish delight were so popular to consume alongside them—they added sweetness to the otherwise bitter flavour of the drink.

Once she'd finished, Ella stood and slipped the photo against the map, deciding to carry both as she set off to find the house. When she arrived, she would show it to Alexandra if she opened the door—it might keep it from being closed in her face if she had something to give her.

*

Fifteen minutes later, Ella stood outside a very pleasant, very large home halfway up the hill. The cobbled paths and pretty shuttered houses reminded her of Skopelos; everywhere she looked there was a picture-postcard scene. Until she'd visited herself, she'd almost wondered if Skopelos could actually be as pretty as it appeared in photos. She could confirm that it most definitely lived up to expectations.

Ella lifted her hand, taking a deep breath before knocking three times against the wooden door.

She waited, trying to focus on breathing calmly, before eventually knocking again. She hadn't really thought about what she'd do if nobody was home. Would she come back the next day? She looked around to see if anyone was watching from the other houses, wondering if she could show the photo around to see if she was at least at the right house, when a voice called out from inside.

Ella wasn't sure what she'd said, but she waited, nonetheless.

The woman didn't sound as old as she'd expected, and she wondered if it could be a housekeeper. Or the wrong house. Trust her luck, to have knocked at the wrong door.

But when the door finally swung open, her breath caught in her throat and she found herself lost for words. The woman had black hair streaked heavily with grey, pulled back into a bun, and appeared even younger than Ella's own grandmother had been. She wore minimal make-up, with a light red lipstick that made her look effortlessly elegant, dressed simply in a silk tank top and slacks. As Ella stared at her, she could well imagine that this woman had come from a privileged background—there was a presence about her that commanded attention, despite her age.

'May I help you?' she asked in perfect English that barely betrayed a hint of an accent.

Ella cleared her throat, not used to being so lost for words.

'Alexandra?' she asked. 'Alexandra Konstantinidis?'

The woman blinked back at her, nodding ever so slightly.

'My name is Ella, and I know this will very likely come as a shock, and I might be entirely wrong, but I was given this photo. From what I can gather, it appears to be a photograph of you and your mother, taken many years ago.' Ella held it out and watched as the woman hesitated at first, as if unsure about taking it at all. She caught her breath, trying to slow down when she spoke the next time. 'Alexandra, I've been led to believe that one of the women in this photo might be my great-grandmother. That perhaps you are related to me?'

The woman took the photograph, her hand trembling as she stared down at it. When she finally looked up, her bottom lip was trembling too, and her eyes were damp with tears.

'You *are* Alexandra Konstantinidis?' Ella asked. 'You are the girl in the photograph? Or have I made a terrible mistake in knocking at your door?'

Ella's brow furrowed as she stared at the woman. She'd expected her to be so much older. This woman couldn't possibly be her great-grandmother.

Ella started to back away. 'I'm so sorry I bothered you, I—'

'I always wondered if this day would ever come,' the woman finally said, reaching out her hand and taking hold of Ella's, gripping her fingers tightly arounds hers. 'I've imagined a thousand times over what this moment would be like.'

She let go of Ella's hand and reached up, touching Ella's face, studying her as if she were a road map that had to be committed to memory.

'You were expecting someone to find you?' Ella asked, puzzled at the way this elegant, beautiful woman was smiling at her as she kept hold of her. 'Because of this photograph?'

'Well, I expected it would be my daughter searching for me, not a granddaughter, but yes, I've half expected someone every day for the past fifty years. And yes, this is a photograph of me with my mother, taken many, many years ago.' The woman let go of Ella, only to wipe her eyes, still holding the photograph in her other hand. 'I'm sorry, I just, I gave up hope many years ago of this ever happening. For a long time, I imagined constantly what it would be like, and then I slowly began to lose hope of ever connecting with my daughter.'

'May I come in?' Ella asked.

Alexandra nodded, before stepping forwards and embracing Ella, gently holding her in her arms as if she wasn't certain whether it was the right thing to do or not. She held her for a long moment, and Ella felt her body soften, hugging her back. 'I would very much like you to come in,' Alexandra said when she finally let go of her. 'It was all just so unexpected, seeing you standing there with that photograph.'

'It was just as unexpected for me, realising that I'd somehow found my way to you,' Ella said. 'To the person in the photograph. I've been staring at it ever since I was given the box, and it drove me crazy wondering what the link to my family was.'

'I'm sorry I didn't write something on the back of it. At the time,' Alexandra said, glancing back at Ella over her shoulder as she walked, 'it was all so overwhelming. I've second-guessed my choices for decades, wishing I could go back in time and leave something more obvious behind.'

Ella followed her into a house that looked every bit as elegant as its owner. She marvelled at the stone walls that were painted the same warm white as the exterior, with an exposed wood ceiling and floorboards to match. The wooden windows were like picture frames for the ocean view, with white drapes billowing in the breeze and adding to the luxurious, relaxed feel of the home. It was stunning.

When Ella turned, she found Alexandra watching her with a curious look on her face, but neither she nor Ella said anything straight away.

'Please, take a seat,' Alexandra eventually said, as she sat in one of the white chairs by the window.

Ella followed her lead and sat across from her. She'd thought so much about what to say when she reached the doorstep, but she'd planned very little after that point. It seemed almost impossible to believe that she'd actually found the woman in the picture.

'Perhaps you can tell me how you came across this photograph,' Alexandra said. 'I mean, I think I know, but it's been a very long time. Was this given to your mother many years ago?'

'Actually, no. We only recently received a phone call, from a lawyer who represented a place named Hope's House.' Ella watched as Alexandra shut her eyes, nodding her head as if she was reliving a memory. 'There was a box with my grandmother's name attached to it, and given that she'd passed away recently, I went to collect it, thinking it was something for her estate. I've only been in possession of it for six weeks or so.'

'I think you'll find it was your mother's name on the box,' Alexandra said. 'My daughter's name. I'm the one who left it there for her.'

Ella shook her head. 'No, that can't be right. I'm certain that it was my grandmother who was adopted.' She paused. 'Could she have been your mother's child? It just doesn't quite make sense to me.' There was no way it could have been her mother who was adopted. Wouldn't she have known?

Alexandra leaned forwards in her chair. 'I gave your mother her name, Madeline, and my only request was that her adoptive parents continue to use it,' she said. 'I named her when she was born, for it was a name my own mother had always loved. Perhaps you were confused, by the initials on the box?'

M James. Of course, her mother and grandmother had the same initials.

'But—'

'Hope refused to tell me much about her, even when I begged her for details, but the one thing she did tell me was that they'd honoured my wish and kept her name."

'My grandmother's name was Margaret,' Ella murmured. 'That's why we presumed that the initial *M* was for her.' Did that make this woman sitting across from her, Alexandra, her own grandmother? Her heart started to race. This was her mother's mother. It was almost impossible to believe. 'When I was contacted by the lawyer to say that something had been left to the estate of my grandmother, I never once thought to question that they had the correct recipient. It was for my mum all along.' Her mother, who seemed to be the only person completely uninterested in the history of the box or what it contained.

'I've thought about the contents of that little box every day for the past fifty years, wishing I'd been less cryptic with my clues.' Tears ran freely down Alexandra's cheeks then. 'And not a day has passed that I haven't prayed that my daughter would forgive me for the terrible thing I did, giving her up for adoption.'

'My mother doesn't know,' Ella told her. 'All of us, we all presumed that it was my grandmother who was adopted, that it was kept secret because of the era. But you're so young, it must have been the early seventies when you were pregnant?'

'It was. And I know what you're thinking, that surely by then the world had become more progressive and young women wouldn't have been forced to give up their babies, but I came from a very conservative family. It would have brought great shame on my father's family if anyone had discovered that I was pregnant.'

Ella could only imagine what it must have been like. She reached into her bag and took out the sheet of music, having forgotten about it when she first arrived. 'You left something else in the box,' she said. 'Something else that helped me to find my way to you.'

'The sheet of music,' Alexandra replied, her hand hovering over her heart. 'I can't tell you how difficult it was to leave that behind.'

'Please,' Ella said. 'Take it. It belongs to you, after all.'

Alexandra reached for the paper, sitting back in the chair and studying it, her hand raised to her mouth now as if to stifle her cries. Gabriel had told her that he wondered if the music had great sentimental meaning, whether it was for an audition or important performance, and seeing Alexandra's reaction told her that he was most likely right.

'A friend of mine plays for the London Symphony Orchestra,' Ella said gently. 'It was through him that I was slowly able to piece together who the mystery "B" was on the note. Until then, I couldn't make head or tail of how it connected to my family.'

Ella watched as Alexandra held the worn piece of paper to her chest. 'Bernard was always writing me notes. He was such a romantic, and whenever I was nervous he'd know just what to say, or what to write.'

'But why this piece of music?' Ella asked. 'Why leave this particular piece behind?'

'Because it meant so much to me. Because it was the last note he ever wrote for me, the last written words of encouragement, and I wanted to leave the thing that meant the most to me behind for my child.'

Ella nodded, watching as Alexandra rose and walked across the room, suddenly appearing agitated.

'I was one of the first women to audition for the London Luminary Ensemble,' Alexandra said, her eyes fixed on something outside the window. 'This was the piece I chose to play, and even though I knew it by heart, I always carried it with me, just in case. Bernard knew that I would look at it, and whenever I did, I was reminded of just how much he believed in me.'

'So you were a member of the orchestra?'

Ella waited for Alexandra to speak, about to repeat her question when she finally replied.

'It wasn't to be,' Alexandra finally said. 'But it was a very long time ago. If I'm honest I can barely remember how to read music these days.'

'And Bernard?' Ella asked. 'He became your husband?'

Alexandra sighed and sat down heavily in the chair again. 'Bernard and I were not meant to be either. At least not then, anyway.'

Ella wasn't sure what that meant, but she didn't want to push for more information than Alexandra was prepared to give.

'You have his eyes, you know. There's something about you that reminds me of him.'

'I have my mother's eyes,' Ella said. 'There's not a lot similar about us, but I've always been told that I have her eyes, and the older I get, the more like hers they seem.'

They both smiled at each other then, and Ella laughed. 'I can't believe I'm sitting in a room with a biological grandmother that I had no idea even existed.'

'It's hard for me to believe too, Ella. After all this time, all those years of hoping, and then losing my Bernard…' Her voice trailed away for a moment. 'I'd all but given up hope.'

She wasn't sure what Alexandra meant by that, since she'd already said that she and Bernard weren't married.

'I thought your mother would have received the box years ago, that was the agreement. She was supposed to receive it when she turned twenty-one.'

'She was?'

'Hope told me that she asked each mother who gave birth whether they'd like to leave something behind. Not everyone did, in fact many chose not to, but she said that when a child turned twenty-one, she would personally send their box to them.'

Ella hesitated. 'Hope passed away some time ago, I don't know how long it was, but perhaps something stopped her from following through with her promise? There were only seven boxes found before the house was scheduled for demolition.'

'Demolition?' Alexandra's voice quavered. 'If only those walls could talk, the tales they could have told. There were many, many boxes, I saw them all when Hope took me into her office.'

Ella didn't have an answer as to why only these seven were left. She imagined the others had been sent out as planned, but something about these last remaining boxes had made Hope want to hide them. Maybe Mia was right, and these were the ones that for some reason weren't supposed to be discovered.

'How about I make us something to drink?' Alexandra said, rising again and gesturing for Ella to follow her. 'Would you stay for the afternoon, to tell me more about your mother? I'd very much like to hear about her.'

'Of course I would,' Ella said as she found herself in a large kitchen, watching as Alexandra took down two glasses. 'But would you mind if I asked you about your connection to the monarchy? Someone mentioned you were forced to leave Greece?'

'We did leave, many years ago, when I was just a girl,' she said with a loud sigh. 'It all seems like such a long time ago. A lifetime ago, in fact.'

'You must have had an extraordinary life in your younger years. Were you in Athens before you fled?'

'I was, and although I can look back and see that it was extraordinary now, back then it was just my life as I knew it. My mother was adored by many, the princess of the equine world, and my father was a man with huge ambition. An ambition that became more important to him than anything else.'

'So then how did you end up in London?'

Alexandra took out a bottle of sparkling water and poured it into each glass, her hand shaking a little as she did so. Ella watched her curiously, wondering how this woman who wasn't even the same nationality as her could possibly be her grandmother. She studied the graceful way she held herself, the elegant fingers glinting with diamonds, the whispering lines around her eyes and mouth. She was certainly youthful for a grandmother, although there was a sense that something had aged her, as if she was carrying a great pain, and Ella wondered if it went beyond having to give up her daughter.

'What happened was that life as I knew it changed in an instant. Suddenly I was in another country, taken from everything I knew and loved, thrown into a new world that I felt a stranger in for so long.' She passed Ella a glass, staring into her eyes as she spoke. 'Until I met Bernard, that is. Then everything fell into place, and I was finally living the life I wanted to live, on my terms.'

Ella smiled at Alexandra. 'Until?' she asked.

'Until my father walked back into my life and stole everything I loved from me,' she murmured. 'For the second time in six years, my father made a decision for me that changed my life forever.'

CHAPTER 25

London, 1973

It seemed as if Alexandra was always having to make it up to Belle for not seeing enough of her. Today they'd been to Harrods for high tea and a spot of shopping, and although it had been a welcome break from the hours she'd been spending practising these past months, she was exhausted. Belle always moved and spoke at a frantic pace, and she shopped with the same enthusiastic attitude, which meant Alexandra was ready to collapse.

'Aren't you supposed to find out by today?' Belle asked as they walked up the steps to their front door. 'I can't believe you haven't mentioned it all day.'

'I've been trying not to think about it,' Alex said. 'Although to be fair, I've done nothing *but* think about it.'

'Well, let's see if anything has been delivered while we were out. Imagine if it's good news!'

'I think they only send a letter if you're being invited to join, although that might just be a rumour.' Her heart fluttered at the thought. She could just imagine the life she and Bernard would live, the countries they might be able to visit as they toured the world.

'We're home,' Belle called out as they walked into the hall, her heels clicking on the wood floor. 'Mother? Has something arrived for Alex? She's—'

'In here, girls.'

Belle gave her an excited look, her eyes wide as she hurried ahead of her. Alexandra followed, her breath coming in shallow pants as she prepared herself. Was that why Elizabeth had called to them? Had it arrived, and she was waiting to give it to her?

But her excitement turned to despair when she stepped into the room and saw that her aunt was seated across from a well-dressed man with a thick head of salt-and-pepper hair and a neatly trimmed moustache. He gave her a smile as one might an acquaintance they hadn't seen in a very long time.

It appeared, after all these years, that her father had returned. Her aunt and uncle had been right to be concerned, after all.

'Hello, Father,' she said, as Belle glanced at her and moved closer, almost protectively. Alexandra had her right hand hanging at her side, and she felt Belle's little finger graze hers, as if to tell her she was there for her.

'Alexandra, I wouldn't have recognised you,' he said, with a smile that took her by surprise. 'You've blossomed into quite the young woman.'

As you would know if you'd been to visit. She wished to hurl an insult at him, but stayed quiet instead. She could rant and rave to Belle later, or to her aunt, who she knew would be most understanding and perhaps even join in.

'What brings you to London?' Alexandra asked politely.

'Your father has expressed an interest in you going to live with him,' her aunt said, before her father had the chance to answer. 'I've been explaining to him how difficult it would be for a young lady to be uprooted from everything she knows.'

'I—' Alexandra faltered, as her father interrupted.

'Regardless of your aunt's protests, I believe it is time for you to return to your family, Alexandra. You've been here quite long enough.'

'Alexandra is eighteen! She can't be moved around as if she's a child any longer; she's an adult!' Belle erupted, earning her a sharp stare from her aunt.

'Belle, please leave us,' Elizabeth said, her tone final as Belle touched Alexandra's shoulder and gave it a quick squeeze.

'I'm sorry,' Belle mouthed to her, before leaving the room.

'She's right,' Alexandra said. 'I am an adult, and you cannot arrive after being absent for almost seven years, expecting me to welcome you with open arms.'

Her father stroked his moustache and sat back in his chair. 'You are aware of what has happened in Greece? Of the situation there?'

Alexandra nodded.

'Then you should also be aware that everything I have dedicated my life to has changed. That we're on the verge of losing everything.' He had the audacity to smile, despite the news he was breaking. 'But you, my dear, are the one thing of value I have left.'

'I am not a horse to be traded for money,' she retorted. 'If that is what you are insinuating?'

'Don't be naïve enough to think that we are the wealthy family that we once were.' His voice rumbled in his throat; she'd forgotten how intimidating he could be when he was angry. 'There was only so much family silver, jewellery and Fabergé gifts to smuggle out of Greece, and they're long gone.'

Alexandra lifted her chin slightly and levelled her gaze at her father—he was speaking of the gifts their family had received from the King and Queen over his years of service, and her mother's years of friendship. 'What of my mother's personal jewellery collections? I should very much like to have those returned to me.'

Her father turned a deep shade of red, his entire cheeks stained as he looked at the ground.

'Nicholas?' Elizabeth asked. 'Your daughter has asked you about my sister's private collection. The collection that was passed to her from our parents, the collection that is her birthright.'

'*My* collection,' he said under his breath. 'She was my wife, and that means the collection was mine to distribute as I saw fit.'

Alexandra knew. She didn't need to be told, didn't need him to confirm it.

'It's gone, isn't it?' Elizabeth said. 'Sold to fund your hedonistic lifestyle these past seven or so years?'

Alexandra had the immediate sensation that she was going to be sick. *Gone. Everything of Mama's is gone.*

'I would like you to leave,' Alexandra said, surprised by the sound of her own voice. She looked at her aunt, who rose and came to stand beside her.

'You're asking your own father to leave?' he spluttered. 'Well, if I'm leaving, you'll be coming with me. You've been spoiled here long enough. It's time for you to marry and do your obligation for your family.'

'No, Father, I won't. I have no intention of coming with you today or any other day, for that matter, and I certainly won't be marrying a man of your choosing. This is 1973, and women in London have a choice in such matters now.'

'Nicholas, to what do we owe this pleasure? Such a sad turn of events in Greece.'

Her uncle glided into the room then, clearly attempting to defuse the situation, and Alexandra took her chance to leave the room. Her stomach heaved and she hurried up the stairs, hearing her aunt behind her but not stopping for fear she might be sick on the carpet.

She ran into the bathroom, heaving up the contents of her stomach into the toilet as her aunt stroked her hair back from her face and held it. Alexandra dropped down to her knees, waiting to make sure the moment had passed before slowly rising.

'I'm sorry, Elizabeth, I don't know what came over me.'

'I can understand how your father's demands could make you feel unwell,' she said. 'But if I'm not mistaken, you were sick the other day too?'

Alexandra nodded and washed her face, taking down a glass from the cabinet in the bathroom to fill with water. 'My stomach has been rather delicate lately. I think it could be an overconsumption of champagne.' In truth, she wasn't certain why she was so unwell; her stomach was usually not so unreliable.

'How about I ask the doctor to call and see you in the morning? Just as a precaution.'

'Of course,' she replied, before suddenly remembering the letter. 'Elizabeth,' she asked before her aunt turned. 'Did anything arrive for me today?'

'Other than your father?' Her aunt asked with a conspiratorial grin. 'Yes, there was. A letter, in fact.'

Alexandra's heart skipped a beat. 'Is it—'

'On the table in the hallway,' her aunt said. 'I'm surprised you didn't notice it on your way in.'

Alexandra barely heard her last words. She raced back down the stairs in such a hurry she almost ran into her father at the bottom as he was leaving the drawing room.

'You've changed your mind already, my dear?'

She completely ignored him and snatched the letter from the hallstand, tearing into it and quickly reading the words as her heart fluttered.

I'm in. Oh, my goodness, I'm in!

'They've offered me a place,' she gasped, laughing as she reread the letter over again.

She'd temporarily forgotten that she wasn't alone, but when she turned she saw that her uncle's face had lit up.

'Congratulations, Alexandra,' he said. 'You've worked so hard for this, I'm so proud of you.'

Her father looked between them. 'Proud of what, exactly? Please don't tell me you're wasting your time applying to universities or such?'

She held her head high. 'I've actually spent much of my time in London dedicated to music, the violin to be specific, and I've just been offered a place in an orchestra.'

'And it's not just any orchestra,' her uncle announced. 'She is to be one of the first women invited to join the London Luminary Ensemble.'

'I shall return tomorrow,' her father said curtly, 'and we will discuss your marriage prospects and what I expect of you. There is a lot resting on your shoulders, Alexandra, and there is no time to fill your head with thoughts of running away with the orchestra.'

I'd hardly be running away, she thought, as she bit down on her bottom lip in an attempt to hide her excited smile.

'With you at my side, we can restore our family name and fortune. I expect you to seriously consider my proposal overnight.'

'Your proposal?' she asked, looking at her uncle, who simply shook his head as if she shouldn't ask any more.

'I have arranged a marriage between you and a gentleman from Athens. He is from a very wealthy family, a family that is most interested in connecting our families in this way,' he said. 'Not to mention they're very well respected in Greece.'

She silently went to stand beside her father, her letter clutched tightly in her hand. Eventually he turned on his heel and made his exit, leaving her with her uncle, who clapped his hand firmly on her shoulder.

'Marvellous news on the orchestra front, Alex. At least it will take your mind off all this business with your father.'

'He can't force me to marry, can he?' she asked, her voice barely a whisper.

'No, he most certainly cannot. And if he tries? Then he'll have me to answer to, and we will stop at nothing to protect you.'

'Thank you,' she said, giving her uncle an impromptu hug. He blustered and patted her on the back, but when she let go he smiled down at her.

'Go and tell your aunt the good news.'

Alexandra ran back up the stairs, but instead of going to her aunt's room, she went straight to the bathroom, turning on the tap so that no one could hear her being sick again. Afterwards, she studied her complexion in the mirror and noticed how pale she looked. Elizabeth was right; it wouldn't hurt to see the doctor in the morning, just to make sure it wasn't something more serious than bad food.

The orchestra was scheduled to go on an international tour the following week, and although she doubted they'd invite her to join them, she would be expected to begin rehearsals immediately. Part of her had hoped that they might invite her to join them if she showed enough promise, so the last thing she needed was to be sick.

*

'Your aunt tells me that you've been unwell?'

Alexandra sat on the edge of her bed, still in her nightgown. She'd felt even worse when she'd woken up, the nausea making it impossible to rise straight away.

'Actually, now that I think about it, I was feeling unwell a couple of months ago, but the feeling passed. But now...' Her stomach lurched and she shut her eyes, wishing it would go away. 'Do you think I could have food poisoning?'

The doctor gestured for her to lie back again, and he gently touched her stomach, his palm pressing across her abdomen, before he took out his stethoscope. He looked her directly in the eye before placing the earpieces in his ears.

'Alexandra, when did you last have your period?'

She frowned, propping herself up on her elbows. 'Well, I don't know. I've been so busy rehearsing, and they're often irregular, but…' *When did I last menstruate?* 'I'm actually not sure.'

He placed the stethoscope on her stomach for a few minutes, before putting it back in his black leather bag and zipping it up, while she watched him expectantly.

'Alexandra, there's no easy way to tell a young woman this, not at your age and with your marital status, but you're pregnant. At least three months along, if I were to guess.'

She felt the colour drain from her face. 'Pregnant?' Her hands immediately reached for her stomach. 'Wouldn't I know if I were pregnant? Wouldn't I…'

'This is never easy news to digest, but I am in no doubt. I heard your baby's heartbeat.'

Her mouth went dry when she opened it, her mind full of all the reasons she couldn't possibly have a child.

'Please don't tell my aunt,' she managed to whisper. 'I would like the chance to tell her myself.'

'Of course,' he replied. 'I can assure you of my discretion, but I would tell her sooner rather than later, if I were you.'

He gathered his things and stood, but it wasn't until he shut the door that she fell apart. *Pregnant?* A baby would mean she couldn't accept her invitation to join the orchestra; it would put an end to all her hopes and dreams. To their dream of what their future would look like.

What will Bernard think? She knew that he loved her, but would he love her enough to marry her if he found out she was pregnant?

Alexandra curled into a ball and pulled the covers over her body, turning her face into her pillow as she began to cry, her hands wrapped protectively around her middle.

She'd only been in bed perhaps an hour or two when there was a knock at her bedroom door. Alexandra sat up as their housekeeper looked in on her.

'I'm fine,' she mumbled. 'I just need to sleep.'

'You have a visitor.'

Alexandra groaned. 'Tell Bernard I can't see him. The doctor said I have the stomach flu, so I don't want to give it to anyone, especially him.'

Bernard was to leave for the overseas tour in six days' time. He would never choose to see her if he thought she had something contagious.

'It's not Bernard; it's your father.'

She flopped back and covered her face with a pillow. 'Tell him I don't want to see him.'

'You will have to try harder if you want to drive me away, Alexandra.'

She removed the pillow from her face and sat up, hating to think how she must look, with puffy eyes and a pale, drawn face.

'Where is Elizabeth? Is anyone else at home?' Alexandra asked the housekeeper, who was wringing her hands as she stood in the open doorway.

'No one is here, only me.'

Her father began to close the door, and Alexandra forced herself to sit up properly in bed.

'How long have you been unwell?' he asked, sitting on the chair across the room from her.

'I'm fine. Please don't worry about me.'

'You know your mother was ill from the moment you were conceived,' he said.

Alexandra knew her face was burning, but she tried to keep her expression neutral.

'The doctor has confirmed that you're pregnant?'

She couldn't see the point in lying—there was only so long before she would have to confess her secret to everyone, unless she chose to find a doctor who assisted in ridding women of unwanted pregnancies. But she knew in her heart that simply wasn't an option.

She nodded, maintaining her father's stare.

'You will leave with me today, without question,' her father said, standing and pacing to the window. He parted the drapes slightly and looked out, sending more light into the room. 'We shall tell everyone that you have gone to a Swiss finishing school for young ladies, which will explain your absence. In the meantime, I shall finalise your engagement, and we will plan for you to meet your intended as soon as the baby is put up for adoption.'

'Adoption?'

'There is a place that takes in unmarried women here in London, and they guarantee absolute discretion. I'm certain you will be most comfortable there until the baby is born.'

Alexandra felt as if a knife had been plunged into her stomach. 'No,' she croaked, tears welling in her eyes, her throat thick with emotion. 'I have a boyfriend, I have my own plans for the future, I have—'

'Tell me, this young man of yours, this *boyfriend*,' her father said, slowly beginning to pace again. 'He has means? He could support you and your child? He has expressed a desire to marry you in the very near future?'

Alexandra hated him. She hated him so much she wished she could strangle him with her bare hands. And how did he even know that such a place existed? Had he sent one of his own lovers there to have his child?

'Bernard would never see our baby given away! He loves me,' she cried, at the same time as a sense of dread began to encircle her.

'You truly believe that this young man would give up his own dreams to save a girl he mistakenly got pregnant? And if he did, you think he wouldn't end up resenting you for ruining his life?'

She was about to answer, but her father barely paused.

'Your young gentleman, he is a musician, is he not? A cellist?'

Alexandra didn't even think to ask him how he knew. What did it matter anyway?

'Would you expect him to give up what he loves in order to provide for his family? To find a home to house you, to look after a wife and child when he hasn't even proposed marriage to you? His love would quickly turn to hate, for the life he wanted to live but was curtailed from enjoying. You would be like a ball and chain following him around. Is that what you want to be?'

Tears ran freely down her cheeks then. Was he right? *Would* Bernard feel that way about her if he found out that he was to be a father?

'And your aunt and uncle, do you think they'd want you here with your cousins once they found out? An unmarried teenager with a bastard child living in their home?' He laughed. 'I certainly think not. That would be pushing even *their* generosity to its limits.'

Alexandra dug her fingernails into the covers, wishing to scream at him and hurl the pillows at his head. But instead she froze, as if she were that little girl again, the twelve-year-old who'd just lost her mother.

'Take a moment to compose yourself, and then pack your things. We leave in an hour.'

'I can't,' she whispered.

'It will spare Elizabeth the embarrassment of asking you to leave herself, Alexandra. You're not a child anymore, you know the right thing to do.'

Bernard. She would go to Bernard. Bernard would know what to do.

CHAPTER 26

'Alexandra!' Bernard swept her into the house and up to his room. She could tell he hadn't slept because his eyes were bloodshot and his things were strewn all over the room, but his bed was still made as she'd left it the morning before.

'You're packing already?'

He dropped the clothes he was holding and opened his arms, and she went straight to him, head to his chest as he held her. She slipped her arms around his waist, not wanting to let go.

'I don't know how, but I had the dates wrong. We're leaving tomorrow!'

'Tomorrow?' She let go of him and stepped back.

'I know, I know,' he said, going back to his packing. 'Apparently they wanted us to have longer to rehearse in China before our performances, somehow I missed the updated schedule, and—' He frowned. 'Alex, I'm so sorry, wasn't yesterday the day you were supposed to hear about your audition?'

She forced a smile. 'I haven't heard yet,' she lied. 'But fingers crossed a letter will arrive today. You know how unreliable the post can be sometimes.'

He grinned. 'Next time we have a tour, you will be packing too. Can you imagine, the two of us travelling the world, with no fixed abode? We will be auditioning for orchestras all around the world, just the two of us.'

Alexandra sat on the edge of the bed and watched him. It was taking all her strength not to burst into tears.

'That sounds lovely, B. It's a life I could have only dreamed of until now.'

He sat beside her and took her hand. 'Something's wrong?'

A tear slid down her cheek then, escaping from the corner of her eye. 'No, nothing's wrong, I'm just going to miss you, that's all.'

He kissed her tears away. 'I'll miss you too. And I promise I wasn't going to leave without telling you, I was going to come to the house on my way to the airport.'

Alexandra quickly wiped her eyes, smiling through her tears as Bernard went back to packing. She knew then what she had to do; he had his whole life ahead of him, had sacrificed so much to follow his dream, and she wasn't going to be the one to stand in the way of that, to stop him from being the man, the musician, he was supposed to be.

When his car arrived to take him to the airport, she would stay behind and write him a note.

I love you. I'm sorry.

Because what else could she say if she didn't want him to know the truth?

CHAPTER 27

Alexandra gripped the door of the car as her father caught hold of her arm.

'You can't make me,' she pleaded, feeling like that little girl again back in Greece, refusing to leave for London. 'I won't go.'

'I don't care if I have to carry you kicking and screaming, you are going inside.' She knew he was barely containing his anger, red seeping into his cheeks as he glared down at her. 'Let go of the car, Alexandra.'

'No!' she cried, as he tugged so violently at her arm she feared he might break it. 'Please, don't make me. Please!'

'You should have thought of that before you brought shame on our family,' he seethed. 'You have done this, Alexandra, and now this is the price you have to pay.'

She went quiet then, still not relinquishing her grip as she stared at him. 'And what of the whores you've been with? Do you think I don't know what you've been doing all these years? While I've been studying and making a life for myself?'

Alexandra didn't see the slap coming. Her father had always had a quick temper, but he'd never struck her before. His palm hit her cheek with such force, she felt as if all her teeth might rattle from her jaw, recoiling as he glared down at her.

'I hate you,' she spat at him. 'I hate you with every fibre in my body. The way you've disrespected my mother, the way you discarded me like unwanted goods until you needed me again. I despise your very existence.'

'How dare you speak to your father in that way!'

'*Father*?' she laughed, wiping at her lip as she realised it was bleeding, the metallic taste taking her by surprise. Alexandra looked down at the ring on his little finger and realised that's why it had hurt so much—it had caught her bottom lip when he'd struck her. 'You don't deserve the title of *father*. It means nothing. I'm only sorry I wasn't the son you so desperately wanted, the son you've spent my entire life wishing you had instead of me!'

He lifted his hand as if to strike her again when a soft voice called out to them, breaking the moment.

'Please be aware of people watching from their windows. I'd prefer it if you didn't make a scene.'

Alexandra hadn't realised she was holding her breath until her father lowered his hand and she exhaled. She stared at him for a moment, still gripping the car door, before slowly turning her head to see where the voice had come from.

'You must be Alexandra? Your father called ahead.' She paused. 'I'm Hope, and this is my home.'

She nodded, studying the woman who was slowly walking towards them. She was dressed in a simple cotton dress with an apron tied around her middle, her hair pulled back into a bun, but it was her smile that Alexandra noticed the most. It was kind, and something about the way she nodded told Alexandra that she wanted to help; the way her eyes seemed to fix on hers as if she knew what her father could be capable of. But she certainly didn't appear afraid of him.

'My daughter is being particularly wilful today,' her father said, taking a step away from her, which allowed her to loosen her hold on the door. Her fingers ached from the grip she'd maintained.

Hope nodded again. 'Would you mind giving me a moment with your daughter?' she asked. 'It would be preferable if we could avoid a scene.'

Alexandra narrowed her gaze and watched her father, saw the way he looked at her with such disgust. Well, she felt the same about him, and she was no longer scared of him knowing it.

'I'll take a short walk,' he said, removing his car keys from the ignition as if he thought she might steal the car. He didn't even realise that she'd never driven a car before.

'Alexandra,' Hope said, quickly coming round to her side of the car and touching her hand. 'I know this is difficult, and this is no doubt the last place you want to be right now, but what I can tell you is that you will be treated with the respect and dignity you deserve if you walk through the door to my house. And no one will make you stay against your will, not once he's gone.'

Alexandra was listening, and she slowly let go of the car.

'Men like your father see women, and particularly unmarried women, as a burden. I have seen countless men like him over the years, and I would much prefer that you were in my care than his.'

'But I don't want to give up my baby,' she whispered, finally breaking, finally saying the words that had been circling in her mind. Alexandra put her hand protectively over her stomach. 'This isn't how it was supposed to be. This wasn't supposed to happen yet.'

Hope stepped forwards and took Alexandra into her arms, soothing her with her touch and her words. 'Once you come with me, everything you do will be your decision. Your father will not be allowed to set foot in my home.' Hope stroked her hair. 'You're safe with me, Alexandra.'

She let herself be held, catching her breath and fighting against her tears. She refused to let her father make her cry; refused to be his victim when she knew in her heart that she'd done nothing wrong. When Hope finally let go, smiling down at her with such warmth that it reminded Alexandra of her mother, she knew what she had to do.

'Can we go now, before he comes back? I don't want to see him again.'

Hope nodded. 'Of course we can. I shall deal with your father.'

Alexandra took the two bags she'd packed from the back seat of the car, letting Hope carry one of them as they walked up the path to her home, past the sign that read HOPE'S HOUSE. The front door was red, and Alexandra stopped at it and looked back, as if to give her father one last chance to change his mind. But when she saw him, standing back beside the car again, she realised that she didn't want to go with him, even if he did. She hadn't been lying; she *did* hate him.

'Go inside and make us both a cup of tea,' Hope said. 'I'll settle things with your father.'

Alexandra didn't need any encouragement—she picked up the second bag that Hope had set down and took them both in, leaving them neatly at the bottom of the stairs before walking through the house in search of the kitchen. She could hear noises upstairs and guessed they were other young women in the same position as her, so she started to sing softly beneath her breath as she found the kitchen and put the water on to boil, not ready to think about where she was or why she was there.

Thankfully Hope didn't keep her waiting for long, joining her in the kitchen and taking over. She brought a plate of biscuits to the table and Alexandra sat down, curiously watching Hope. She wasn't entirely certain how old she was, but she guessed she could have been a grandmother, perhaps in her late sixties, perhaps even early seventies.

'He's gone,' Hope eventually said.

'Until when?'

She gave Alexandra a long look before bringing over her tea and sitting across from her.

'Apparently he has a marriage arranged for you. For after the baby is born?'

Alexandra's face burnt, with shame and anger, and tears welled in her eyes. 'I had a life here in London,' she whispered. 'I was to be a musician, I was in love, I—'

'Found yourself pregnant,' Hope said gently. 'Babies have a way of changing plans and turning lives upside down.'

'No,' Alexandra said. 'What happened was that my father returned for me, because I was the only way for him to live the life he wants. I'm nothing more than a pawn for him to use to his advantage.'

'Alexandra, what you'll come to realise here is that I don't pressure the girls in my care to do anything they don't want to do. You will have the time to consider your options.'

'Even though my father has paid you handsomely to have me here? You would truly have me believe that anything is my choice?'

Hope nudged her mug of tea closer to her. 'Trust is something that is earned,' she said. 'And over time you will learn that you can trust me.'

Alexandra curled her fingers around the hot mug, flinching when it burnt her.

'Your father has paid me to house you for the coming months and to provide birthing services,' Hope explained. 'Families such as yours like my discretion when it comes to who stays here and the adoptions that I arrange, but this is not a prison. You are free to walk out the door whenever you want. I only ask that you tell me if you're not returning, so I can give your bed to another young woman in need.'

Alexandra took a sip of her tea, her heart finally slowing, her body no longer telling her to flee. 'I can really leave?'

Hope nodded. 'You can leave.'

She reached for a biscuit and slowly looked up at Hope. 'My mother would never have sent me here.'

'Your mother is dead?'

Alexandra nodded, nibbling at the edge of the biscuit. 'When I was twelve.'

'And what of the baby's father?' Hope asked gently. 'Does he even know you're expecting?'

Alexandra shook her head. 'No.'

'Well, there's plenty of time for you to tell me your story, when you're good and ready,' Hope said. 'How about we finish our tea for now, and then I can take you up to show you to your room?'

It wasn't that Alexandra couldn't tell how kind Hope was, and she was already inclined to trust her. Her problem was that all she could think of was Bernard, and every fibre in her body was telling her to run to him, to let him hold her in his arms and tell her that everything would be all right. Only Bernard was gone. And the only other place she wanted to go was home to her aunt and uncle's, but she knew she couldn't do that either. She was pregnant and unmarried; the last thing she could do was to be an embarrassment and a burden to them, not after everything they'd already done for her.

*

Five months later, Alexandra walked along the street, stopping outside and staring at the Royal Festival Hall. She'd come during the day, so there was little chance of seeing anyone, and it was the only place she felt close to Bernard. She'd been tempted to go to his flat once she knew he was home from the tour, to bravely march up to his door and knock early one morning or late one night, to confess what had happened, but something had kept holding her back.

You will ruin his life. Her father's words echoed in her mind every time she thought of Bernard. In her heart, she believed they were far from the truth, but still she couldn't bring herself to find him. And it was the same with her aunt—she'd been so close to going to her so many times, but somehow she'd always stopped herself. *They took you in out of the goodness of their hearts, but even they aren't soft-hearted enough to take in a girl with a bastard baby on the way.* She hated that she kept hearing his words, but he'd been right on both counts, as loath as she was to admit it.

She touched her palm to her rounded stomach and shut her eyes, as the sun shone from high above, warming her skin as she stood in front of the building where she'd first met Bernard. The place she'd been destined to play, the place she'd imagined performing in ever since she'd first seen Bernard perform.

When she opened her eyes, she looked around, as if expecting someone to be watching her. But there was no one. Alexandra sighed and smoothed her hands down her skirt before quietly walking away.

She would catch the bus home soon, arriving back well before dark so as not to worry Hope, but for now she was going to sit on the steps and finally read the letter from her father. She'd been carrying it in her pocket for days, almost too afraid to see what he had to say.

All those months and then years she'd waited for a letter from him, when she was younger at her aunt's house; all those birthdays she'd prayed that he would remember her and send her something as simple as a note.

Alexandra,

I trust you are well and that your condition is not too overbearing. Soon this will all be behind you, and we can move forwards with the plans I've put in place.

You are to be married to Peter Andino in the autumn,
which I hope brings you great joy. It is an arrangement that
suits both of our families, although I am certain you will
find happiness with your new husband. He is a widower
in search of a companion, and I have assured him that
once you return from your studies abroad, you will be an
excellent match.

Finally, I ask that anything of value of your mother's
that you may have in your possession be sent to me at once.

Regards, your father

Alexandra screwed the letter up into a ball, holding it in her fist as she thought about what a beast her father was. He'd been happy to forget her for years until he needed money, and now he wanted what little she had of her mother's so that he could sell it.

She fingered the diamonds in her lobes, the earrings she'd worn every day since her aunt had gifted them to her. There were so many items she wished she'd thought to pack when she'd left Greece—rings or necklaces, even her mother's wristwatch—but she'd only been a girl and the only thing that had meant anything to her then had been her mother's perfume, so she could still smell her.

When Alexandra stood, she heard something that made all the tiny hairs on her arms rise. *It's him.* She knew it the second she heard the lilting sound of bow against string, the deep, enchanting notes of the cello that came to her on the wind, as if the music was embracing her as she stood and listened.

She hadn't expected anyone to be there, had thought they'd be practising elsewhere. Alexandra walked slowly towards the open door, surprised it had been left open. She could only guess that they were trying to let the fresh air in, which had inadvertently let the music out.

A little voice in her head told her to turn and catch the bus, but her feet seemed to be acting of their own accord. She walked as quietly as she could, glancing around to make sure no one saw her, but there was no one there, not so much as a cleaner mopping the floors. Alexandra kept her eyes down as she hurried to the door that led into the theatre from the foyer, the soloist still playing, the music as haunting as it was beautiful.

Her final step took her to the edge of the door. She pressed herself against it, trying to make herself invisible, her eyes trained on the stage. It had been months since she'd seen him now, months of only remembering what he looked like; of imagining his fingers against her skin; of inhaling and trying to recall the scent of his aftershave.

The music abruptly stopped, and Alexandra found herself holding her breath. But then it started again, from the beginning, and she continued to watch, indulging in the way his hair flopped slightly over his forehead when he dipped his head low to play. She gave herself a few more minutes, listening and telling herself that the only person she was harming was herself.

Bernard had no idea she was there, couldn't see her from his position on the stage, even if he was looking. And as much as she wished that he could somehow sense her presence, she knew that it was a childish thought.

Alexandra turned before the end of the piece. It seemed sadder today, the deep notes pulling her into their darkness, and the lighter notes barely releasing her. But however they did or didn't make her feel, the way Bernard played them was flawless.

She took a few steps backwards before ducking her head and turning to leave, but as she did so she saw a man walking quickly towards her. It was the conductor; she'd performed her audition in front of him.

'Hello there! I'm sorry, no one is allowed in here!' he called out.

'Sorry,' she mumbled, lowering her head even more as she hurried to the door, not looking back, refusing to wonder if Bernard might be walking from the stage, about to take a break. If he was, they would have been hardly a handful of steps apart.

Go back. Tell him what happened. Show him what happened.

Alexandra began to cry then, walking as quickly as she could back to the bus stop, one hand placed slightly beneath her stomach to support it. It felt lower all of a sudden, and a sharp pain kept coming and going across the side of her abdomen. She estimated she still had about another three or even four weeks to go before the baby arrived, so she put the pains down to her heartache and the pace at which she'd been moving down the street, but when she boarded the bus, the sharpness made her pause.

'Are you all right?'

A concerned older woman stared at her from one of the seats on the bus, but Alexandra just nodded, finding a vacant seat and gritting her teeth. It was a twenty-minute journey back to Hope's House, although it felt much longer, every bump making her pain intensify, and if she wasn't imagining it, the pain was coming in faster waves now than it had before.

When the bus finally pulled up to her stop, she forced her feet to move, pausing every few seconds before getting off the bus and hobbling down the road. She pounded against the front door when she finally reached Hope's House, as she tried to open it.

'Hope!' she cried.

Alexandra stumbled inside, leaning back against the door as the biggest wave of pain she'd experienced yet grasped hold of her, as if a fist had tightened inside her stomach.

'Alex?' Hope came rushing down the stairs then. 'Alex! What's wrong?'

'I think,' she said through gritted teeth, her breath hissing from her lungs, 'that the baby is coming.'

Hope frowned and rushed closer, placing her hand over Alexandra's stomach. 'It's a bit earlier than expected, and—'

A loud, guttural groan escaped from Alexandra's lips, her legs almost buckling as pain gripped her abdomen again.

'Let's get you to your room,' Hope said, her voice soft and calm as she took hold of her arm and guided her up the stairs. 'It appears that this baby of yours is in a hurry to see the world.'

CHAPTER 28

Six Days Later

Alexandra was numb. She stared out of the window, her fists clenched so tightly that her nails may well have drawn blood. *Six days*. Six days she'd loved and nursed her little girl, six days she had known what it was to be a mother, and now it was over as if it had never happened at all.

Her bags were packed, both neatly placed near the door, but she didn't want to leave the room. It smelt of Madeline; her sweet, milky, newborn scent seeming to waft around her. Her breasts hurt, aching with the milk that she would never feed her with, but most of all her arms ached from not holding the baby she already loved so fiercely with all her heart.

It was only now that she understood why her mother had looked at her with such tenderness, why she'd sometimes caught her watching her when she was reading or playing: it was the same way she'd found herself staring at her own child. If there was a gift born from her pain, it was that becoming a mother had brought back so many memories of her own mama, memories that she'd once feared had been lost.

'Alexandra?'

Hope's soft voice on the other side of the door pulled her from her thoughts. She quickly wiped her cheeks and cleared her throat. 'Come in.'

Hope entered and came to sit down beside her, taking her hand.

'She's gone?'

'Not yet,' Hope said. 'Alexandra, the mother has asked to meet you. She would like to speak to you before they leave.'

Alexandra looked up, meeting Hope's warm gaze. 'I don't,' she swallowed, trying to get her words out, 'I don't think I can.'

'And that's perfectly fine,' Hope said, gently squeezing her hand. 'But not many girls get the opportunity to meet the woman who will raise their child. So I'll give you a few minutes in case you change your mind. We'll be just downstairs.'

Alexandra nodded, sitting silently and listening as Hope closed the door behind her. She stood and looked out of the window, parting the curtains and looking down at the smart Ford Cortina parked outside the house. That was the car her daughter would be leaving in.

She took a deep breath before turning and hurrying across the bedroom. *If I don't meet her, if I don't do this, I'll regret it forever.*

Alexandra walked down the stairs, hearing voices, and she paused outside the sitting room for a moment, listening. She could hear them, this couple who had adopted her daughter.

'Sorry to interrupt,' she said, as she found the courage to step into the room.

'Alexandra,' Hope said, immediately coming to stand beside her. 'My dear, thank you for coming down. I'd like you to meet Margaret and Simon.'

'Hello,' she managed, finding it almost impossible to speak as she stared at the woman in front of her, holding her baby. She fought against the desire to snatch her daughter back, to tell them they couldn't have her. Alexandra stared at the dark sprinkling of hair on her head, the perfect little pink, Cupid's bow lips, her tiny fingers reaching out over the blanket as she stretched.

You are my heart, little one. I love you more than you could ever imagine.

'Thank you for coming down to meet us,' the woman said. 'Could we have a moment in private, just me and Alexandra?'

Hope looked at her and Alexandra nodded, and soon they were standing in the room, just the two of them.

'I want to start by saying thank you for the gift you've given us. We've been trying to start a family for three years, so this little one has truly made our dreams come true.'

Alexandra hated the way she looked down at *her* baby with such contentment, but she knew that was wrong. She should have been grateful that the other woman was so immediately smitten with her.

'Promise me that you'll give her the life she deserves,' Alexandra whispered, stepping forwards and touching the backs of her fingers to her daughter's warm, soft cheek.

'We will. But in turn, I want you to promise me one thing too.'

Alexandra studied the woman's face. 'What could I possibly promise you? I've already given you my baby.'

'I want you to promise me that you'll never come looking for her. She's our daughter now, and from the moment we walk out through that door, you'll have to let her go.'

Silent tears ran down Alexandra's cheeks as she forced herself to nod.

'There will be no photos sent to you, no contact whatsoever, and we have no intention of ever revealing to our daughter that she was adopted. Do I make myself clear?'

'Yes,' Alexandra whispered.

'Good,' the woman said. 'Now that's settled, would you like to hold her one last time?'

Alexandra would have preferred to cry and tell her how cruel she was, but instead she held out her arms. This was the very last time she'd hold her baby. 'I would very much like that. Thank you.'

The moment her daughter was in her arms again, the pain that arrowed through her was more excruciating than child-birth. It took every ounce of strength not to call Hope in and tell her that she'd changed her mind, but she'd already gone through this countless times. If she were to keep her, where would she go? How would she find a job and care for her daughter all on her own? She could beg her aunt to take her in, but the last thing she wanted was to ask such a thing of another.

Alexandra pressed a kiss to her baby's forehead, her lips lingering as she inhaled, committing the smell and feel of her to memory. 'I love you,' she whispered. 'I love you so much it hurts.'

And as her tears started to fall all over again, she passed her back to the other woman and turned away, hurrying back upstairs so she didn't have to witness them leaving with her. For once they walked out of that door, her daughter was gone forever.

*

'Thank you, Hope.' Alexandra gave her a long hug, wishing she didn't have to say goodbye to the woman who'd come to mean so much to her.

'What you've been through is not something I would wish upon anyone, but you've handled it all with such grace.'

Alexandra sighed—a deep breath that shuddered with emotion as she let it go. 'I wish things could have been different.'

'As do I,' Hope said, reaching out to smooth a strand of hair that had slipped down.

She had her long hair tied back again, now back to the length it was before she'd followed Belle's advice and cut it short. It felt like a lifetime ago when she'd been out shopping and giggling with her cousin; and it was as if she'd aged a decade instead of eighteen months.

'Alexandra, may I ask, what did she say to you earlier?' Hope said. 'It's unusual for an adoptive mother to request a private conversation. Usually they want nothing to do with the birth mother. I've always thought it's because they don't truly want to confront the fact that they're taking another woman's baby.'

Alexandra looked into Hope's eyes, as always seeing such kindness shining from her gaze, and she did something she'd rarely ever done in her lifetime before. She lied.

'She only wanted to thank me for the gift I'd given her,' Alexandra said. 'She mentioned it had been very hard for them to conceive.'

Hope patted her hand. 'Well, that's lovely to hear, because you *have* given them the most beautiful gift.'

Alexandra forced a smile.

'Don't forget, if your daughter wants to find you one day, I will have the box to give her,' Hope said. 'And if she doesn't come looking before her twenty-first birthday, I shall make sure it's sent to her, just in case.'

She wanted to say something. It was on the tip of her tongue to tell Hope that the box should never be given to her daughter, that she was never to know she was adopted, but she didn't. She couldn't.

'I'm just glad you kept those diamond earrings instead of putting them in the box,' Hope said. 'A woman never knows when she might need something of value, how her circumstances might change.'

Alexandra hugged Hope again, not able to find the right words to say, and so embracing her instead. If it hadn't been for the conversation earlier, she'd have insisted on adding the earrings to the tiny box of clues, but now she knew there was little point. The mother of her child would make certain her daughter didn't receive it.

She closed her eyes as Hope rubbed her back in big, comforting circles, thinking of what she'd left. The photo had been one of her favourites, and one of the only pictures she had of her mother. And the sheet of music; it held her heart. It was the only thing she'd had left that connected her to Bernard, so it felt right to leave it behind.

Alexandra heard a car pull up outside and forced herself to let go of Hope.

'I hope you have a wonderful life,' Hope said, as she kissed her cheek. 'And I hope one day you can forget the pain of this past week.'

She only nodded and collected her bags, one in each hand, and walked down the steps to the waiting car. A driver stepped out, and when he opened the back door, she could see that there was no one else inside. Her father hadn't bothered to come and collect her himself.

Once she was settled in the back seat, the driver looked at her in the rearview mirror.

'Do you have instructions for where to take me?' Alexandra asked.

'Yes, miss,' he said, taking something from the passenger seat and passing it back to her. An envelope. 'I'm to take you directly to the airport.'

She tore at the envelope and took out an airline ticket. *Athens. After all these years, I'm finally going home.*

It was strange that now she had the opportunity to go home, all she wanted was to stay in London. *When my heart was in Greece, all I wanted was to go back. But now my heart is here, with my daughter. With Bernard. With Elizabeth, Belle and Will.*

Only her daughter would never know she even existed, and Bernard thought she'd vanished into thin air. She didn't know what her aunt and cousins had been told, and she hadn't been brave enough to tell them herself, too ashamed of what had happened.

'Can we please take a detour on the way?' she asked.

The driver cleared his throat. 'Miss, your father was very clear with his instructions that I was to transport you directly to the airport.'

She stared at him when he looked in the mirror at her, hoping her gaze was as cold as her words.

'Unless you want me to throw myself from the vehicle, we will be taking a detour,' she said.

The driver didn't say anything in reply, only gave her a curt nod, and she leaned back in the seat as he pulled away from the kerb and Hope's House disappeared into the distance.

'Where should I go, miss?' he asked.

'I would like to drive slowly past the Royal Festival Hall,' she said.

'So you won't be exiting the vehicle?'

'No,' she murmured. 'I won't be.'

I need to drive past one last time. I need to see the place that connects me to Bernard, to that part of my life. I need to see it again one last time before I leave.

Alexandra was tempted to visit her aunt and uncle too. To say goodbye to Belle and explain why she'd left so abruptly and not been in touch since—she'd been like a sister to her, after all—but she knew it would be easier to simply disappear. For all she knew, they'd as good as forgotten about her already.

CHAPTER 29

Present Day

Ella sat and digested everything Alexandra had told her. It was a lot—a story of two young people who'd been manipulated into believing that their life together was never meant to be. Fate had been cruel to her grandmother, of that she was entirely certain, but what she hadn't told her was how they'd found their way back to each other.

'May I ask you a question?' Ella said, softly. 'And please, I'm not making any judgement, I'm just trying to understand the past.'

Alexandra nodded, her eyes bright as she sat forwards in her chair. She was younger than the grandmother she'd known her entire life, but there was something about her, something that still reminded Ella of the photograph she'd been carrying around. There was an enchanting youthfulness to Alexandra that had most certainly taken Ella by surprise.

'When you and Bernard were reunited, why didn't you look for my mother? Didn't you both want to find her?'

She received a smile in response. 'Ella, if we were younger, perhaps we would have, but it felt too late by the time we found each other again.'

Ella's eyebrows rose in wonder. 'Too late?'

Alexandra laughed. 'By the time we reconnected, we'd both been married and widowed. It wasn't a few years but a few decades between when my father sent me to Hope's House and when I found my dear Bernard again.'

'Decades?'

'Oh, yes, we were quite a sight when we were at last reunited,' Alexandra said, her eyes sparkling as she sat back in the armchair. 'We must have looked like a pair of star-crossed lovers, but we were old and grey, the pair of us. There was still something about him that took my breath away, or perhaps in my mind I still saw the young, dashing man that he once was.' Alexandra paused, smiling, although now with a faraway look in her eyes. 'You see, when you get older, you don't *feel* old. You still feel like someone thirty years younger, or at least I certainly do. It's just the mirror that deceives you, making you look so much older than you are inside.'

'Would you be so kind as to tell me how you met, after all those years? What was it like?'

Alexandra stood then, walking to the window again, her knuckles brushing the glass as she lifted a hand. Ella wondered for a long moment if she wasn't going to say anything, if perhaps she'd asked too many questions, but when Alexandra turned, she knew that she was finally going to hear the last part of her grandmother's story.

'Promise me something, Ella.'

She nodded. 'Of course.'

Alexandra walked over to her and sat down, taking her hands and folding them on her lap as she held them. 'I want you to follow your heart, and not let anyone tell you how to live your life.' Tears filled the older woman's eyes as Ella stared back at her, blinking and finding herself nodding. 'Someone once asked me what advice I'd give to my younger self. An innocent question at the time, of course. But I'd tell her with all my heart not to let anyone stand in the way of what she wanted to do, and not to fear the reaction of someone she loved.'

Ella squeezed Alexandra's hands. 'I don't think it was so easy for you then. Not like it is now, for my generation. I can't even imagine being sent to a home for unmarried mothers.'

'Perhaps not, but I wish I'd tried harder to resist. Turned to those who loved me and asked them for help, perhaps. Trusted that they loved me enough to do anything for me.' Alexandra sighed. 'I don't often dwell on the past, so forgive me. No one likes to hear an old lady moan.'

'Maybe not,' Ella said. 'But I would very much like to hear about how you and Bernard crossed paths again. I'm sure it's terribly romantic.'

Alexandra's smile lit her face. 'Would you believe that it involved music?'

'Given your history, how could it not?'

Alexandra wiped her eyes, and Ella hoped it hadn't all been too much for her.

'How about we call it a night,' she suggested. 'It's been quite the day, hearing all about you and your Bernard, but I can always come back tomorrow? I'm in Greece for another week, so there's no hurry.'

Alexandra's eyes met hers. 'You will come back?' she asked, reaching for her hand and holding it tightly. 'I don't want to lose you when I've only just found you.'

Ella blinked away her own tears then, seeing how much it meant to Alexandra to be reunited with her, with a family member who she'd clearly long since given up hope of meeting.

'I promise I'll come back,' she said. 'Why don't I take the late-morning ferry tomorrow, and you can tell me all about how you found your way back to Bernard?'

Alexandra began to cry then, and Ella wrapped her arms around her, holding her until she stilled, instinctively knowing she needed to be held. She was clearly still grieving the man she'd loved almost all her life, the man she'd spent so many years yearning for, and so few years with him at her side.

'He would have loved to meet you, Ella. After we were reunited, he often said that he would have loved a daughter or a granddaughter. It was our greatest regret that we didn't have that chance.'

'I'm sure I would have loved him too,' Ella said, rubbing Alexandra's back in big circles with the palm of her hand, before standing back a little and holding her at arm's length, hands to her shoulders. 'And if you don't want to talk about him tomorrow, if it's too painful to remember—'

'Tomorrow,' Alexandra repeated, nodding her head and looking away again, as if she could see something that Ella could not. 'Tomorrow, I will tell you all about it.'

Ella made sure that Alexandra was settled and had everything she needed, hesitating before leaving but knowing that if she didn't go soon, she'd never make the ferry.

CHAPTER 30

Ella took out her phone as she walked, having just arrived back on Skopelos from seeing Alexandra for the second time, walking from the dock back to the house. She called Kate, smiling with relief when her aunt picked up on the third ring.

'Hello, traveller.'

She sighed. 'Is it strange that we're not biologically related now?'

'Strange? Yes. But does it matter? Not a bit.'

'It's so nice to hear you say that.' It had been the only part of the entire journey that had made Ella deeply uncomfortable, finding out that Kate, the family member she felt so connected to, wasn't actually a blood relative.

'It's that whole nurture-over-nature thing, right? We've nurtured each other for years, so this doesn't mean anything. Other than being an incredible story that I can't wait to hear more about.'

'It's a story, all right. I can't wait to tell you all about Alexandra. She's an incredible woman, but that's not why I'm calling.'

Kate was silent at the other end of the line.

'I'm worried about Mum, and how she's taking it all. Have you heard from her?'

'Not since she left. How have you found her?'

Ella frowned. 'What do you mean? I haven't spoken to her since…'

Ella almost dropped her phone, her eyes wide.

'Ella, your mother—'

'Is here,' she finished for Kate. 'I'll call you back.'

She slipped her phone into her pocket and hurried the last few steps up to the house, where her mother was standing. She'd been sitting, her back against the door, her suitcase beside her. She was wearing a large sunhat and a dress, items of clothing Ella had never even seen her in before.

'Mum, what are you doing here?!' she said, giving her a hug. 'I love the Meryl Streep vibe.'

Her mum hugged her back, before gesturing to the door. 'Please tell me you have wine in there, because I'm in need of a very large glass.'

Ella nodded and opened the door, taking her mum's bag and wheeling it in. The fact that her mum wanted wine and was dressed so differently, for her, told Ella that something was very, very wrong. Her mother wore beige trousers and silk shirts no matter the weather, with the rare exception of particularly cold days when she changed into beige cashmere.

She went to the fridge and found half a bottle of wine, taking down two glasses and filling them. 'Mum, I know all of this must be very hard for you, finding out that—'

Her mother held up her hand. 'Ella, I have to tell you something.'

She gave her the glass and went to sit down on the sofa, tucking her legs up beneath herself. 'Okay.'

She watched as her mum took a large sip, closing her eyes for a moment before finally meeting Ella's gaze.

'I knew.'

Ella frowned. 'Knew what?'

'I knew that if you figured out those clues, you'd find out that it was me who was adopted.'

She leaned forwards and set her wine glass on the table, carefully watching her mother. 'This wasn't a surprise to you? Everything I've discovered these past few weeks?' Ella recoiled. 'You *knew*?'

'You have to believe me when I say that I didn't know anything about my birth mother or the story of my past, but I did know that I was adopted, and when you were given those clues—'

'You told me to forget about the little box, because you knew I'd find out. Because you didn't want me to know?' Her mum had come all this way to tell her this? 'You know, you could have told me over the phone. You didn't have to come all the way here.' Ella bristled.

Her mother stood and went to the window, staring out, her back turned to Ella. 'Your grandmother told me just before she died,' she said in a quiet voice. 'I was holding her hand, sitting there with her, and she whispered to me that she'd adopted me when I was a baby.'

Ella folded herself back into the sofa, listening intently to her mother and trying not to be angry.

'I wasn't certain she was lucid, she'd been saying all sorts of strange things that day, but she kept telling me what a darling little baby I was, and that the moment she saw me, she knew I would be her daughter.'

'Why didn't you say anything?'

Her mother sighed and slowly turned around. 'At first I didn't believe it, but then some things started to make sense. Little comments she'd made over the years, and the fact that I was so different to Kate. But she gripped my hand and told me not to tell anyone, that it was a secret.' She laughed. 'It's ridiculous, but even as a grown woman with an adult child, I still felt like a little girl being told what to do by her mother. I'd never disobeyed her before, and I wasn't about to start then.'

'So you tried to stop me from searching because you didn't want anyone to find out the truth?'

'In the beginning, when I first heard about the box, I wanted to stop you so I could keep Grandma's secret.' She crossed the room and sat on the sofa beside Ella, taking her hand and slowly looking up at her. 'But in truth, I don't think that was why. I didn't want anything to change. I didn't want to take anything else away from our family.'

Ella's anger dissipated and turned to sadness. 'Our family is still our family, Mum. This doesn't change that. *Nothing* changes that.'

Her mother wiped away tears. 'I know that. Logically as a sane, intelligent person I very much know that. But to find out that Kate wasn't my biological sister, that she wasn't your biological aunt, I suppose I was afraid that we might lose her like we lost Harrison. I wanted to keep the secret for my own selfish reasons, to keep our family together.'

Ella laughed, even though her own eyes were brimming with tears at seeing her mother's pain. She didn't mean to make fun, but she couldn't help it. 'Kate isn't going anywhere. I don't think we could get rid of her if we tried!'

'Would you think I was silly if I said that I thought she might cut ties with me when she knew she wasn't my real sister?' Her mum laughed too, as if she could hear how ridiculous she sounded, until they were both half laughing, half crying. 'I've always felt like Kate only puts up with me because I'm her sister. I thought the minute she found out we weren't truly related, she'd run for the hills!'

'Mum, Kate loves you,' Ella said. 'She loves both of us, and she'd do anything for us, whether we're related by blood or not. Nothing will ever change that.'

'You truly think so?'

She patted her mother's hand. 'I don't think so, I know so. Kate is stuck with us, whether she likes it or not.'

They both sighed, then laughed at their joint reaction, before sipping their wine.

'So tell me, what is my birth mother like?'

'She's amazing,' Ella said. 'Honestly, I feel like she's been waiting her entire life to meet you. She was forced to give you up when she was nineteen, and I don't think she's ever forgiven herself for having to leave you.'

'Did you tell her how lovely my parents were? That I'd had a wonderful childhood?'

Ella smiled. 'I think that's something you can tell her yourself,' she said. 'Tomorrow morning, I'll take you to meet her. I can't even imagine her reaction when she discovers not only her long-lost granddaughter is in Greece, but also her daughter.'

Her mother was silent for a long moment. 'Thank you, Ella.'

'For what?'

'For being brave enough to uncover the past. I don't tell you often enough, but I'm so proud of you.'

Neither of them said anything for a moment.

'Whatever you choose to do with your life, whatever decisions you make, I believe in you, Ella. I'm only sorry I haven't told you that before.'

'Thank you,' she said, her voice cracking with emotion as she leaned into her mother. 'I needed to hear that.'

Her mum put her arms around her, close in a way they hadn't been in so long.

CHAPTER 31

The moment Alexandra opened the door, Ella knew that she'd done the right thing in bringing her mother with her. Travelling all this way, refusing to give up on the clues, and bringing her mother to meet Alexandra—it was one of the most special moments she'd ever been part of.

Alexandra was silent as she stared at Ella's mother, her fingers gripping the door so tightly that Ella could see her knuckles turn white. The two women simply looked at each other, not moving, until Ella spoke.

'Mum, I'd like you to meet Alexandra Konstantinidis,' she said in a soft voice. 'Your birth mother. Alexandra, this is Madeline.'

'Madeline,' Alexandra whispered, taking a shaky step forwards and lifting a trembling hand to her daughter's cheek. 'All these years, I've imagined what you might look like.'

Her mother was silent, her jaw falling slightly open as if she wanted to speak but couldn't find the words.

'How about we have a coffee?' Ella suggested. 'Shall we go inside?'

Alexandra looked at her then as if she'd only just realised Ella was even there. Her face was devoid of all colour, and Ella took her arm, giving her mother what she hoped was an encouraging smile as she beckoned with her head for her to follow.

'All these years,' Alexandra repeated, clearly still in shock at seeing the daughter she'd given up over fifty years ago.

'Come on, sit down here and I'll make us coffee,' Ella said. 'Mum, sit down here by Alexandra.'

'Your eyes,' Alexandra whispered, shaking her head as she stared at Madeline again, as if she still couldn't believe she was sitting in front of her. 'You blinked up at me before you were taken, as if you were telling me that everything would be all right.'

Ella spoke when she realised her mother still hadn't found the right words. 'And it *was* all right, wasn't it?' she said, prompting her mum. 'My grandparents were wonderful. They raised my mother with love, and she has a sister who is a few years younger than her.'

Her mother finally cleared her throat. 'I'm sorry, this is all just so hard to process. But yes, my parents were lovely people. I couldn't have asked for a nicer family.'

'I wanted to find you,' Alexandra said. 'Goodness knows, I cried myself to sleep so many nights. But Hope wouldn't tell me where you were, even though I went there every year to ask her. I even thought about breaking into her office to see if I could find your records, but by then she'd passed away and the house was derelict. You must have been one of the last babies born there, because it shut less than six months later.'

'And yet I had no idea you even existed,' her mother murmured. 'It's seems almost cruel to know that you were in so much pain, and I was oblivious all these years.'

'I want you to know that I didn't willingly give you up,' Alexandra said, tears in her eyes as she leaned forwards in her chair. 'Now, when I look back, I know I should have fought harder. I should have been braver.'

Silence rested between them for a moment.

'No,' Madeline said. 'You did the right thing. I was raised by a family who loved me, and I wouldn't change that for the world.'

'Mum—' Ella murmured, seeing the way Alexandra's face had crumpled.

'No,' her mother said, her voice more even now, stronger. 'I'm so grateful to be sitting here today, meeting you, Alexandra, but you need to forgive yourself and know in your heart that your decision was the right one.' Her voice softened then. 'You did the right thing for your daughter, and I can only imagine the level of bravery that took.'

'I was only nineteen,' Alexandra whispered.

Ella watched as her mother rose and sat beside Alexandra, taking her hand in hers. 'You were only a child. It must have been so traumatic.'

'To lose you, to hold you for such a short time and then to have to give you up…'

Alexandra cried then, and Ella watched as her mother wiped her tears, gently using her fingertips to clear them. 'I too know the loss of a child. My son passed away when he was only twenty-one years old, and I've never forgiven myself, even though in my heart I know there was nothing I could have done to prevent it.'

Ella swallowed, tears forming in her eyes now too as she listened to her mother speak. She'd never realised her mum blamed herself, but now it made sense. The way she'd changed, grieving in a way that had never ended, taking the joy from everything, even so many years after Harrison's passing.

'Then we both know how to stay alive while dying of a broken heart,' Alexandra said.

'We do. But we are fortunate enough to be sitting here together today,' Madeline said. 'I certainly never expected to be in Greece, meeting my birth mother, so I would like to turn today into a celebration.'

'I wholeheartedly agree!' Ella said, relieved at how positive her mother was being. 'I, for one, am thrilled to have another grandma. Most especially one with a house in the Greek islands.'

'Shall we have a glass of something special to celebrate?' Madeline asked. 'Champagne, perhaps, instead of coffee?'

Alexandra rose then, disappearing for a long moment before returning with something curled into her hand. It most definitely wasn't a bottle of champagne. She sat on the edge of the sofa, slowly opening her palm.

'These were given to me by my aunt, who raised me following the death of my mother,' Alexandra said. 'She told me on the eve of my eighteenth birthday that they were special family heirlooms, passed down from my own grandmother, and that they were to stay in our family forever.' She smiled. 'I've waited a very long time to do this. May I?'

Ella edged forwards, gasping when she saw the size of the diamond solitaires that Alexandra was gently placing in her mother's ears.

'They're beautiful,' Ella whispered. 'Absolutely beautiful.'

'I wanted to leave them behind in the little box of clues, but Hope wouldn't let me. She said that I might need them one day, and I knew that what she meant was that if I ever left my father and had to fend for myself I might have to sell them. But I could never have parted with them, they were too special.'

'Alexandra,' Madeline said, as Ella watched the gentle way she touched her lobes, her fingertips grazing the diamonds there. 'Was he a good man? My father?'

Alexandra sat straighter then, even though Ella thought such a question might make her falter. She looked first at Ella, then at Madeline, before rising and going to a table in the far corner of the room. She returned with two framed photographs, one of a young man on stage, holding a cello, and the other an old man with a head of thick white hair, laughing as he sat on the beach.

'This was your father, Madeline,' Alexandra said. 'And your grandfather, Ella.'

Ella leaned forwards and looked at the photographs, even though she'd already seen them before. She heard the sharp intake of her mother's breath, saw the way she reached for the picture of the older man, holding it close to her face as she studied it.

'Bernard was the love of my life,' Alexandra said. 'I loved him as a young woman, and I loved him as an old lady. My feelings for him never changed, despite the years that passed. '

'You were so fortunate to have found him again,' Ella said. 'I'm only sorry I wasn't given these clues a year ago, so we could have met him.'

'Alexandra, Ella has told me that you found your way back to Bernard. How, after all those years apart, did you manage to find each other again?'

'I'd travelled to London to see the orchestra, would you believe? After all those years of refusing to go to a live performance, I'd decided it was time to let go of the past and find my love of music again. In the audience of course, as an observer.'

'So it was a chance meeting? Seeing Bernard again?'

'Fate had been most unkind to us in our younger years, Ella, but that night, it was almost as if it were meant to be.'

CHAPTER 32

London, 2012

Alexandra stood in the foyer of the Royal Festival Hall and looked around in wonder. It had barely changed since the first time she'd been there, or perhaps it had merely been so long that she simply couldn't remember. It had been the eve of her eighteenth birthday, after all; a performance and a night that had changed the course of her life. The glittering dresses and the dapper men; the bubbles of champagne on her tongue; the breathless anticipation as the crowd had waited for the orchestra to begin. It washed over her as if no time had passed, and if she closed her eyes she truly believed that she'd look down and see the young, slender body of her youth, wearing the dress that she and Belle had gone shopping for all those years ago. Her cousin Belle would be to her left, Will to her other side, her aunt and uncle smiling and watching them as if they couldn't have been prouder to be taking them out for the evening.

'Aunt Alexandra?' She looked across at her niece, taking a moment to realise who was saying her name. Thankfully she'd reconnected with her mother's side of the family after her father had passed away, realising how foolish she'd been not to turn to them in her hour of need, even if she hadn't been able to see that at the time. Her greatest pleasure had been her relationship with Belle's children and then grandchildren. Jessica was the only granddaughter, and Alexandra visited London at least once a year to see her.

'Sorry, darling, I was suddenly a million miles away.'

Jessica just smiled and took her arm. 'Are you feeling all right?'

'I'm perfectly fine,' she said. 'It's just being here, after all these years, it's all coming back to me.'

'How long ago?'

'Decades,' she replied. 'Only a few years after our family had been effectively exiled from Greece.' Alexandra patted her niece's hand, smiling down at her. 'Back then, we thought the monarchy would be restored within months, that the exile was only a temporary thing.'

'It's almost impossible to imagine that you grew up in Greece with the royal family as friends.'

It did seem surreal. Alexandra thought back to her childhood, and it was almost as if she were recounting a fairy tale rather than real life. For a while, she'd held on to the memories of her mother ferociously, terrified of letting her go, almost believing that one day she'd walk through the door and it would have all been a mistake. But then, something had changed inside her, and she'd decided it would be easier to forget, to try to make the pain go away. And eventually, it had.

Alexandra looked around the room, sighing as she reminded herself that this was another time. There would be no giggles with her cousins, or dreaming about a boy she'd just laid eyes upon; tonight she was here with her niece to listen to the orchestra, not to remember what had once been.

'I can't believe it's been a year since you were in London,' Jessica said, hugging her arm as they slowly walked, following along beside everyone else. 'We have so much to do while you're here. Should we go shopping tomorrow?'

She nodded as she reached for the programme that was passed to her. 'Shopping sounds lovely. So long as you remember I'm an old lady who needs to be well fed and watered along the way.'

Jessica laughed. 'Point taken.'

They were standing in the queue now, and Alexandra took her glasses from her bag and put them on, looking over the programme.

'I'm sure it's going to be a wonderful evening, I've heard they're just fabulous.'

She was listening to her niece talk as they moved forwards in the line and showed their tickets, and when they stopped again she turned the pages of the programme, until she suddenly stopped. Her eyes stayed fixed to one sentence at the very bottom of the last page, to one name that had made her feel as if she might faint.

BERNARD GOLDMAN.

Alexandra's heart began to race, her body trembling as she reread the name over and over, as if she might have made a mistake.

'Alexandra?'

She gripped the handrail on the staircase, dropping the programme and then having to fumble for it, bumping into someone behind her.

'Alexandra, what's wrong? You've gone very pale and—'

'I, I—'

'Come on, let's sit down, you don't—'

'I'm perfectly fine,' she said, surprised by the sudden strength in her own voice. 'I just saw a name, someone from my past, and it took me by surprise.'

Jessica didn't look convinced, and the couple in front of them had turned around as if to see whether they could offer assistance.

'You're certain you're okay? If you'd rather take a seat or—'

'Would you excuse me for just a moment?' Alexandra said. 'Please, go ahead and take your seat. I just need to use the bathroom and I'll be right back.'

Alexandra gave her niece what she hoped was a reassuring smile and walked through the crowd of people to the counter by the front door. Everyone had been admitted now, so there was no queue, and she went straight up to the woman seated there.

'I was hoping you might be able to help me,' Alexandra began.

'Do you need assistance finding your seat?'

'I'm afraid it's a little more complicated than that,' Alexandra said, taking out the programme. 'I would be very grateful if you could tell me how to find this man.' She pointed at Bernard's name. 'I know this is a strange request, but…'

The young lady was watching her with a disinterested look on her face. *I lost you once, B. I'm not going to make the same mistake twice.*

'I'll be honest with you. This man was my lover many years ago. We had a baby when we weren't married and my father forced me to give her up.' She took a breath, noticing that the woman was suddenly sitting straighter in her chair, not blinking. 'We've been parted for decades, and it would mean the world to me if you would help me find him, if you could reunite us.'

'This man?' the woman said, tapping on Bernard's name. 'This man was your,' she hesitated, lowering her voice, '*lover*?'

'This might be the only chance I have of finding him again,' she confessed, as tears filled her eyes, as she saw him standing before her, heard him whispering in her ear and encouraging her to play for him, and for the world.

'Tell me your name,' she said. 'If I can help you, I will.'

'Alexandra,' she hesitated, almost saying her married name but quickly stopping herself. 'Alexandra Konstantinidis.'

The woman reached for her radio, giving Alexandra a long look before pressing the button and speaking into it.

'I need someone to take over the desk,' the woman said.

'Alexandra!' Jessica appeared at her side, looking flustered, as if she'd been running around looking for her. 'What are you doing?'

'Finding someone from my past,' she said, as the woman who'd been helping her disappeared, leaving Alexandra clutching the programme and hoping her niece didn't think she'd gone completely mad. Or that she wasn't about to be hauled out of the venue by security.

Everyone else had long since filed out of the foyer and taken their seats, and Alexandra could see that Jessica was starting to shift her weight from foot to foot, impatient at the delay.

'Please take your seat, darling. I don't want you to miss any of the performance.'

Jessica gave her a thoughtful kind of look. 'Is there a chance that this is all a big misunderstanding? That perhaps—'

Alexandra turned away from her niece then, as the woman returned with a man by her side. He had a full, thick head of white hair and a neatly clipped beard, and he was walking quickly, as if he were agitated. But the moment he saw her, the moment their eyes met, he stopped.

Her heart began to thud as she stood, staring, looking at a man who should have been a stranger to her. But he wasn't. Even after all these years, he wasn't.

'Alexandra?' Bernard's voice carried to her as she opened her mouth to say something, *anything*, but found herself still standing, silent.

'Alexandra!' he repeated, loudly this time, as she began to walk towards him, her hands outstretched.

She couldn't see anything else, couldn't hear anything, could only focus on the man coming towards her.

'It's you,' he said, when they were barely a few metres apart. 'It's truly you.'

'Oh, Bernard, look at you. Look at you!'

He took her hands and they stood, their fingers wound tightly together as they stared into each other's eyes.

'As beautiful as the last time I saw you,' he whispered. 'How many years has it been?'

'Forty years,' she said, letting go of one of his hands to place her palm against his cheek. 'It's been four decades, Bernard. A lifetime.'

He put his arms around her then, holding her as they stood there, as if they were the only people in the room, as if they weren't in the foyer of the concert hall. She pressed her cheek to his shoulder, inhaled the unfamiliar scent of his aftershave, the feel of his body against hers. There were so many things she thought she remembered about him, but she was also realising how much she'd forgotten.

'Alex,' he said, finally letting her go and standing back to look at her. 'All this time, I can't believe you're standing here in front of me.'

'You're…' she said, her eyes suddenly fixed on the gold band on his finger.

'Widowed,' he said gently. 'Three years ago.'

She wished she didn't feel relieved, but she did. After all this time, she couldn't imagine finding out that he belonged to another.

'You just left me, Alex. All those years ago, you just disappeared, and no one would tell me anything, other than that your father had returned for you. But I could never accept it.' He shook his head. 'Even after all this time, I've never forgotten my broken heart.'

Tears caught in her lashes and she did her best to blink them away. Of course he was angry; she'd always felt as if she was the one whose heart had been broken, without thinking how much it must have hurt him.

'Alexandra?' Jessica appeared at her side then, giving her a strange look. 'This is an old friend of yours, I gather?'

Alexandra took Bernard's hand in hers, her eyes still fixed on his face, wondering how a man could look so handsome after so much time had passed.

'This isn't just any friend, Jessica,' she said. 'This man was the love of my life.' *And somehow, still is.*

'Well, I'm very pleased you've been able to reacquaint your-selves, but I fear we might miss our opportunity to be seated.'

'Follow me,' Bernard said, gesturing back the way he'd come. 'It just so happens that I can take you to the best seats in the house.'

Jessica gave them both a puzzled look, and Alexandra saw the way she glanced at her hand in Bernard's, but bless her, she never said a thing. But when they reached the backstage door, Alexandra turned, forgetting everything and everyone else as she looked up at Bernard.

'I know it's too late, but I've waited a lifetime to say this,' Alexandra said.

Bernard's eyes were on hers, his hand raised to touch the small of her back as he'd been about to usher her through.

'I love you with all my heart, Bernard. And I'm so sorry. I'm so sorry that I didn't fight hard enough for us. It will forever be the biggest regret of my life, but if you can find it in your heart to forgive me…'

A tear escaped from the corner of his eye, and she lifted her hand to brush it away, catching it against her fingertip.

'I forgive you,' Bernard said, leaning forwards and touching a kiss to her cheek. 'You're here now, and that's all that matters. I was always going to forgive you, Alex, I just never had the chance until now.'

Warmth spread through her when his lips whispered against her skin, as his words settled, as the sound of the orchestra beginning hummed through the air. It had taken four decades, and it had broken her heart a hundred times over, but here, somehow, after all this time, she'd found her way back to the man she loved. She only hoped it wasn't too late.

'I'm sorry,' she whispered, again, the tears choking in her throat.

He moved her slightly in front of him, just inside the door to the backstage area, as the stringed instruments burst into life, as the music swept around them.

'I'll never let you go again, Alexandra Konstantinidis,' he whispered into her ear, still holding her hand, taking her back to the last time they'd stood backstage, when he'd murmured words of encouragement to a scared young woman.

She turned and searched his eyes in the almost dark of the space. 'Even after all this time?' she whispered back.

'Even after all this time.'

Suddenly Alexandra was eighteen again with her life stretching ahead of her. Full of dreams and hope, and without the broken heart that she'd spent almost all her adult life nursing.

CHAPTER 33

Present Day

'What happened after that night?' Ella asked, sitting beside Alexandra on a little stone wall not halfway between the beach and her grandmother's house. They'd decided to take a walk as Alexandra shared the story of the past with her and Madeline, but they'd slowed and eventually come to a complete stop. 'How did you stay in touch?'

Alexandra smiled, her gaze fixed in the distance. 'We never spent a night apart ever again.'

'So after all those years, you just picked up as if nothing had happened?'

'No,' Alexandra said, turning to face her. 'Not as if nothing had happened. I felt guilty for not fighting against my father, for so blindly believing him and letting him control my life, and Bernard felt guilty for not searching for me, for not trying harder to find me when he returned from his tour. But we were together, and we were both determined to make up for lost time.'

'You were back in Athens by the time he returned? After you'd given birth to me?' Madeline asked.

'No, I was still in London when he returned. I was at Hope's House having you, our daughter.'

'You were in the same city all along?'

'We were,' Alexandra said with a sigh. 'But that's all in the past now. I sometimes look back and think how naïve I was, how easily I could have made a different decision and found my way back to Bernard. But it wasn't to be.'

Ella stared out at the tourists walking by, and looked up at the sun shining down on the water in the distance, wondering how Alexandra could be so calm about such a sad turn of events. Yet there she was, living in a time when women could supposedly do anything, worried about pleasing her own parents and not letting anyone down.

'I'm sorry,' Ella said, her voice low. 'No one deserves the kind of heartache you endured.'

Alexandra turned to look at her—to truly look at her—and Ella angled her body to face her. Her mother was beside her, and she could hear her shallow breathing, knew how hard it must be for her hearing the story from the past.

'I was more fortunate than most, Ella. I had a kind husband who never questioned why I couldn't give him my heart and eventually, I had Bernard again.' She sighed. 'We had ten beautiful years together, and I wouldn't swap that decade for anything in the world.'

'Even though you missed out on so many years together?'

Alexandra looked away again. 'Who knows what would have happened if I'd run back to Bernard, pregnant and penniless? Perhaps I was right all along, and he would have eventually resented the wife and child he was tied to. Maybe our love wouldn't have been enough.'

But maybe it would have been. Ella couldn't help but think those words, even though she would never say them to Alexandra.

'Alexandra, did you ever play the violin again?'

'I did,' she said, laughing softly as if at a private joke. 'Bernard was so cross with me when I told him I'd never played again after I left London, so I did start again. But only for him. My music was only ever for an audience of one.'

Ella wished she could have heard her play—maybe one day she'd be brave enough to ask her. But for now, it was enough being able to spend time with her, to get to know the woman she'd been so fortunate to meet.

'Shall we go for lunch?' Alexandra asked. 'I have a hankering for clams in a white wine sauce.'

Ella stood and offered Alexandra her arm as they began to walk again, something she'd once done with her other grandmother. 'That sounds delicious.' She only had a short time left in Greece, and she planned on soaking up every second in her grandmother's company and eating the best food she could find.

And then she was going to go home and decide what she truly wanted from life. Because if there was one thing Alexandra's story had taught her, it was that she had to make her own decisions about her life, and to be sure to follow her heart when she needed to. And hadn't her own mother told her only the night before that she would believe in her no matter what decisions she made?

'Now tell me, what makes your heart race, Ella? What is your great love?'

'Art,' she said, without hesitation, smiling across at her mother as she said the word. 'I'm…' She paused, turning the word over in her mind. 'I'm an artist.'

'Well, I shall have to see some of your art. Do you have any photos you could show me?'

Ella shook her head. 'No, but I've been working on a new piece since I've been here in Greece. I'll show it to you before I leave.'

'You have?' her mother asked.

'I have.'

Or perhaps I could give it to her as a gift?

'I would like that very much.'

One more week. One more week of sunshine, of being this new version of me, of discovering my past. She only wished she had longer, because Alexandra didn't even want to think about her going home, not yet.

'And tell me, do you have a special someone?'

'I'm not sure if he's my special someone yet,' Ella said, feeling her mother go still beside her. 'We haven't known each other very long, but I hope he becomes that person. I'd love for you both to meet him one day.'

'Well, all I can say is that if he lights up your eyes and makes your heart skip a beat, if he makes you feel like home, then don't let him go. Take it from an old lady who made many mistakes where love was concerned.'

They strolled arm in arm, with a warm wind blowing against their skin, the sun still high in the sky as they made their way down to the cluster of restaurants near the water. Suddenly Ella had the most overwhelming longing for her brother, and she put her arm around her mother's shoulders and squeezed her gently. It made her grateful for the journey the little box had brought her on. Not only had she discovered a grandmother she'd never known existed, but it had also brought her closer to her mum in a way she hadn't felt since Harrison had passed.

I wish you were here, Harry. Every adventure was better with you, and this one would have been no different.

Two hours later, the three women sat in Alexandra's home, their bellies full from the most delicious food Ella had ever eaten, cheeks sore from all the smiles and laughter. But now that they were back at the house, surrounded by photos of Bernard and

Alexandra together, there was still part of the story that she was waiting to hear. And when her mother stood and took one of the photos down, staring intently at the man in the picture, she knew it was the right time to ask.

'Alexandra, did Bernard only recently pass away?' her mother asked, looking up from the photograph.

'He did. We didn't have long together after reuniting. It seemed that we were never destined to be together for long, as if a cruel twist of fate stopped us from having our time together later in life too.'

Ella and her mother waited as Alexandra dabbed her eyes, taking back one of the photographs, the one of Bernard as a young man, and smiling down at it. 'But we made the most of every day when we did find each other again. There wasn't a day that passed that he didn't tell me he was the luckiest man alive. He was a beautiful man, and he treated me the way every woman deserves to be treated.'

'He suffered from an illness?' Ella asked.

Alexandra looked out of the window, clearing her throat. 'My Bernard had cancer. By the time they found it, it had spread everywhere, and we only had months from when he was first diagnosed until the day we said goodbye.'

Ella moved closer to Alexandra so she could put an arm around her, looking at her mother and hoping she'd know the right thing to say. But her mum was still studying the photograph.

'He does have my eyes,' Madeline suddenly said with a gasp. 'I feel like I'm looking back at myself. I can't…'

'That's why I couldn't stop looking at you before I gave you up,' Alexandra said. 'Because it was as if I were looking at my Bernard.'

'Alexandra, would you tell us, what happened in the end? Were you able to stay by his side through his illness?'

Alexandra laughed, softly, under her breath. 'The doctors and nurses knew better than to try to part us. After all those years separated, I wasn't going to leave his side for so much as a night.'

'Yours was a true love story,' Ella said.

'And your mother here is evidence of just how much we loved each other,' Alexandra said. 'Even at the end, when he was ready to take his last breath, we wondered about you. You were never far from our thoughts.'

Ella watched the way Alexandra reached forwards to touch her mother, as if she couldn't quite believe her daughter was sitting in front of her. She watched as she stroked her hair back from her face, traced her fingertips across her cheek, shook her head in wonder. It was the most beautiful moment to be part of.

'What happened to your family, Alexandra?' Madeline asked.

The smile dropped from Alexandra's lips then, as if a dark shadow had passed over her. 'I never spoke to my father again, not after I was married. I never saw anyone from his side of the family, not ever, not after you'd been adopted and I moved back to Greece.'

'And your mother's side of the family?'

'They are my true family,' she said firmly. 'They took me in after my mother died, and loved me in a way my father never could. But I was so ashamed of what had happened that I never told them about my baby, about *you*,' she said, gesturing at Madeline. 'In hindsight, I should have. They would have known what to do, and would have cared for me, but at the time I was so young and scared, my father made me believe that I'd brought great shame on my family, and that it was my duty to restore our wealth by marrying well, as if I had something to repent for. In truth, I think he simply wanted his status in society restored, and that was the only way he could see to make that happen.'

'I wish I could have met Bernard, my father,' Madeline said. 'I can't believe that he's already gone.'

'I want you to know that your father was loved and cherished until his very last breath. I was with him right until the end.'

Ella couldn't take her eyes from Alexandra as her face came to life talking about the man who she'd clearly loved with all her heart.

CHAPTER 34

Athens, 2022

Alexandra touched her palm softly to Bernard's cheek. His skin was still soft beneath her fingertips, but it was a different type of soft now, with gentle wrinkles creasing it slightly. His hand rested against the small of her back, and as the music played they circled in little shuffles across the floor, their feet barely moving.

'Once, we would have been as light-footed as elves,' he whispered into her ear.

That made her laugh. She leaned back in his arms and looked up into his eyes, the way he looked at her as passionate now as it had been fifty years ago when they'd first danced.

'Do you remember when we met?'

'On your eighteenth birthday,' he replied. 'How could I ever forget?'

Alexandra smiled up at him once more, before moving closer so that she could touch her cheek to his. On the left side of his face there was an oxygen tube, their reminder that what they shared was coming to an end, that after so many years of being deprived of each other's company, they were now on borrowed time.

But Alexandra didn't want to dwell on the years they hadn't spent together; she wanted to soak up every moment of being with Bernard. The man who'd told her that everything she'd ever dreamed of was possible; that she was capable of being the greatest musician in the world, if only she could believe in herself. Sometimes she tried to remember what it had felt like, to be so young and innocent, to truly believe that anything *was* possible. But when she did that, all she could remember was Bernard, and the way he'd made her feel.

Bernard's movements became even slower then, and she could tell that he was tiring. Alexandra held him more firmly in her arms and gently steered him back towards the bed. The nurses had been so kind to them, letting her stay by his bedside at all times of the day and night, and not batting an eyelid when she arrived with a stack of music to play all his favourite old songs. They most likely had a giggle at the two old people doing their shuffle dance in the hospital room, but bless them, they never tried to interrupt them or tell Alexandra to get him back to bed. They also never told her not to bother when she arrived with his favourite meals each night, even though he was scarcely able to swallow more than a mouthful or two. The cancer had ravaged his body, but she was determined to remind him of all the things he loved, of all the things they'd loved together; she still had so much to make up for. He was an old man made to appear even older by his illness; now an old man so close to the end that no one was brave enough to take away what little time they had left.

Alexandra helped to lower Bernard, fluffing the pillows behind him to make sure he was comfortable. But when she went to move away, his fingers closed around her wrist, still firm despite his frailness. But it was the way he looked at her that reminded her of the man he still was, his eyes still bright as they met hers.

'Don't go,' he whispered.

'I won't,' she said. 'Remember what I told you, B? I'm never leaving you ever again. You will never have to be in this room alone, I promise.'

He smiled and relaxed back into the pillows, his eyes fluttering shut. She reached across to stroke his face, tenderly tracing her fingertips over his cheeks and down his shoulder, leaning forwards to press a kiss to his forehead. Her lips lingered, not wanting to pull away, even as her tears slid down her cheeks and wet his face.

So many years had been taken from them. *Stolen from us.* But no one could take this time from them. No one could steal these final moments they had together. Every second was precious, and they both knew it, which was why she would never leave his side.

She saw how dry his lips were and reached for an ice cube, gently touching it against his mouth and watching as his lips parted. She would have done anything for him, *anything* to ease his pain, to take away some of what he was feeling.

'Play for me,' Bernard murmured, barely audible as she placed what was left of the ice cube back in the cup beside his bed.

And so she stood and went to her case, which was on the other side of his bed, taking out her violin and bow. Bernard's eyes were still shut, but she knew that he would listen intently as she played. She was only pleased that he couldn't see the pain on her face from playing for him, how much it hurt her to do the one thing she'd always done for him, to remember what it was like to play for him and only him when they'd both been young and so full of dreams. When anything had seemed possible.

Alexandra blinked away tears as she lifted her bow, positioning her instrument between her chin and shoulder, and taking a deep breath before beginning the piece. She played what she always played, the song she'd practised with Bernard all those years before, when she'd performed with his words of encouragement ringing in her ears. The piece of music she'd never been able to listen to in all their years apart without thinking of him, but that she'd remembered every night until they'd finally found each other again.

When she looked up, she saw that a group of nurses had gathered in the doorway, with not a dry eye among them, all silently watching as she played the song until the very end. Her heart ached with every stroke, but she didn't stop. And when she'd finished, she moved on to another song he loved, and then another, as if she were on a stage with a collection of music to play. Because sometimes it was easier to lose oneself in music, that's what her aunt had taught her—to play when your heart hurt the most, to distract yourself from life for at least a moment.

When she finally finished, her arm sore from holding the violin for so long, out of practice after so many years of not playing, she closed her eyes and let her breath shudder from her body. The pain of nursing Bernard, the anger at the time they'd lost, the desperation of wishing there was something she could do to ease his suffering—it all surged through her as her bow slid from her fingertips. Because the room suddenly felt empty.

When Alexandra looked over at Bernard, her heart stuttered; for she knew. He was gone. The love of her life had left the world listening to the pieces he loved the most, the music that had been as special to him as it had to her. She could feel that he was no longer there, that he'd been taken from her for good this time.

Alexandra went to his side, placing her violin beside him on the bed as she lowered herself over his body, her cheek to his chest. A hand touched her back, soothing her, a gentle palm against her spine, but she didn't turn. She wasn't ready to concede to anyone else that he'd gone yet, not even his nurses. Her tears wet the front of Bernard's shirt, leaving him damp as her fingers curled around his hand, wishing they'd had more time, wishing she could have had even one more hour, one more day, one more week with the man she loved.

All those years they'd lost, all those decades she could have held him in her arms; the memories they could have created together.

The children we could have had. The love we could have shared. The world we could have explored.

But in the end, it wasn't the years they'd missed but memories of the years they'd shared that wrapped around her now, like the warm embrace of a lover. The day she'd seen her Bernard after decades parted—the moment she'd met his gaze and been reunited with the man she'd loved for her entire adult life—that was when her life had truly begun all over again.

And those were the memories she was going to hold on to until her own dying breath.

My darling B, my heart, my soul. I only wish we'd had longer.

I only wish we'd had longer to search for the daughter that I should never have given up. The daughter that I should have been brave enough to keep, brave enough to tell you about, brave enough to tell the world about.

She would have to live with that regret for the rest of her life, wondering what had become of her beautiful little girl, with eyes as bright as her father's, who'd stolen her heart in the short time she'd held her in her arms.

And she would always wonder if her child would one day come looking for her, so that she could tell her what a beautiful soul her father was. A man who'd taken her hand when she was just a girl of eighteen and promised to never let go, who'd stood in the wings and told her to be brave, who'd have stood by her side when she was alone and pregnant, if only she'd given him the chance.

CHAPTER 35

Present Day

Ella walked along the beach, barefoot and with her sandals hanging from her fingertips. Her mother was back at the house, packing—she'd managed to get on the same flight as Ella going home—but Ella was having a hard time even thinking about returning to London. Greece had changed her in a way she could never have imagined. She'd arrived on holiday with a thought of what she wanted to do, with dreams of painting and filling her spare time with trying to understand the clues in her little box. But her time away had been so much more than a holiday.

She'd gained a grandmother, which in itself was almost impossible to process, but she'd also begun to understand herself and what she truly wanted from life. She was re-energised about going back to work at the gallery; being away had made it clear to her that she loved her work, but she no longer wanted it to be her entire identity. She wanted to paint and find that creative part of herself again; she wanted time to be herself and fall in love, to see what might develop between her and Gabriel. Suddenly, she couldn't imagine her life without him in it.

Ella wasn't yet sure if he was her Bernard, but she wanted to take the time to nurture things between them and see if perhaps he might just be to her what Bernard had been to Alexandra.

She stopped walking then and took the little wooden box from her pocket, bending low and scooping some sand and pebbles into it. Alexandra had the sheet of music and the photo now, both returned to her on the day she'd met her, but Ella hadn't felt ready to part with the box. Without it, she would never have come to Greece, and she wanted to keep a little piece of Skopelos with her at home. She would give it pride of place somewhere so that she could always look at it and smile, remembering the days she spent on the beautiful island.

Ella traced her thumb over the box one last time before putting it back in her pocket, knowing it was time to do one last thing before she went back to the house. Gabriel would be leaving the next day for his tour, and she didn't want to miss her chance to wish him luck.

The phone rang at least eight times before going to voicemail, and although she hesitated and considered hanging up, Ella instead clutched the phone tighter, staring out at the sparkling blue ocean stretching before her.

'Gabe, it's me. I told myself that I was calling to tell you to have a wonderful time on tour, but to be honest I'm calling because I wanted to hear your voice. Maybe I'm mad, maybe it's hearing about Bernard and Alexandra and getting carried away with their story, but I miss you already. Anyway, this is me, saying that when you get back, I can't wait to see you.' She hesitated, before forcing out the words. 'Because I think that I might love you.'

Ella laughed at herself as she finally ended the call. She was mortified, but also happy that she'd been honest. Alexandra would have been proud of her, she was certain of it.

And as she strolled back down the beach, past rows of umbrellas and loungers that had been abandoned now that the sun was going down, Ella felt her phone vibrating. She glanced at the screen and saw that it was Gabriel.

'So you think I'm your Bernard?'

Ella burst out laughing. 'I really wish I hadn't left you that message.'

'Ella, I'm at the airport, we've just boarded, but I saw your voicemail and listened to it just as—'

'Sir, please turn off your mobile device.'

Ella could hear the flight attendant reprimanding Gabriel in the background.

'I miss you too,' he said quickly. 'I promise I'll call, but if I don't go now I'm going to be removed from the flight. I love you too.'

The line went dead then, but Ella didn't care. She smiled to herself all the way up the quaint stone path that she knew she would miss walking up every day, barefoot with her sandals in one hand. She could hear the faint sound of laughter and the clinking of glasses—either tourists celebrating their holiday in paradise or locals happy to be sharing a meal together.

Her mother opened the door when she arrived back, as if she'd been waiting for her.

'That's a lovely big smile.'

'I think I've found my Bernard,' she blurted out.

'Well, then, I can't wait to meet him. Where is he?'

Her mother looked out the door, as if perhaps expecting that he was waiting to come in behind her.

'He's in London. Actually, he's on a plane.' Ella groaned. 'It's a long story.'

'Let's have one last dinner by the water, and you can tell me all about it.'

Ella stood and stared out at the view, at the wooden easel she'd left outside in the hope that someone else might discover it, at the endless blue ocean that stretched as far as the eye could see.

Greece was part of her soul, she could feel it, and she knew that she would return, no matter what.

'Dinner sounds wonderful. Let's go.'

They closed the door behind them and set off down the path again, arm in arm, enjoying the balmy night air as Ella committed to memory the way Skopelos made her feel. After years of not knowing what to paint, now she had a notebook full of inspiration. Just as Alexandra had been Bernard's muse, Greece had become hers.

EPILOGUE

One Year Later

'Ella.' Alexandra opened her arms and welcomed Ella into her home. Part of Ella had wanted to rent the same house she'd stayed in the last time she'd been in Greece, imagining days painting in the courtyard and walking down to the little restaurant she'd quickly come to love. But when Alexandra had called and invited them to visit over the summer, she'd known there was nowhere else she should be than staying in her home with her. It was quite something to have a bonus grandmother, and Ella intended on making the most of it while she could.

'It's so good to see you again,' Ella said, holding Alex in her arms for another moment before letting her go. 'I can't believe it's been so many months since we were last together.'

'It's wonderful to see you again too,' Alexandra said. 'Who would have thought my home would be filled with family, after so long alone?'

Ella stood back as Gabriel hugged Alexandra, kissing her cheek.

'Thank goodness you've brought this gorgeous man with you,' Alex sighed. 'Take those bags upstairs and then come down and tell me all about the orchestra. I'm dying to hear.'

'Your home is so beautiful, Alex,' Ella said, linking their arms. 'I'd almost forgotten how stunning it is. How stunning Greece is.'

'From the moment I left Greece as a child, I vowed to come back one day,' Alex said as they walked slowly together into the living room that looked out at the sea. 'I loved London, but when I couldn't be with Bernard, I knew that Greece was the only country that could truly make me happy. It was like a feeling in my bones that made me yearn to be back here.'

'You never did tell me about your husband, Alex. You came back to Greece to marry him?'

'I did.'

She smiled at her grandmother. 'Was he a good man? Was he kind to you?'

'He was,' Alex said, taking a seat and gesturing for Ella to do the same. 'He was generous, and he was understanding. A good husband, despite the fact that we were never in love. The night before our wedding, I intended on telling him I couldn't go through with it, that I was going to make my own decision about who I would marry, but in the end we came to an understanding and we were married the next day.'

'Did you ever tell him about Bernard?'

'Oh, Ella, of course I did. It was obvious my heart was already taken, and he was a widower, still in love with his late wife.' She sighed. 'In a way, we were the perfect couple, both in desperate need of companionship, and yet not having to pretend we were passionately in love. And without him, I would never have what I have now. He gave me back the life and belongings that my father had frittered away, even down to my mother's jewellery that had been sold to pay my father's debts. He found it all and bought it back for me, as well as this house. It was gifted to my mother by the Queen herself, but even that hadn't deterred my father from disposing of it. I owe so much to my husband, even if he wasn't the love of my life.' She smiled. 'He even convinced me to start reading again, after years of not picking up a book, but that is a story for another day.'

'Alex, do you regret any of it? Do you sometimes wonder what would have happened if your father hadn't returned for you when he did?'

'I'm an old lady, Ella, which means I have all the time in the world to wonder what could have been.' Alexandra looked away, as if lost in her own thoughts. 'The truth is, I'll never know. Perhaps Bernard and I would have had a lifetime together, but then perhaps he wouldn't have been the same man. He toured the world with the orchestra, he was able to live his dream. If I'd found him, maybe he wouldn't have been the man I fell in love with, twice over.'

Ella didn't say anything, leaning into Gabriel, who'd come to sit on the arm of the sofa beside her. They hadn't had a night apart since he'd returned from his tour, and she still had to pinch herself when she thought of how they'd met, how everything in her life had changed since the day she'd received that little box of clues.

'Perhaps if I hadn't become pregnant, we'd have toured the world together and become the greatest of musicians. But it wasn't to be, and if I had, I wouldn't have a beautiful daughter and granddaughter to share the next week with, would I?'

They sat for a moment in silence, before Gabriel stood and held out his hand first to Ella and then to Alexandra. It wasn't lost on Ella how lucky she was—she didn't have to choose between motherhood and her career, and yet her grandmother's life had changed because of her pregnancy.

'Ladies, I think it's time we went out for lunch,' Gabriel said. 'I'm ready to enjoy the best food the island has to offer.'

'Promise this old lady that you'll play for her when we get home, would you?' Alexandra asked.

'I shall play *with* you,' Gabriel said, winking at Ella over the top of Alexandra's head. 'That's my only condition.'

'My Bernard would have loved you,' Alexandra said with a sigh. 'I haven't played since the day he died, but it would be my honour to play alongside you.'

Ella couldn't remember a time she'd been so content. Perhaps her last summer with her brother; that was probably the last time she'd felt as if being happy came so easily, without effort. She'd come close over the past year, but something about today felt different.

'Now tell me all about the baby,' Alexandra asked as they let themselves out of the house and began to wander slowly down the cobbled path that linked all the homes. It would take them perhaps fifteen minutes to walk to the restaurant at this pace, but Ella felt as if she could walk all day, it was so pleasant. 'Do you know what you're having?'

She glanced at Gabriel. They did know, but they'd promised to keep it a secret between them. He gave her a smile and a nod of his head, before mouthing: *tell her.*

Ella took a deep breath. 'You're the first person we've told,' she began, 'that we're having a little girl.'

'A girl?' Alexandra's eyes became misty with tears as she stopped in the middle of the path.

She reached out a hand to touch Ella's stomach, hesitating at first, as if waiting for permission. Ella closed the distance, holding her hand over Alexandra's.

'A beautiful little girl,' Alexandra said, looking into Ella's eyes. 'What a wonderful blessing. I shall very much like having a great-granddaughter.'

'We actually had something we wanted to ask you,' Ella said, as they began to slowly stroll again.

'We were going to wait until after lunch,' Gabriel said, 'when everyone was together, but—'

'We would like your blessing to be married here, in Greece,' Ella interrupted. 'We'd very much like to be married on the island, and celebrate at your home afterwards.'

Alexandra stopped again, this time looking between them. 'A baby and a wedding? Santa Maria,' she said, throwing her slender arms into the air. 'How did I get to be so lucky?'

Ella bent down to kiss her cheek, wishing that Alexandra knew how fortunate they felt to have found her. To discover a grandmother she'd never known existed, and to be spending time with her like this, was almost impossible to believe.

Almost as impossible, she thought as she glanced over at Gabriel, as the fact that she was soon to be married, or that she'd just had her first showing at the gallery, and sold all but one piece from her Greek-inspired collection.

She blew Gabe a kiss when he caught her staring at him, and he just shook his head and laughed. It was going to be the holiday of a lifetime—a wedding and a babymoon, all rolled into one. Somehow, her life had changed in the most unexpected of ways, and she was loving every second of it.

*

Six days later, Ella stretched out in the sun, relishing the warmth on her skin. There was something about being on the beach in Greece that agreed with her; she knew it would forever be her perfect holiday destination, the place that she felt deep in her soul she had a connection with. It also seemed to be the place that inspired her best work, which would give her a very good excuse to return each summer. She would remind Gabriel of that if he ever tried to convince her to travel elsewhere.

She touched her palm to her rounded stomach then, smiling as she thought about the holidays they would be able to have with their little one when she arrived. It would be quite something to share the Greek islands with a daughter toddling around after them. Her phone pinged then and Ella rolled over, reaching for it and holding it up to try to see the screen in the sunlight, smiling when she saw that it was Mia.

After they'd had coffee together, she'd made sure to stay in touch and let her know how everything had progressed, excited to tell her how her clues had led her to Alexandra. Mia had seemed to love the updates, and Ella hoped that it would go some way to reassuring Mia that she'd done the right thing in reuniting the little boxes with their respective families.

How's Greece?

Ella peeked over the top of her sunglasses and stared at the water for a moment, before replying. If only she could describe the beauty of the islands. It would be impossible to do it justice.

It's amazing. There's nowhere in the world I'd rather be.

She repositioned herself and waited for Mia to reply, wriggling so that her torso was shaded more by the overhead umbrella, her legs still warmed by the sun. They'd become firm friends over the past year, linked by the past but finding that they were both similar in so many ways. Only last week they'd had Mia over for dinner, and she had been one of the few personal friends she'd invited to her showing at the gallery.

I've just had news from the contractors demolishing Hope's House.

Ella felt her heart skip a beat as she watched the little bubbles appear on the screen, waiting for the next message. What news could they have for Mia?

> *They found a box of things that I'd missed, hidden in the attic. There were papers and other things that don't make sense to me yet, but I also found Hope's personal diary. It was tucked among the things in the box.*

Ella shouldn't have been so curious, not now that her grandmother's story had been pieced together so clearly, but the whole history of Hope's House fascinated her. She would have been lying if she'd said she didn't want to know more; if anything, finding Alexandra had made her even more curious about the past, and she also felt a deep connection to Mia.

> *Have you discovered something of interest? Have you read the diary yet?*

'Ella, come on, we'll be late for lunch!' Gabriel called out from farther down the beach.

She waved to him, but kept staring at the screen, waiting for Mia's response.

> *I think your grandmother was the last woman to give birth at the house, and I also think that Hope might have been adopted herself. I think it's why she did so much for unwanted babies. But there's more.*

'Ella, what are you doing? Your mum and Kate will be waiting.' Gabriel appeared by her side, blocking the sun as he towered like a shadow over her.

'I just have to read one more message,' she said, smiling up at him and reaching to touch his arm. 'Can you just pack my book and towel into my bag? I won't be a minute.'

She mentions that she never made sense of what had been left for her. That she decided to store the things away for safekeeping. It's made me wonder if there were clues left in the little box bearing her name, but perhaps she took them out and never bothered to return them.

'Ella?'

There's also another granddaughter who's reached out to me for assistance. I was thinking we could both meet her? Her name is Georgia. I think she's the woman who walked out of the meeting at the lawyer's office that day. The one who seemed uninterested in what was left for her.

Ella stood and slid her phone into the pocket of her shorts, her mind full of Mia's last message as she slipped her hand into Gabriel's and walked back down the beach by his side. She would respond to her properly later, but she knew without a doubt that she would most definitely be saying yes to helping the other granddaughter who'd received a box. How could she not, after the way it had changed her own life?

'Was that work?' he asked. 'You know the gallery can survive without you, don't you?'

Ella smiled up at him, standing on tiptoe to press a kiss to his cheek. 'No, it was Mia.' Gabriel groaned. 'Oh, no, don't tell me you have another hidden family member we have to search for? I don't think my brain could stand to decipher any more clues.'

Ella laughed and tucked herself closer to his side. 'No, but I think maybe she does. It sounds as if Mia has her own family mystery, and this <u>other</u> woman, when we get back to London—'

'Come along, wife. Everyone is waiting to see the newlyweds,' Gabe said. 'We can talk about this later, because I know there'll be no stopping you when we get home.'

Ella grinned up at him and he kissed her, his lips grazing hers as they slowed to a stop outside the restaurant, his hands moving to her waist as she kissed him back.

'I think we'd best go inside,' he murmured, turning her slowly around so she could see her family waving, seated at a table inside the restaurant.

Ella waved back. She would tell Gabe all about it another time. For now, she was going to soak up the afternoon with her loved ones. Maybe tonight she'd call Mia though, and see if she couldn't offer some advice on finding the clues that had been left to her.

She touched one hand to her stomach as Gabriel pulled out a chair for her, and Alexandra smiled at her from across the table. After all, without Mia, she wouldn't have any of this.

Helping her is the least I can do.

A LETTER FROM SORAYA

Dear reader,

Thank you so much for choosing to read *The Royal Daughter*!

I do hope you loved reading it as much as I enjoyed writing it, and if you did, I would be very grateful if you could write a review. I can't wait to hear your thoughts on the story, and it makes such a difference in helping new readers to discover one of my books for the very first time.

This was the third book in The Lost Daughters series, and I'm looking forward to sharing more books with you very, very soon. If you haven't already read *The Italian Daughter* or *The Cuban Daughter*, you might like to read both of those books next, and enjoy being swept away to Italy and Cuba, and falling in love with some truly unforgettable characters.

One of my favourite things is hearing from readers—you can get in touch via my Facebook page, by joining Soraya's Reader Group on Facebook, or finding me on Goodreads or my website.

Thank you so much,
Soraya x

🖥 www.sorayalane.com

Soraya's Reader Group:
🄵 groups/sorayalanereadergroup

ACKNOWLEDGMENTS

In previous novels, I usually start my acknowledgements by saying that I have a very small group of people to thank, but when it comes to The Lost Daughters series, I actually have quite a long list! As always, I'd like to acknowledge editor Laura Deacon for taking a chance on this series when I first pitched the idea to her—Laura, it's been such a pleasure working with you! I can't believe we're already publishing book three though; it seems like we were only just talking about the idea for The Lost Daughters yesterday, and yet here we are with three books completed.

I would like to thank the entire Bookouture team for their support, with special mention to Peta Nightingale, Ruth Tross, Jess Readett, Saidah Graham, Melanie Price, Noelle Holten, Kim Nash and copyeditor extraordinaire Jenny Page. But my biggest thanks go to Richard King, who is the rights director at Bookouture. Richard is the reason this series is available in so many languages around the world, and I will be forever grateful to him for pitching my books with such passion. Thank you, Richard—I wish I could express to you how incredibly grateful I am to have you in my corner, and I hope that this is just the beginning of what has already proven to be a very successful relationship. At the time of writing, The Lost Daughters series was being translated into twenty-one languages. Special thanks also to Saidah for the markets she has sold the books into!

I must make special mention and thanks to the other editors and publishers who will be publishing The Lost Daughters series around the world. Thank you to Hachette; to my UK editor Callum Kenny at Little, Brown (Sphere imprint); my New Zealand Hachette team, with special mention to Alison Shucksmith, Suzy Maddox and Tania Mackenzie-Cooke; US editor Kirsiah Depp at Grand Central; Dutch editor Neeltje Smitskamp at Park Uitgevers; German editor Julia Cremer at Droemer-Knaur; editors Päivi Syrjänen and Iina Tikanoja at Otava (Finland); and Norwegian editor Anja Gustavson at Kagge Forlag. I would also like to acknowledge the following publishing houses: Hachette Australia, Albatros (Poland), Sextante (Brazil), Planeta (Spain), Planeta (Portugal), City Editions (France), Garzanti (Italy), Lindbak and Lindbak (Denmark), Euromedia (Czech), Modan Publishing House (Israel), Vulkan (Serbia), Lettero (Hungary), Sofoklis (Lithuania), Modan Publishing House (Hebrew), Pegasus (Estonia), Hermes (Bulgaria), JP Politikens (Sweden) and Grup Media Litera (Romania). Knowing that my book will be published in so many languages around the world by such well-respected publishing houses is truly a dream come true.

Now, back to my usual small group of wonderful people! Thank you to my long-time agent Laura Bradford, who I'm so proud to have representing me. Special thanks also to Lucy Stille for reading *The Italian Daughter* and joining the team! Thank you to my incredible writing friends Yvonne Lindsay and Natalie Anderson—what would I do without you girls? To my parents, Maureen and Craig, thank you for your constant support. And finally, to my wonderful husband Hamish and my gorgeous boys Mack and Hunter—I'm so lucky to have you all.

And finally, a huge thank you to all my readers. I wouldn't be here without you, and I'm so grateful that you've chosen to read my book.

Soraya x

Don't miss the next heartbreaking novel
in The Lost Daughters series, out now.

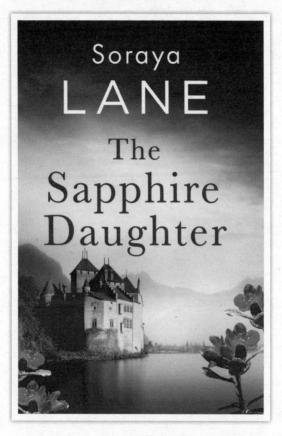

Soraya
LANE

The
Sapphire
Daughter

Turn over for an extract!

PROLOGUE

LAKE GENEVA, SEPTEMBER 1951

SUMMER RESIDENCE OF FLORIAN LENGACHER

Delphine stretched out beside the pool, her silk robe slipping from her shoulder and leaving it bare as she lay in the sun, smiling as she heard Florian's footsteps coming closer. She held out her hand for the drink he'd promised, but instead of a glass, he slipped his palm against hers.

She opened her eyes, sitting upright when she saw his serious expression and turning to face him. In the distance the lake shimmered, the late sun reflecting off the water.

'You look worried,' she said, reaching out her other hand to cup his smooth cheek as he lowered himself to the seat beside her, his dark hair falling forward as he leaned in. 'Tell me—what's wrong?'

'Nothing's wrong,' he replied, smiling as he squeezed her hand. 'On the contrary, I have something to show you.'

Delphine smiled back, only too happy to play along. Their stolen moments together brought her such joy, made her forget all the heartbreak that had come before, and she patiently waited for him to continue.

Her curiosity was piqued when she realised he was holding a box in his other hand. 'What do you want to show me?' she asked.

'This,' Florian said, dropping her hand in order to take the lid off the box, 'belonged to the former queen consort of Italy. I had a feeling you might be familiar with it?'

'The pink sapphire tiara,' Delphine said, her breath catching in her throat as she looked up at him, hardly able to believe what she was looking at. 'I know it well. In fact, I admired it when the queen wore it to a wedding I attended after the war. I don't think there's a woman in Italy who wouldn't recognise it.' She shook her head, leaning forward to better see the stunning jewels. It took her back to her time in Italy, of the years she'd spent going to glittering parties and rubbing shoulders with Italian nobility during the early years of her marriage. 'How has it come to be in your possession?'

'The family discreetly sold some unique pieces from their collection after they left Italy, and my personal curator made certain I was the successful buyer. Most of the other pieces were entrusted to the Bank of Italy in Rome for safekeeping, which makes the few pieces they sold even more special,' he said, holding it up between them so Delphine could look at it more closely. 'I've collected many beautiful diamonds and pieces of art over the years, but this tiara? There is nothing in the world to rival the history and the beauty of such a piece.'

It was certainly unique, and the fact that he'd been able to purchase it reminded her just how well-connected Florian was. The stones caught the light as he turned the tiara in his hands, the sapphires appearing the most vivid pink one moment, and then almost purple the next, made even more brilliant as the sunshine reflected against them. He was right that it was perhaps one of the most coveted and stunning pieces of jewellery he could have invested in.

'This tiara was held in the Italian royal family from the 1800s until they were forced into exile five years ago,' Florian said. 'And now it shall remain in my family for generations to come. This is one of those pieces that I never intend to part with.'

'I hugely admire the former queen,' Delphine said. 'I recall her saying that her only regret during the war was not killing Adolf Hitler herself when she was in the same room as him, and I've always presumed she was quite capable of it. She's one of those rare women who is both feminine and forthright, so it's fitting that you've chosen her favourite tiara. I imagine it's absolutely priceless.'

'I couldn't agree more,' Florian said. 'And you're right, it is priceless. It is to be the jewel in my personal collection, for want of a better expression.'

'It's stunning, Florian. Thank you for showing it to me.' She tucked her legs up beneath her as Florian smiled at her, his expression hard to read.

'I showed it to you for a reason, Delphine,' he finally said, placing the tiara beside him and reaching for both her hands. 'I would like you to choose one of the sapphires so that I can have an engagement ring made for you.' Florian kissed her knuckles, his dark brown eyes never leaving hers as his voice lowered to a whisper.

'Florian—' she began.

'I want us to spend the rest of our lives together, Delphine. I don't want to hide any more. I want the world to know you are to become my wife, and this is my way of showing you what you mean to me.'

Tears filled her eyes, a solitary drop sliding down her cheek as she looked away, wishing it were so easy, wishing she was free to make her own decisions in life. The tiara caught her gaze, and she wondered what heartbreak it had seen, what love it might have been witness to; what sorrow.

'You know it's not so easy as my simply saying yes. If it were…' She couldn't bring herself to finish the sentence. When they were together like this, it felt as if they were the only two people in the world. But outside the walled gates of his compound, of the beautiful, secluded property by the lake that had been their private oasis these past few months, they couldn't be seen together freely.

Florian nodded, his hands guiding her closer until she was curled on his knee, her arms around his neck, tucked tightly to his chest. The tiara would be nothing without one of its sapphires, its value hugely diminished if it were ever to be offered for sale with a missing stone, but she knew that was what he was trying to tell her: that he would break up the most valuable piece in his collection, the piece that meant the most to him, for her. It was abundantly obvious that he had the funds to buy her the most expensive diamond from Tiffany's, and yet he was willing to sacrifice one of the precious sapphires as a gesture of his love.

'I am nothing without you,' Florian murmured into her hair. 'Please, say yes. Let me find a way for us to marry.'

Neither am I, Florian. Without you, I too am nothing.

Delphine looked up at him, her fingers grazing his cheek as she pressed her mouth to his in a long, slow, warm kiss.

'Yes,' she eventually whispered against his lips. 'I will marry you, Florian. If you can find a way, then I promise you. I will marry you.'

CHAPTER 1

LONDON, 2022

Georgia stepped out of the taxi and hurried down the narrow London street, double-checking the address on her phone. Older-style buildings stretched down both sides, with the exception of a modern, glass-fronted design sandwiched between the brickwork at the very end, bearing a discreet sign announcing that it was the law firm she was looking for—Williamson, Clark & Duncan. She'd told herself all morning that she wasn't going to go, right up until the moment she'd walked out of her office, convinced the letter she'd received was a hoax. *And yet here I am*.

She inhaled, squared her shoulders and marched into the lawyer's office, giving the receptionist her name and taking a seat in the chair closest to the front desk. She was surprised to see that there were other young women also waiting, and one glanced up at her before quickly looking back down to her magazine.

When Georgia had received the letter, stating that her presence was required to collect something left to her family's estate, she'd been somewhat caught off-guard. But as the last remaining family member, she'd decided that it would be foolish not to go, especially when her assistant had assured her that the law firm was legitimate.

What she hadn't been expecting was for her name to be called along with five others soon after she'd arrived, and for them all to be ushered into a conference room together. Her heart began to race as she glanced around at the other young women and she shifted uncomfortably. *They weren't all about to be told they were related, were they?*

Georgia took a sip of water from the glass on the table to soothe her suddenly dry throat as she sat, glancing around the modern office as a well-dressed woman stood and introduced herself as Mia Jones. It wasn't that she was uninterested in what the woman standing before her was saying; she simply needed to be elsewhere, and when her phone vibrated in her bag, she knew there was no way she'd be able to stay for more than fifteen minutes. Georgia picked up the bag and placed it on her lap, hoping she might be able to disguise the sound. But even with her arms pressed onto her bag, it was impossible not to hear the vibrations.

Would it be rude to ask to come back another time?

Georgia started to tap her foot as the man who'd introduced himself as the lawyer cleared his throat and began to speak. She recognised his name as the lawyer who'd sent her the letter and, as distracted as she was, she was also very curious about why she'd been summoned. She looked around at the other women there, still not sure what the connection was. There was the pretty brunette with freckles across her nose who'd glanced at her in the waiting area, another brunette and a very attractive blonde, who had both been quick to smile at her across the table when they'd sat down. One of the other women had dark blonde hair and a big smile, emphasised by a shock of bright red lipstick; and then there was another woman, with hair almost as dark as Georgia's, who kept her head down, her fingers worrying the edge of the table.

It wasn't until she looked away from the last woman, as Mia began to place little wooden boxes that were perhaps twice the size of a ring box on the table in front of them, that Georgia had an inkling as to why she was there. Her eyes were drawn to a name that was familiar to her, a name she hadn't seen in years, tied to a piece of string, which was in turn attached to one of the small boxes. *Cara Montano*. Was that why she was here, to receive the tiny box? She glanced at the other women, wondering if they'd recognised the name, too, but no one else appeared to have seen it, or if they had, it didn't seem to mean anything to them.

Georgia sat a little straighter as the woman named Mia, the woman clearly responsible for summoning them all, continued to place the small boxes out on the table, lining them all up in a row as she spoke.

'As you've just heard, my aunt's name was Hope Berenson, and for many years she ran a private home here in London called Hope's House, for unmarried mothers and their babies. She was very well known for her discretion, as well as her kindness, despite the times.'

Hope's House? Georgia had no idea what that had to do with her, but she couldn't take her eyes from the little box, from the name of her grandmother—Cara Montano—staring back at her as plain as day. Her spine stiffened and she involuntarily dug her fingernails into her palms. If she'd known this was about her grandmother, she may not have come at all.

After all these years of wishing she'd come for me, of wishing she wanted me, her name still has a way of hurting me.

She continued to ignore the vibrations from her phone as she listened to Mia, who was telling them about how she'd found the little boxes beneath the floorboards of her aunt's house, and her decision to reunite them with the descendants of the women they'd been intended for. It was fascinating, and if it had been another day, she would have loved to have heard more about it.

Georgia dragged her eyes from the little handwritten label and looked up at the lawyer as he spoke again.

'When Mia found these, she brought them straight to me, and we went through all the old records in her aunt's office. Hope's documentation was meticulous, and although those records should have stayed private, in this case we chose to search for the names on the boxes, to see if we couldn't reunite them with their rightful owners. I felt an obligation to do what I could.'

'Did you open any of them?' asked one of the women seated across from Georgia.

'No.' Mia's voice lowered, much softer now than when she'd spoken before. 'That's why I asked you all to be here today, so you could each choose whether to open them or not.' Her eyes filled with tears, and Georgia watched as she quickly brushed them away. 'To keep them hidden all these years, they must have held such importance to my aunt, but what I don't understand is why she never reunited the boxes with their intended during her lifetime. I felt it was my duty to at least try, and now it's up to each one of you whether they remain sealed or not.'

'What we don't know,' the lawyer said, planting his hands on the table as he slowly rose from his chair, 'is whether there were other boxes that were given out over the years. Either Hope chose not to give these seven out for some reason, or they weren't claimed.'

'Or she decided, again for reasons of her own, that they were better kept hidden,' Mia finished for him. 'In which case, I may have uncovered something that was supposed to stay buried.'

The lawyer cleared his throat as Georgia's phone started to buzz again. She sighed and finally reached for it, seeing that it was Sam, her business partner. *Of course, it was Sam.* She was only going to keep calling if Georgia didn't answer—it was shaping up to be one of the most exciting days of both their careers, which was the reason she hadn't intended on coming to the meeting at all—which in turn meant she needed to go. Georgia listened to the conversation, waiting for a break so she could excuse herself.

'Yes,' the lawyer said. 'But whatever the reason, my duty is to pass them on to their rightful owners, or in this case, to the estates of their rightful owners.'

'And you have no idea what's inside any of them?' another woman asked from across the room.

'No, we don't,' Mia replied.

Georgia stood then, taking her chance and slipping her bag over her shoulder as she cleared her throat. No matter how fascinating this was, she had to go.

'Well, as interesting as all this sounds, I have to get back to work,' she said, hoping she didn't sound as rude as she felt. But when she looked at the other women seated, she realised that was exactly how she came across. 'If you could pass me the box labelled Cara Montano, I'll be on my way. I'm sorry I can't stay longer.'

'Thank you for coming,' the lawyer said, nodding to her. 'If you have any questions, please don't hesitate to contact me. We will be more than happy to discuss the matter with you at a later date.'

Georgia nodded, signing the piece of paper that Mia nudged towards her and rummaging in her bag for her wallet so she could show her identification. Her cheeks heated a little as she felt everyone's eyes on her, but she didn't look up from the task at hand.

'Thank you,' she murmured to Mia, touching her hand to the other woman's arm. 'I can see how much this all means to you. I'm only sorry I can't stay longer.'

Mia gave her a small smile before passing her the box, and Georgia took it and dropped it into her bag, before crossing the room and pushing open the door as she reached for her phone.

Sam answered in a tone as clipped as Georgia's heels on the tiled floor.

'G, where have you been? I need you! The investor—'

'I'm on my way,' Georgia said as she waved down a taxi and stamped her feet against the cold as it circled round for her. 'I'll be back in the office in twenty minutes. I'll come straight in to see you, I promise.' She ended the call, sliding into the taxi the second it pulled up to the kerb and giving the driver the address.

Georgia rested her head back and took a breath then, trying to process what had just happened. Sometimes she felt as if she hadn't truly rested in years, every minute of every day filled with work and her nights spent answering emails and sitting up in bed until she fell asleep with her laptop, before it started all over again. It was as if she'd been exhausted for as long as she could remember.

She leaned forward and reached into her bag for the little box she'd just been given. Georgia turned it over in her hand, blowing away a little dust that had gathered against the string as she wondered whether she even wanted to know what was inside. She'd spent the past ten years accepting the fact that she didn't have a family, proving to herself and to the world that she could succeed despite everything she'd been through, that she could move past the grief of her teenage years. And yet the idea of opening the box felt almost as if she'd be unravelling the carefully constructed barriers she'd so painstakingly built around herself.

Just open it. Don't overthink it, just open it.

It took her a moment to untie it, her nails catching on the string as she tried to pull the knot. Eventually it gave way and she discarded it along with the tag, lost to the depths of her oversized bag, before pulling back the lid and finding an enormous gemstone resting inside. She gasped, not having expected anything quite so extravagant, especially knowing the decades the box had spent hidden beneath floorboards, gathering dust in an old house. She put the box on her lap and took out the stone, turning it over in her fingers, marvelling at the sheer beauty of it and wondering whether it was a rare gem or possibly even a diamond, its pink hues so radiant they were almost purple as it caught the light. The size was almost impossible to comprehend—it was at least twice the diameter of the largest engagement ring she'd ever seen.

Beneath it was a newspaper clipping, and she reluctantly put the stone back inside the box and took the yellowed paper out. It was in a language she didn't recognise, and so she folded it again, taking out the stone so she could place it all back carefully inside. Her grandmother had been wealthy—that was one of the only things she really knew about her—and she'd held that wealth as tight as could be until her death. But this stone was possibly something her grandmother didn't even know about; or if she had, was it something she'd been searching for throughout her lifetime? Had her grandmother even known she was adopted?

'Miss, this is as close as I'll be able to get you,' her driver said.

Georgia looked up, having lost all track of time as she inspected the little box, realising they were almost at her office. As her phone began to vibrate again, she quickly secured the box and put it back in her bag, nodding her thanks to the driver as she paid him at the same time as answering the call.

'Sam, I'm here. I told you—'

She touched her hand to her bag, her mind still on the stone she'd found as her best friend and business partner positively squealed down the line, her excitement palpable, and told her that they'd been called in for a final meeting within the hour to discuss the proposed buyout of their company. Georgia crossed the road and hurried towards her building, deciding to grab them both very strong coffees at the café downstairs before going up, even though Sam had insisted she come straight to her office. But despite Georgia's excitement at what they were about to achieve, for once it wasn't work on her mind as she stood and waited for their espressos. After all these years, all that time yearning to have more reminders of her family, to discover more about the loving parents she'd never stopped mourning, and now she'd finally been given one.

She only wished that the one reminder she'd now been given didn't belong to the one family member she'd have preferred to forget.